Just then,
Manuel Escobar gulped for breath.
Trina turned quickly,
fearing it would be his last.
He was trying to speak.
"City . . . sands," he said in a faint whisper.
Louder now, he repeated the words.
Suddenly, he screamed with a terror
so unspeakable that Mark wanted
to yank Trina out of the room.

"City . . . under . . . sands!"

CITY UNDER THE SANDS

Wallace Henley

LIVING BOOKS
Tyndale House Publishers, Inc.
Wheaton, Illinois

ACKNOWLEDGMENTS

The exploration of the most frightening chambers of the world of biotechnology would have been quite impossible had I not been accompanied on this expedition.

I am grateful to James and Marti Hefley for encouragement and the application of their considerable literary talents in improving the first draft of *City under the Sands.*

My wife, Irene, has spent countless hours before a word processor, typing the final manuscript.

Joyce Ellis and other editors at Tyndale House, like precise sculptors, have chipped off the rough edges and shaped the final product.

I thank several authors whose work contributed to my understanding, and whose research shows that the projects described in *City under the Sands* are not limited to the world of fantasy. These authors and their works include: Jeremy Rifkin, *Algeny,* New York: The Viking Press; Ted Howard and Jeremy Rifkin, *Who Should Play God?,* New York: Dell; Maya Pines, *The Brain Changers,* New York: Harcourt Brace Jovanovich.

Above all, I give praise to the Maker of parables.

First printing, May 1986
Library of Congress Catalog Card Number 85-52351
ISBN 0-8423-0286-7
© 1986 by Wallace Henley
Printed in the United States of America

Humankind . . . faces two crises simultaneously. The earth is running low on its stock of burnable energy and on the stock of living resources at the same time. We are at a turning point in the history of civilization, and it is at this critical juncture that a revolutionary new approach to organizing the planet is being advanced, an approach so overwhelming in scope that it will fundamentally alter humanity's entire relationship to the globe.

After thousands of years of engineering the cold remains of the earth into utilities, human beings are now setting out to engineer the internal biology of living organisms. . . . We are moving from the age of pyrotechnology to the age of biotechnology. The transition is indeed staggering.

Jeremy Rifkin, *Algeny*, New York: The Viking Press, p. 6.

MANUEL ESCOBAR staggered through the Valley of Fires. *Hell is as hot as promised*, he thought, as his feet shuffled through the blistering sand, which felt like hot ash. Manuel wanted to run. But his living nightmare was like the fantasies of the most terrifying night. For some reason he couldn't run. His legs were sticks of lead, becoming molten in the fires seeming to rise from the ground.

Manuel yearned to close his eyes, to blot out the screeching, angry sun. He had not expected the fiery ball to blast into hell, but there it was. *Perhaps*, he thought with that tiny part of his parboiled brain that could still concentrate, *hell is really an asteroid scant miles from the sun.* Regardless, the heat had welded his eyelids open.

Manuel wandered goggle-eyed through hell as his body screamed for shade, for anything cool.

Not conscious of his actions, Manuel lifted his bare, blistered arms, groping for an oasis. The flaming sand at his feet tripped him. Manuel fell. The grains pierced his naked groin with the rage of a million spears. Almost impossibly, Manuel heaved himself up again, his hands as well as his feet now burning from the hot sand.

As horrible as the fire was the fact that Manuel was alone. He was the only human being in hell. And behind him was a terror even greater than where he now limped. A jagged range of mountains stretched across the back of hell like the spikes on a dragon's back. The mountains had eyes and teeth. They pursued Manuel. He knew he must escape the evil mountains, for beyond them lay the *Jornada del Muerto*—the Journey of the Dead. The mountains would hurl him over their fanged peaks and he would be trapped, forced to walk the *Jornada del Muerto*.

But hell had unspeakably monstrous surprises for him. As he peered ahead with his frantic, unblinking eyes, Manuel saw two giant tarantulas speeding toward him. One was taller than he, the other only a third of the size of the first. But both were large enough to entwine Manuel totally in their hairy spears of legs.

If only I could run. . . . Why can't I run? Manuel's tortured mind screamed for escape. He turned from the tarantulas, staggering again toward the mountains and the *Jornada del Muerto*. But the tarantulas rode on jet-empowered feet.

The hot sands did not blister them, did not slow them down. Manuel wanted to scream, but he could utter no sound. He had been mute since that day he was vomited into this place from some unknown origin.

Now the tarantulas were at his back. He moved his leaden legs a few more anguished steps. He could feel the blistering breath of the beasts on his back. They shrieked at him.

Then the tarantulas were on him. The larger one knocked Manuel to the ground, and they rolled in the singed sand. Manuel knew he must keep the leg-spears from tearing into his body. Consciousness began to slip away. The last thing Manuel Escobar heard before he plummeted into oblivion was the large tarantula speaking to the smaller one.

"This guy looks like a zombie," said the giant tarantula.

Manuel Escobar didn't know that the giant tarantula manufactured by his confused brain was Mark Tilman, a man who had only chased him through the desert to try to help him. Had Escobar known, there would have been no need for Tilman to throw his 264-pound, six-foot, three-inch frame at Manuel. The tackle had been as rough on Tilman's forty-six-year-old body as it had been on Manuel.

Not that Mark Tilman hadn't already felt the desert floor of New Mexico's Valley of Fires. The night before, Tilman and his ten-year-old son, Danny, had slept on that ground in sleeping bags.

It was mid June—Saturday, June 16, to be exact. The camping-hiking trip in the deserts of New Mexico had become an annual ritual for Tilman and his son. For a few days, Tilman could escape the endless yelping of telephones and cold, staring computers in the newsroom of the *Albuquerque Evening Star*. And Tilman could also escape the painful memory of Donna.

He and Donna had been married thirteen years and seven days when she died. Danny was only two years old then. Donna had also been a reporter for the *Evening Star*. One sun-soaked day eight years ago, she had helicoptered to Santa Fe to cover a story at the state capitol. During her return trip, the helicopter dropped like a stone to the ground near Santo Domingo Pueblo. No survivors. For eight years, Tilman had raised his son alone. He thought that no woman could ever replace Donna. He couldn't even enter the newsroom where they had met and worked together without thinking of her. But that was eight years in the past.

For the present, Mark Tilman focused on the strange, zombielike man he encountered in the desert.

"He's real sick, son," said Tilman to Danny. "We've got to get him to Carrizozo. Maybe the sheriff there can help us."

Tilman covered the naked babbling creature with a lightweight jacket and lifted him into the back of the borrowed jeep that he and Danny used on their treks into the desert. As they rushed into the small town of Carrizozo, Danny rode in the back to keep their patient steady. Tilman parked

at the Lincoln County Sheriff's station at Carrizozo, and a deputy, sensing trouble, came running.

"We found him out in the desert," Tilman explained.

"This guy's in bad shape." The deputy called
to his coworker, "We've got to get him to Alamogordo fast!"

Tilman and Danny watched as two deputies
loaded the zombie into a patrol car. One of the
deputies tossed Tilman his jacket and threw a
sheet over their passenger.

As the patrol car wailed up the street toward
Alamogordo, Tilman stood in its dusty wake, assuming he had had his last encounter with the
pitiful human found in the sands.

Carey Martin, chief of the *Evening Star* copydesk,
looked up from his computer screen just as Mark
Tilman entered the newsroom. "Hey, Tilman,
you don't look bad for the whale that swallowed
Detroit." Martin endlessly kidded Tilman about
his weight. Momentarily forgetting the copy he
was editing on the screen, Martin shook his head
as he surveyed Tilman's appearance: rumpled
clothes, bird-nest hair, and his ever-present
brown lunch sack.

Steve Poole, a copy editor, joined the kidding.
"Whatcha got in there to eat today, Tilman?
Some iguana eggs you picked up in the desert?"

Tilman was one of those people who invited
jest. The big, bumbling man loved it as much as
his colleagues did.

"Nope, Steve," Tilman gibed back. "First, iguanas don't lay eggs. Second, I'm packing turkey eggs I collected in *your* backyard."

Reporters around the copydesk smiled but shook their heads at Tilman's corny joke. No one could ever remember Tilman tossing anything but corn. His clownish appearance and dry humor made almost anything he said seem funny.

Not until lunchtime would anyone know what Tilman had in his lunch sack. Then it would be revealed he had brought a bag full of raw vegetables, his latest fad diet.

As Tilman sat down behind his desk, Carey Martin walked over and perched on the corner of Tilman's desk. "When did you get back from the desert?" he asked.

"Late last night," answered Tilman, turning his desk calendar to Monday, June 18. He winced as he saw the reminder on the calendar. Warren Baxley, the Sunday editor, wanted a feature piece on the father-son desert venture for the Sunday "New Mexico Living" section.

"How was the Valley of Fires?" asked Martin, who occasionally hiked and camped with Tilman.

"You'll know soon enough," Tilman answered. "I'll be shooting you ten pages of copy on it for Sunday."

"Tilman, I wouldn't edit ten pages for Shakespeare, let alone some desert bum," Martin kidded.

"You might just be interested in what I'm going to say this time," Tilman responded. "Danny and I bumped into a real weirdo out there, just wandering naked through the sands. Must have been on drugs or something. Anyway, we took him to the Lincoln County Sheriff's Office and they rushed him to the hospital. They said they didn't know who he was, but I managed to snap a photo of the guy. I'm going to try to get Warren to run it with the story. Maybe somebody'll recognize the crazy guy."

"If it's a missing person story, you probably ought to run it today," Martin suggested. "We've got time for the afternoon locals. Let's get it in."

By 3:30 P.M., the afternoon local edition bearing Manuel Escobar's picture and Tilman's story, "Encounter in the Desert," was on the street. At 4:30, Tilman's phone rang. "Tilman," he answered tersely.

The voice on the other end was a woman's. "Mr. Tilman, my name is Trina Escobar. The man in your article today . . . I think he's my brother . . . but he looks so *different.*"

"When did you last see your brother?" Tilman sat up straight and began taking notes.

"Two weeks ago. I visited him at . . . uh, county jail," she stammered with a slight Mexican accent. "He had, uh, robbed a convenience store."

Tilman stretched backward in his chair. "Well then, the man I found in the desert couldn't have been your brother," he told the woman. It's a long way down to the Valley of Fires. Besides, if he's locked up in the Bernalillo County Jail, he sure couldn't be wandering around in the desert."

"But that's just it," she protested. "I got a call

last week from the sheriff's department. Sheriff
Jeters told me my brother—his name is Manuel—
Manuel had walked away from a work detail.
They didn't know where he was, and the sheriff
wanted me to call if Manuel came to my house."

When Mark Tilman, who had won two awards
from the *Albuquerque Evening Star* for enterprise in journalism, sniffed a story, he was like an
eagle tracking a rabbit. Tilman leaned forward on
his desk. "Miss Escobar, would you ride down to
Alamogordo with me tomorrow and see if you
can identify the man?"

"I don't know if I can tomorrow. I'm a waitress
at El Condor Mexican Restaurante. And . . . and I
don't know if I can get off that quickly. . . . But
this is so important . . . yes. Yes, Mr. Tilman, I'll
just tell my boss I have to go."

"Great!" said Tilman. "Can you come to the
reception desk on the first floor of the *Evening
Star* around eight in the morning?"

"Yes, I'll be there," Trina Escobar promised.

Tilman rushed to the city editor's desk to alert
him of the possible story. Moving like a leviathan
in a fairy castle, Tilman managed to spill the Styrofoam cup of cold coffee on Cleve Stringer's
desk.

Stringer jumped up to dodge the rancid, day-old
coffee. "Tilman, you clumsy idiot!" he barked.

"Sorry, boss. But look, I've got to go down to
Alamogordo tomorrow. I have a possible follow-
up of that weird guy I found in the desert."

"Tilman, it'll be such a delight to get you out

of this newsroom for a day, I don't care if you go to Nome, Alaska," Stringer hollered angrily.

Ten years earlier, when Dr. Ernst Singlelaub devised the plan enabling U.S. President Prentiss Pearson to impose martial law on the nation,* Singlelaub had been able to hold the thermostat on his perpetually boiling anger. But the failure of his plan, the impeachment of Prentiss Pearson, plus Singlelaub's own near-tragedy, had eroded his cool control. Now his anger often boiled over, scalding those around him with his red-hot words.

"What do you mean AB-2 has escaped?" Singlelaub yelled at his assistant.

"I have no details, Dr. Singlelaub. All I know is that one of the ablation subjects escaped from the Desert Center. There was a story with his photograph in an Albuquerque newspaper."

Singlelaub stood up behind his desk and cursed. "Get Shelley, Porteous, and Stelmetz in here. I want them to brief me on this AB-2, whoever the crazy fool is!"

On Tuesday morning, June 19, Tilman arrived at his desk at 7:45. At 8:00, the receptionist phoned him. Miss Trina Escobar was waiting for him in the lobby.

Tilman never ran *up* the stairs to the second floor newsroom. Too much bulk to lift. But

*See *The Roman Solution*, Tyndale House, 1984.

whenever he was in pursuit of a story and the elevator lagged, he took the stairs *down*. As soon as he burst through the stairway door, Tilman could tell he would enjoy the ride to Alamogordo. There were no other visitors in the lobby. The petite, dark-haired woman had to be his guest.

"Miss Escobar? I'm Mark Tilman."

Trina Escobar nodded a tense greeting.

Tilman just stood there, looking at her for a moment. In the years since Donna's death, Tilman had had little interest in women. In fact, it bothered him that he would always come just short of involvement. After Donna's death, Tilman plunged into a period of introspection. Looking for answers, he began to read the Bible and eventually became a "born again" Christian—another chunk of fodder for the kidding machine in the newsroom.

Once, Tilman confided in his pastor about his problem with women and discovered the source. Tilman realized that he feared any involvement that might end in that unbearable pain he had felt at Donna's loss. Still, understanding hadn't brought a solution.

That didn't keep Tilman from finding women attractive—even desirable. He was still a man. At forty-six, his sex drive hadn't waned, though his new commitment kept him straight. Trina Escobar was appealing, her beauty marred only by a mouth that was a little too large. Her dark Latin skin and raven hair contrasted sharply with the delicate peach-colored blouse and white pants she wore. Tilman, his hair in its usual just-awake jumble, found himself tucking in his shirttail, which habitually strayed over his straining belt.

While apologizing for not being able to provide a very comfortable drive, Tilman escorted Trina to his eight-year-old green compact car. The fender on the driver's side bore a dent haloed in rust, and the whole car needed a good wash.

Tilman headed the heap south on the interstate, and they traveled five miles in tense silence. The sun had just hurdled Sandia Peak, and its rays highlighted the green stands of trees that teased at the mountain's crest. Tilman scanned the uncluttered horizon, punctuated here and there with stark, flat buttes. He felt reticent to disturb his focus on the sparkling New Mexico morning, but he knew he would have to take the lead in breaking the silence.

"It's about two hundred miles down to Alamogordo from here. I guess we could use this time to get acquainted."

Trina smiled and said nothing.

"Well, since you asked," Tilman teased, "I was born in Carlsbad. Grew up right on the river." He glanced at Trina. She still held her mouth in the same taut smile. "OK, your turn," he said.

"I . . . I'm from Deming," Trina answered, ducking her head as if she wanted to hide her origins.

"Hey, that's way down south. I had a fraternity brother at the University of New Mexico who was from Deming. Used to go down and visit him. His father owned a dry goods place there. Ever hear of Mitchell's Department Store?"

"No, Mr. Tilman. Actually we moved to Albuquerque when I was three. I don't remember much about Deming."

For fifteen minutes there was silence. Tilman didn't want to push conversation on Trina. *Maybe*, he thought, *this business about her brother has her preoccupied.*

Trina's mind, spurred by Tilman's probing, began a painful trek into the past. She saw her brother, Manuel, as a scrawny Mexican child, sobbing as he told her of his classmates' taunting. She remembered the anger that took root in him as he built a shell to protect himself from the gibes of the Anglo kids.

Trina had always been stronger than Manuel. She had been able to dismiss the kidding they threw at her. But as the years passed, Trina's strength and sympathy for Manuel had turned into maternal protectiveness, which Manuel cultivated and manipulated, at times unknowingly.

Trina winced as she pondered her beginnings. She had not been honest with Mark Tilman. "I lied to you," she said suddenly.

"About what?"

"About Deming. I wasn't born there. I was born in Mexico. My parents waded the Rio Grande when I was three and Manuel was five. We lived in Deming for only six months, then moved to Albuquerque."

Tilman sensed anger. Maybe he had pried too much. "Hey, I'm sorry if I put you on the spot."

"I'm sorry I lied to you."

"That's OK. I mean, it's your business. . . ."

"No, lying is wrong. I shouldn't have done it."

"Well, you must be one of the few human beings on Planet Earth who has a conscience about lying," Tilman remarked.

"That's because I don't live by the rules of Planet Earth, Mr. Tilman."

"What does that mean?"

"That means I live by the rules of heaven, which are written down in the Bible."

"You're a Christian?"

"Yes."

Tilman wasn't really surprised. He had detected a steadiness of spirit in Trina, even with the hefty stress she carried, that had already caused him to conclude there was something different about her.

"I am, too," Tilman declared.

His words were like a blowtorch on an ice cube. Immediately, Trina's cold attitude melted.

"You look relieved," Tilman said.

Trina laughed. "Mr. Tilman, the only reporters I've ever seen have been in the movies. They were heavy drinkers and always chasing women. Honestly, I dreaded this ride with you, but it was the only way I could find out about my brother."

For the rest of the journey, Trina Escobar seemed at ease, sharing her life history with Tilman. Like Tilman, she had turned to God after bitter tragedy. She had married at seventeen because she was pregnant. Prospects of motherhood propelled her into a spiritual search. The father of her child soon abandoned her. Then, on a drinking spree one night, he was killed in an automobile accident. In spite of his rejection, Trina still loved him, and the shock of his death caused a miscarriage.

Trina Escobar retained her maiden name and focused the rest of her life on two things: the evangelical church she had joined and her brother—trying to keep Manuel out of trouble. On the latter, Trina had to admit failure. Manuel had a bent for trouble and an addiction for robbing convenience stores.

As Trina talked, Tilman realized that the trials she had passed through were strengthening rather than breaking her.

"And that brings us up to this drive to Alamogordo," Trina said. "Now, Mr. Tilman, I am curious about you—especially how a newspaper reporter became a real Christian."

"Actually, I'm a living relic," Tilman joked. "I grew up in a pretty wealthy home down in Carlsbad. At eighteen, I decided to chuck it all and run away."

"Problems at home?" Trina asked.

"Problems everywhere. By the time I was eighteen, I already weighed 243. Everybody—my dad, my teachers, the coaches—they all thought I ought to be playing football. They acted like it was a sin that somebody my size wasn't out on the field killing people every day. I couldn't get anybody to understand that I'd rather spend my time in a library or writing. . . ."

"You couldn't get your dad to understand?"

"Especially him. He had this idea that I was

going to follow in his footsteps: be a football hero, then become a hot lawyer. I just had to get away."

"What did you mean when you said you're a living relic?"

"Oh, that." Tilman grinned. "I was a flower child. Remember the hippies? I had long hair, a guitar, and a sleeping bag. For a whole year, I hitchhiked around the country. Somewhere out there I came to my senses and decided I really ought to make something out of my life. So I came to Albuquerque and enrolled at the University of New Mexico."

"Is that when you became a Christian?"

"Heavens, no! I was a hard-eyed agnostic in those days. I didn't become a Christian until after Donna died."

"Donna?"

"My wife. She was a reporter, too. Killed in a helicopter crash. If I hadn't had a small son to raise, I might have done away with myself. I guess God used Donna's death to break through the barrier of pride that had kept him out of my life. Anyway, two years ago, I realized that I couldn't go on without something more. That's when I really opened my life to the Lord."

Tilman had erected a firm bridge between Trina and himself. For two more hours, their conversation crossed and recrossed the bridge of faith, comparing experiences and affirming beliefs. The time passed quickly, and soon they pulled into the hospital parking lot at Alamogordo.

Walking into the building's sterile corridors,

21

the two identified themselves and were directed to the intensive care unit. Trina gasped at the figure stretched on the bed. She knew she would need all the strength her thorny past and steely faith had produced in her.

CURLING, plastic serpents of tubes intertwined around Manuel Escobar's swollen body. His skin had a strange, mottled appearance. His head seemed a little too small, and his eyes stared, reflecting the panic in what was left of his mind.

Battling tears, Trina leaned over him. "Manuel, can you hear me?" she begged.

He stirred. His eyeballs shifted toward his right hand, which had been punctured by an IV and strapped to the bed. Then his eyes found her. The cardiac monitor showed that his heartbeat quickened. His blood pressure shot up. But he did not speak.

Trina could stand no more. She turned away and clung to the man she'd known only a few hours. "Mark, Mark, this is what I've been dreading—what I've been fighting. I've tried so hard to keep Manuel from being hurt," she wept. "Now he's been destroyed."

Just then, Manuel Escobar gulped for breath. Trina turned quickly, fearing it would be his last.

He was trying to speak. "City . . . sands," he said in a faint whisper. Louder now, he repeated the words. Suddenly, he screamed with a terror so unspeakable that Mark wanted to jerk Trina out of the room. "City . . . under . . . sands," Manuel screamed, trying to yank himself from the bed.

The cry brought a nurse running. She quickly ordered Tilman and Trina outside.

In a few moments the nurse emerged from the cubicle, shaking her head at Trina Escobar. "I've given him a heavy sedative. He'll rest better now," she said. "They've scheduled a brain scan in the morning to try to find out what's wrong. Maybe the tests will show us how to help your brother."

At the Albuquerque airport, a tall man wearing a neatly tailored, conservative dark suit disembarked from a plane and made his way through the terminal building. A sinister darkness smoldered in the slender man's gaze. He barely noticed the Indian decor of the unusual airport lobby as he quietly asked an attendant about his connection to Alamogordo.

Within two hours, the stern-looking visitor had boarded the connection, flown to Alamogordo, and begun preparations to fulfill an important assignment at the hospital there. His assignment was Manuel Escobar. His was not a mission to help.

Manuel was tumbling down a long, looming shaft. The walls shot by dizzily. Soon he would thud at the bottom, his limbs the chaotic jumble of a discarded marionette. Manuel tried to fight back, but his body felt welded to a slab plunging down the shaft with him.

"Be still!" a voice commanded. It sounded far-away. The strident tones echoed in Manuel's mind against the cold walls of the shaft.

Actually, the voice came from an attendant at the Alamogordo hospital who was wheeling Manuel down the hall for a CAT scan.

The illusion of falling down a shaft existed only in Manuel's addled brain. He lay flat on his back, gazing up at the ceiling, which rushed by as he was pushed down the corridor. To Manuel, the ceiling appeared to be the wall of the shaft. His panic grew. The only words that would emerge from his terror were "city . . . under . . . sands."

It took three technicians to get Manuel Escobar on the table of the CAT scan machine. To Manuel's hallucinating brain, the huge round opening of the device appeared as the jaws of a shark. He struggled to keep from being shoved down the beast's gullet.

"We've got to stabilize his head as tightly as possible," said the chief CAT scan technician.

Almost violently, another technician pinioned

Manuel's shaved head against a pillow of Styrofoam using wide sheets of nearly unbreakable tape to hold him in place. The rest of his body was also strapped tightly to the table. The technicians left Manuel's side and went into the monitor room.

Soon Manuel could hear the shifting jaws of the shark. Manuel's body slid forward until his head was within the jaws, which now shifted back and forth taking more than two hundred readings of Manuel's brain with each degree of rotation. Manuel writhed in a futile effort to escape the jaws of the shark that he was convinced had swallowed him.

The CAT scan stopped its clunking rotation. Manuel Escobar lay on the table, now so fearful that he couldn't move even if he hadn't been strapped and taped.

In the monitor room, the machine's computer awakened. It zipped through more than thirty thousand calculations of tissue thickness. The video screen blinked brightly. Slices of Manuel Escobar's brain were now visible in sparkling colors of red, yellow, and green. Although the CAT scan technician was not a neurosurgeon, it was obvious that Manuel Escobar's brain was seriously damaged. As the CAT picture slipped down through Manuel's forebrain, it passed into the region known as Wernicke's area—the brain cells enabling speech comprehension. The region was streaked with lesions. Further down, Broca's area, the cells enabling speech production, showed no damage. That explained why Manuel seemed to understand nothing, but could still endlessly say, "City . . . under . . . sands."

As the picture on the computer screen sank deeper into Manuel's brain, the technician blinked at what he saw. When the picture was complete, he punched the print button on the computer console in front of him. The neurosurgeon would want to examine this strange phenomenon inside Manuel Escobar's brain.

At the Alamogordo motel seven miles from the hospital, Ernst Singlelaub's sinister-eyed representative pulled from his briefcase a blue-toned copy of the floor plan of the hospital. He already knew Manuel Escobar was in the intensive care unit. Now he plotted how to get past the nurses' station and into Manuel's room. Once there, he knew what he would do. A taut little smile popped briefly onto his face.

At the same motel, the telephone in Trina Escobar's room rang. She dashed out of the bathroom in a robe, toweling her dark hair. It was a nurse at the hospital. Dr. Clay Bunting, Alamogordo's best neurosurgeon, wanted to see her at 11:00 A.M. Trina immediately phoned Mark in his room and asked him to hurry.

At 11:00 Trina and Mark sat before Dr. Clay Bunting in a small conference room at the hospital. "Miss Escobar," the doctor began, "has your brother ever had surgery on his brain?"

Trina frowned in confusion. "No, Manuel's never even been in the hospital," she replied.

"You're absolutely positive?" the neurosurgeon persisted.

"Dr. Bunting, I've spent virtually all my time looking after my brother. I'd know if he'd been in the hospital for even a day."

"Then I'm afraid what I'm going to tell you may be shocking," the doctor said, trying to prepare Trina.

"What do you mean?" Tilman blurted.

"There's a tiny organ in the brain known as the amygdala," the physician began. "There's evidence that it controls much of our emotional response. The anterior of Mr. Escobar's amygdala has been ablated."

"I'm sorry, doctor. I don't understand," said Trina.

"I apologize," said Dr. Bunting. "What I'm trying to tell you is that the front of your brother's amygdala has been *surgically removed.*"

"But how . . . ?" Trina asked softly.

Mark reached over to comfort her.

"I don't know, Miss Escobar," Bunting continued. "But the surgery was recent."

"What can be done for him?" Tilman asked.

"Nothing can be done to reverse the brain damage. Whoever did the surgery didn't use much caution. There are scars all over his head. About all we can do is get them healed and release him to you. Frankly, I think you're looking at a longterm care situation."

"You mean in a nursing home?" Trina asked.

"Yes," answered the doctor. "That or some other kind of institution."

Seven miles away, the sinister-eyed man was in his rented car, already driving toward the hospital. If he succeeded in his mission, Trina Escobar wouldn't have to worry about long-term care for her brother.

In the hospital cafeteria, Trina Escobar picked at her food. Mark Tilman, perpetually hungry, wolfed his down.

"Mark," puzzled Trina, "I just don't understand. The last time I saw Manuel, two weeks ago, he was in the Albuquerque jail. How could he have been operated on?"

Tilman, who regretted his appetite was stimulated by excitement, shook his head. He continued to eat and listened as Trina reasoned aloud.

"Why, Mark, *why* would anyone want to operate on my brother's brain? The police said he escaped from a work detail. Where did he go when he escaped?"

Momentarily, Tilman paused, wiping his mouth. "Wherever it was, it was close to the Valley of Fires where Danny and I found him."

"What's close to the Valley of Fires?" Trina asked.

"Not much more than wasteland, except for the little town of Carrizozo. And White Sands Missile Range, of course."

"Dr. Bunting wanted me to try to keep talking to Manuel. He thinks that even if Manuel can't understand my words, he might at least recognize my voice. Maybe I can comfort him a little," she said.

There would be no comfort for Manuel Escobar. As Trina and Mark Tilman talked in the cafeteria, a tall, slender man dressed in hospital whites entered the intensive care unit where Manuel Escobar slept under sedation.

The unit clerk behind the nurses' station scribbled busily at her paperwork. A technician watched the cardiac machines pulsing with the heartbeats of her patients. The white-clad orderly carrying a basket of medicines and specimens seemed to be from the hospital lab. No one paid any attention to him as he entered Manuel Escobar's cubicle.

Silently and swiftly, the imposter slipped into surgical gloves and replaced Manuel's IV bottle with another. The clear liquid resembled glucose, but its transparent sparkle was deceptive and as deadly as a snake's venom.

The sinister-eyed representative adjusted the drip, and the new liquid began to flow into Manuel Escobar's arm.

Fifteen minutes later, the ICU cardiac monitor technician suddenly had a straight line on one of her machines. The monitor emitted a strident tone, alerting medical staff. Cardiac arrest.

On cue, the unit clerk squawked into the hospital intercom, "Code Blue, ICU. Code Blue,

ICU." A resident physician and other nurses dashed into Manuel Escobar's cubicle, but it was too late. The man Mark Tilman called a zombie, Ernst Singlelaub's team had labeled AB-2, and Trina Escobar knew as her brother, was dead.

On the edge of Alamogordo, the sinister-eyed representative, again attired in his blue suit, made a phone call from an outdoor phone booth.

The man who answered switched the call to the office of Ernst Singlelaub's chief assistant.

Hearing the aide's voice, the representative spoke tersely into the telephone. "AB-2 is terminated."

"Good," replied the assistant. "Return to base."

"I want an autopsy," Trina Escobar sobbed.

An hour before, Trina and Tilman had been summoned from the hospital cafeteria. Having heard the Code Blue on the public address system, they were shocked to hear that the code had been for Manuel. Sitting in a small conference room in the ICU with a resident physician and hospital chaplain, Mark questioned her decision.

"Are you sure you want an autopsy?" he asked. "Your brother was a very sick man. I'm sorry. . . ." He fumbled for words. "But his death shouldn't surprise us."

"Mark, the doctor says Manuel's cause of death was cardiac arrest. My brother had many weaknesses, but I know he had a strong heart. I can't believe his heart just stopped."

Within a few hours, Trina and Tilman were sitting in another hospital conference room with the chief resident, Dr. Bunting, and Jason Guinn, the hospital administrator.

"I have some bad . . . and . . . frankly . . . confusing news," Dr. Bunting said, holding Manuel's autopsy report.

"The news couldn't be any worse than it already is," Tilman said.

"Miss Escobar," Dr. Bunting said, shifting his gaze toward her, "I'm afraid your brother may have been murdered."

Trina gasped.

"The autopsy showed traces of a poison that causes cardiac arrest. We have the IV bottle. It was full of the stuff," Bunting continued.

"You mean someone in the hospital murdered Trina's brother?" Tilman asked.

"We don't know," Guinn answered. "The unit clerk in the ICU vaguely recalls a lab messenger entering the ICU shortly before Mr. Escobar died. But there's no record of a lab messenger being sent to the ICU at that time. And the IV bottle is definitely not the same one Mr. Escobar's nurse installed earlier."

"We assure you, Miss Escobar," Bunting broke in, "we're going to do all we can to find out how your brother died. The police will be here soon, and they'll conduct a joint investigation with our hospital security people."

As Mark listened, he knew that he, too, would conduct an investigation.

Trina Escobar had stirred in him feelings he

had not felt since Donna's death. At first Tilman had resisted the feelings. But they washed over him like a warm wave, drowning his cool detachment from women in the depths of his affection for Trina.

Tilman had two weeks of vacation coming. He would use whatever time it took to unearth the roots of Manuel Escobar's tragedy. The only clue Tilman had was Manuel's strange utterances about a city under sands. The roots of Manuel's tragedy must be buried somewhere in those "sands."

THE roots that choked the life from Manuel Escobar were ten years long. Ernst Singlelaub had seeded, cultivated, and lullabied them into healthy growth. He had not given up his vision of using those stifling roots to encircle as much of human society as possible.

But Singlelaub had some tidying up to do before his dream became reality. Tremors of rage shook America when it learned that President Prentiss Pearson had planted a detention center in the Mojave Desert for recalcitrants, had had former president Riley Torrance killed there, and had conspired in the murder of General Royston Wade.

Singlelaub grimaced as he remembered the horrible night at the Hollywood Bowl, when what was to have been a tribute to Pearson was turned into his indictment. Jeremiah Durkin, Pearson's former top assistant, had grabbed the podium and exposed to the world what Pearson had done. Pearson was impeached and found guilty of conspiracy to commit murder. Ernst Singlelaub felt like a man with a noose around his neck waiting for someone to kick away the stool on which he stood. For Singlelaub had masterminded the whole scheme. Only his extensive contacts in the Congress saved him from a prison sentence.

Liberals who controlled congressional committees investigating the Pearson debacle had always enshrined Ernst Singlelaub. He had sold himself as the patriarch of enlightenment. And there was only the word of religious fanatic Jeremiah Durkin—a known enemy of Singlelaub—implicating Singlelaub in the Wade murder conspiracy. Secret parleys and a few well-placed payoffs finally snipped the rope from around Singlelaub's neck.

Singlelaub went into seclusion for six months to write a ponderous, self-serving book: *America at the Chasm*. The title, plus the massive advertising budget supplied by Singlelaub's fawning publisher, produced a best-seller. In it, Singlelaub humbly informed the world that if he had not been at Prentiss Pearson's side, the abuses would have been even greater.

Furthermore, proclaimed Singlelaub, society was in serious need of new goals. There was a need to recognize that human beings couldn't continue to govern if they remained finite. Singlelaub called for the acceptance of a "posthuman" concept. Through biological engineering, a new species would be artificially evolved—a species above evil, above the corruption that had devoured Prentiss Pearson.

After sniffing the bouquets tossed at him from his admirers in *academe* and the media, Ernst Singlelaub turned his mind to creating the new society and the new organism that would inhabit it.

So one June day, almost ten years prior to the day Mark Tilman and Trina Escobar drove to Alamogordo, Singlelaub went to work.

As Americans splashed in ocean surf, zipped along on heart-thumping theme park rides, and toiled in the summer heat, Singlelaub's associates arrived one by one at La Guardia airport in New York. Then by helicopter they rode to an isolated span of Long Island, gathering at the exclusive Glades of Bacchus. There, the first seeds of Ernst Singlelaub's deadly plan were sown.

"What is this place?" asked Dr. James Shelley as he walked into the reception area of the Glades of Bacchus.

"Call it a retreat for the Platonist elite," answered the attendant Singlelaub had ordered to greet each guest personally.

Shelley scanned the massive building they had just entered. Heavy, rustic beams hoisted the ceiling thirty feet above him. A natural rock fireplace, attended by plush sofas and chairs, yawned at one end of the room. At the other end of the rectangular reception quarters, large windows and double doors opened onto a sprawling wooden porch overlooking Huntington Bay, the choppy waters of Long Island Sound beyond. The rustic look was strictly for atmosphere, Shelley noted, watching uniformed waiters and waitresses carry drinks to men on the porch.

"Not many people get invited here, you know," the attendant said as they moved to the reception desk. "For years, the Glades of Bacchus has served as one of the two places in America where our most powerful people can get away and do whatever they like without fear of snoopers. The West Coast counterpart of the Glades is the Bohemian Grove in California."

Shelley grinned. "What do you mean 'do whatever they like'?" he asked, waiting for the reception clerk.

"Just that," the escort answered. "All of us have . . . er . . . preferences that might not be acceptable to everyone. America's leaders and opinion makers live in glass houses. Some of their exotic indulgences might seem, well, somewhat scandalous to narrow-minded people. Yet our leaders live under immense pressure. They deserve to be able to get away and, you know, do their own thing."

Dr. James Shelley knew exactly what the attendant was talking about. The tall, bronze-toned neurosurgeon had lived a relatively quiet existence until fame had descended on him. Shelley had written a book called *Brain Frontiers*, which was an argument for surgical, chemical, and electrical experimentation with the brain. In chapter after chapter he had espoused that only by improving the brain could man hope to survive an increasingly perilous future. Shelley's book had brought him to the attention of the nation and of Dr. Ernst Singlelaub, which was the reason Singlelaub had invited Shelley to the Glades of Bacchus.

Shelley had been despised by fellow hospital employees because of his arrogance. Even his patients' families hated him. He was often seen talking to them after surgery, still in his surgical scrub suit but bearing a book like *1001 Ways to Win in Las Vegas* under his arm.

Shelley had gone into neurosurgery for the money. Highly skilled, he easily financed his new life-style of womanizing and gambling.

The nattily attired physician had been warned by Ernst Singlelaub that the gathering at the Glades was business. But Singlelaub had also promised pleasures his guests would long remember.

Shelley smiled as he filled out the registration card.

Dr. P. T. Montgomery, the president of the American Society of Educational Theorists, had made the same discovery James Shelley was about to make: once past the reception clerk with the plastic smile, guests at the Glades of Bacchus would encounter the dazzling toga-clad staff, young men and women who were there to serve every whim of the self-inflated guests.

Montgomery's sexual preference was young men, a fact he had carefully concealed throughout his career as an educator.

In educational theory, Montgomery's preference was the behaviorist school. Montgomery dreamed of controlled classrooms stuffed with wide-eyed children sitting in uniform rows, their faces bathed in the gray-green dawn of a computer screen.

In Montgomery's vision, these children would have been predesigned through biological engineering to be the fastest learners a society could produce. They would work endlessly through learning programs, chaining bits of information together one after another. The pupils in Montgomery's fantasy would be reinforced at each success, encouraged to go on to the next link in the knowledge system programmed into the computers by the children's masters.

Montgomery had been honored with an invitation to Ernst Singlelaub's affair at the Glades because Singlelaub had once heard Montgomery speak. He had been impressed with P. T. Montgomery's dreams for American education. He understood, as Montgomery did, that if university education departments adopted Montgomery's text on teaching, then Montgomery's system could become the wave of educational theory immersing America.

At age fifty-five, P. T. Montgomery was the opposite of Dr. James Shelley. Their only similarity was the fact that they were both tall, Montgomery rising to six feet one inch. But beneath his pin-striped suits sprinkled with dandruff, Montgomery hid a broad girth. Because his fat collected just below his waistline, twenty years earlier his irreverent high school students had called him The Pear. His appearance often hindered sexual conquest at the homosexual bars he frequented during out-of-town speaking engagements. But P. T. Montgomery knew it wouldn't matter to the staff of the Glades of Bacchus. They were paid to overlook such trivialities.

Dr. Shelley didn't have to worry about professional efficiency from the Glades staff. The young woman who awaited him in his quarters after he checked in would be his willing servant.

"I'm Jana, a priestess of the Glades," she said to Shelley as he entered the room.

Shelley looked at the ravishing woman dressed in a toga. "You're a priestess? I didn't know this was a religious retreat." He smirked.

"Oh, but it is," she answered. "We worship your desires."

L. Archibald Porteous's only desire was for a glass of the richest wine he could find. Porteous sat now in his suite at the Glades, two doors north of James Shelley, and meditated on the fragrance of a Chateau Avignon 1932. Porteous, when not on duty as executive director of the National Association of Physiological Psychologists, was one of America's leading wine experts. Were it not for his commitment to eradicating superstition from the world, he would be a full-time wine connoisseur.

That was one reason he'd accepted the invitation of his longtime friend, Ernst Singlelaub, to come to the Glades conference. Singlelaub had promised Porteous a sampling of the rarest, most treasured wines, and an intellectual challenge. Porteous had worked with Singlelaub on many projects through the Institute for Human Advance. Singlelaub had never failed to spark the neurons connecting to the learning centers of Porteous's brain.

Porteous's love of wine was appropriate to his view that man was little more than an organism responding to stimuli. The small, balding man agreed with the famed scientist Sir Francis Crick that all newborns should be tested to determine if they qualify to be human.

Porteous had been angry all his life. He had decided long ago that the development of cells in the anger centers of his brain had been over stimulated by the childhood taunting he had received because of his dwarfish size. But Porteous converted that anger into a determined antagonism toward any lurking notions that there might be more to man than bone, flesh, and blood.

He had also discovered that ample amounts of his cherished wine would calm the neurons leading to the anger center. The synapses of his neurons would be quiet. No neurotransmitters would leap across the microscopic gaps between the neurons, carrying electrochemical stimuli to the brain.

Porteous's only problem was that his alcoholism became increasingly difficult to hide.

Concealment was also on Buck Prather's mind. His hands shook as he sought a hiding space somewhere in his suite at the Glades. Travel had become troublesome. At home, Prather had easily carved out his secure niches. In the dark basement of his house in Aspen, Colorado, no one would find his treasures. But now, far from Aspen and his secure basement, Prather wondered where he would stash his pouch of cocaine.

America's best-selling novelist lit a cigarette and scanned the suite. As the cigarette hung lower and lower in his mouth, a trail of ash followed him wherever he walked. Unaware that Singlelaub would have urged him to use his cocaine openly at the Glades, Prather swore in a frustrated, raspy voice. All mellow tones had been eroded by the smoking he had done for forty-five of his sixty years. Swearing was as common to Prather as eating. His profession was irreverence, and American sophisticates adored him for his cynical literary skill.

Prather was of medium build, his sallow, creased face crowned with shocks of gray hair hovering wildly over him like sinister thunder clouds. The hair, which seldom knew a comb—not even when he had gone to Stockholm to collect the Nobel Prize for literature—might have served as a warning of the perpetual lightning streaking through Prather's brain. He couldn't remember being free of hostility in thirty years. The origins of his hurricane of hate were lost.

TV talk-show hosts loved Prather. He always guaranteed a fiery, verbally explosive interview, full of bleeps the home audience could fill in.

The American press also lauded Prather, who had once been a crusty wire-service reporter. Although a number of newsmen were aware of his cocaine snorting, they concealed it, giving Prather many other platforms for his views in addition to the lavish stage set by his books.

Lately, his target had been religion. As a child, Prather was taken to church Sunday after Sunday. Unfortunately that church had been only a social institution. The edifice sat high on the slope looking down on the Monongahela River and downtown Pittsburgh. That was exactly the way the members regarded their city: they looked down on it in smug disdain. If a smelly slum dweller crawled up the slopes to the ornate church, the ushers blocked his entry into the building. Minorities were also banned.

Prather assumed the character of his childhood church to be the attitude of all organized religion. Ignorant of those churches putting their institutional life on the line every day, he generalized that all churches were twisted.

In novel after novel, Prather assaulted religion—especially Christianity. His massive tome on Tahiti depicted all missionaries as dour overlords who had come to crush the local culture.

Every pastor was a cunning, devious Elmer Gantry in Buck Prather's world.

Prather's skill in expressing his various hatreds had made him attractive to Ernst Singlelaub. Once Prather's fuse was lit, no one could stand up to him in debate. Not even Ernst Singlelaub.

Dr. Hyman C. Stelmetz toyed with the occult—not that he believed in it—but he was fascinated by apparent coincidences: astrologies that perfectly described persons by their star signs, prophecies that came true, ESP that really seemed to work. Stelmetz's hobby was to use his scientific genius to unlock the secrets of occult practices.

Although the brilliant geneticist didn't know it, a dark force had already found entry into the spiritual vacuum of his life. Like the man in the biblical parable, Stelmetz had long ago swept his house clean of the supernatural. He broke his parents' hearts when he turned from the Orthodox Judaism of his youth.

Unknowingly, Stelmetz had swept God from his life and opened a small crack in his spirit. Like water seeking its level, demons now poured into the crack they had blasted into a cavernous entry. By turning to the occult, even as a scientific curiosity, Stelmetz had unwittingly offered his life to the demons.

Stelmetz had gained entry to Singlelaub's soiree at the Glades of Bacchus because he knew more about genetic engineering than any man alive. From recombinant DNA to test-tube embryos, Stelmetz was the expert. Like Buck Prather, Stelmetz was a Nobel laureate. Stelmetz's award came for developing a 95-percent-accurate method to select the sex of a fetus *in utero*. His discovery had set off a series of other innovations putting him on the threshold of a method for determining body type—tall, short, lean, chunky. In short, a human race could be built to specifications.

All that was needed were the elite who would design those specifications. Stelmetz accepted the invitation to the Glades because Singlelaub promised him that he could become part of that elite.

But Stelmetz came to the Glades with a bias. He would design human beings who resembled himself.

As Stelmetz stepped from the shower in his plush suite, he dried his body in front of the full-length mirror on the bathroom door. He smiled, admiring what he saw. Hyman Stelmetz was sixty-three and looked forty-five. His body was lean and pliable. No stiff joints. No puffy pockets of fat. No choked arteries. In fact, he had showered because he had just finished his daily five-mile jog.

The breeze off Long Island Sound and the lightness of his step on the deep carpet made Stelmetz feel he was walking in the clouds. He pulled a robe over his venerated body and glided to a table where he had set up a Ouija board. Stelmetz believed that the answers spelled out by the board resulted from unconscious manipulation by the human subject, not some supernatural spirit. Still, it was fun to experiment.

"Will I create the human race in my own image?" Stelmetz asked the Ouija, closing his eyes. As he lightly touched the moveable pointer, it seemed to float across the face of the board. Finally, the pointer stopped on the word *yes*.

At that moment, a noise at the door caused Stelmetz to look up. A small white card appeared on the carpet, and he walked over to pick it up. Fingering the expensive card, he read:

Dr. Ernst Singlelaub
requests the pleasure of your company
at dinner
7:00 P.M.
in the Forum Room of the Glades of Bacchus.
A briefing will follow.

Ernst Singlelaub obviously intended the elegantly engraved invitation to be a souvenir. Stelmetz sensed the meeting he was about to attend would be historic.

THE image before Hyman Stelmetz sent tremors through his Jewish psyche. *Dr. Goebbels*, he thought. Stelmetz had never seen Ernst Singlelaub in person. When his host entered the Forum Room, Stelmetz was shocked at his resemblance to Josef Goebbels, Hitler's minister of propaganda.

Stelmetz scrutinized Singlelaub's wiry appearance. The man's leanness was not that of a runner. There was little muscle tone. Singlelaub appeared almost emaciated. His sharp nose and chin looked like the points of mountain peaks that had been chiseled into razorlike symmetry through years of exposure to hard winds. The white plain of Singlelaub's narrow face ascended into a tightly slicked head of black hair.

At Singlelaub's side, holding his arm, was a young woman with similar features. On Singlelaub, the appearance was sinister. Molded into a female face, the features produced a fragile beauty. The sharpness became delicacy, precision. The thinness became lithesomeness.

"Gentlemen," Singlelaub spoke. "I thank you for giving me your time for these few days. I welcome you to the Glades of Bacchus. The time we spend here may be the most significant in your lives. But we will discuss that after dinner. First, I want to introduce to you the most important person in my life."

James Shelley's hearing sharpened as he listened to Singlelaub's taut voice. Shelley knew he must discover the identity of the dark-haired, tempting sprite at Singlelaub's side.

"This is my daughter, Megan. She, of course, is not a guest at the Glades. The only women allowed to reside here are staff. She will, however, play a vital role in our meetings as she joins us during the day. Now, let's enjoy the meal the Glades has prepared for us, and after dinner, I'll tell you why I've asked you to come here."

"The issue that draws us together tonight is the world's survival," began Ernst Singlelaub. His guests, full of the Glades' most savory cuisine, had moved from the Forum Room to the library. They sat now in a semicircle of fat, leathery chairs with Ernst Singlelaub and his daughter at the center. Behind them stood an easel draped with a white cloth.

Hyman Stelmetz beat back his irritation at P. T. Montgomery's cigar, which smelled like a rope soaked in a septic tank. Montgomery's cigar had inspired Buck Prather to light a cigarette, adding to Stelmetz's rankle.

Dr. James Shelley continued his intense visual study of Megan Singlelaub.

"We have come to that moment in history," Singlelaub continued, "when, as Winston Churchill predicted before the House of Commons in 1955, 'safety is the sturdy child of terror, and survival the twin brother of annihilation.'

"As I speak, I need not remind you that the world's superpowers are poised to destroy the planet, if need be, to save their own frontiers from violation. Thomas Huxley, you may recall, described it all as a vast game—a game, I might add, in which there are no winners."

Singlelaub paused dramatically, then continued. "The game, said Huxley, is chess, and the world is the chessboard. The chess pieces are nature's phenomena—like the atom. The rules are the *laws* of nature. We cannot see our opponent. We know our adversary never fails to take advantage of any mistake we make. One slip and the world is crushed."

Tension built in the room. Prather lit another cigarette. James Shelley's eyes shifted to the left, away from Megan and toward her father. Montgomery discarded his rancid cigar as a smelly chunk of cold cinder. Porteous sipped slowly on his brandy. Stelmetz turned his attention from the works of Nostradamus, which held an honored position on the shelves just behind Singlelaub, and sat forward slightly.

Ernst Singlelaub revved up their motors for the daring proposal. "What makes all this so frightening—" Singlelaub took a breath for emphasis, "is that the chessboard of the world is trembling. It is impossible to predict where a knight, or king, or pawn will slide. The tremors are caused by expanding population, by growing economic disparity between rich and poor nations, by shrinking supplies of natural resources, by famine. Any one of these circumstances could light the fuse of nuclear conflict. We have come to the moment when all other concerns must be subordinated in the interests of survival."

Buck Prather, his natural cynicism stoked by his distaste for listening to speeches, removed the cigarette from his mouth and interrupted. "There's not a person in this room who doesn't know all that, Dr. Singlelaub. The problem is that nobody has an answer for it. It's a waste of time to go over the morbid state of this world one more time."

"But if you will be patient, Mr. Prather, I'm going to propose a solution—one in which you could have a role."

Singlelaub's guests eyed one another, some in disbelief, others in anticipation.

"All of us would agree," Singlelaub continued, "that we must have a new world order. And the central coordination of this order must be benevolently controlled and planned."

There was total agreement in the room with that position. Singlelaub had chosen each of his guests, partly because he had read their works or heard them favoring world government.

"I propose, however, to take the solution to the next step, which is absolutely essential for the new order's success," Singlelaub said, his voice building in intensity. "Nature moves too slowly. I propose that we come to its assistance and speed up evolution, build a bridge into the posthuman era. I propose that we create a new man to occupy the new order!"

Plunged into a chasm of silence, the guests pondered Singlelaub's statement.

"What do you mean by *posthuman?*" Montgomery asked.

"I believe Dr. Stelmetz can answer that for you. He has pushed genetic research to its most progressive extremes," replied Singlelaub.

"Posthuman," Stelmetz said, "refers to an organism with twenty-five times the intellectual ability of a genius with a 150 IQ occupying a physical structure in which even the brain cells replenish themselves."

"The brain cells?" Prather asked.

Now Porteous leaped into the enthralling discussion. "As the human body is now constructed, Mr. Prather, you have ten to thirteen billion brain cells. Those are all you'll ever have. When they die, they are irreplaceable."

Montgomery's interest piqued. "Dr. Singlelaub, how do you propose to create this world of posthumans?" he asked.

"Our friend Stelmetz is close to that technology now, and Dr. Porteous has the ability to develop the ideal psychological structure," responded Singlelaub.

"Then every person in society would be required to undergo the, uh, developmental program?" Montgomery asked.

"Correct," answered Singlelaub. "With birth processing clinics, every woman would be required to check in as soon as she discovered she was pregnant. Her fetus would be genetically adjusted *in utero*, and the baby would be delivered at the clinic."

"And what if the adjustment fails?" Porteous asked.

"A newborn would be tested at birth," Singlelaub replied. "If it failed the requirements, it would not be classified as a person, and it would be disposed of."

"I assume some type of board would determine the guidelines," Montgomery probed. "Won't that elite group be subject to corruption, throwing the world back into the instability you're trying to avoid?"

"That's why we must help nature develop the posthuman," Singlelaub responded. "I was in a position to closely observe that fool Prentiss Pearson. I know how a man can weaken. That's why we must have a new being for the new order."

A slight frown creased James Shelley's brow.

"But what about individual rights, Dr. Single-laub?" he asked. "Can you really force people to undergo genetic engineering?"

"Rights?" Singlelaub smirked. "In the new order, there will be no room for individual rights. In fact, they are irrelevant now. We must all sacrifice rights."

"Dr. Singlelaub," Hyman Stelmetz cut in, "do you have a structure for this new order?"

Singlelaub beamed. "That's why my daughter, Megan, is here. She earned her Ph.D. in political theory from the Ivy Brook Center for Strategic Studies. Her postgraduate study focused on developing political structures for an increasingly destabilized world. I'll let her respond."

James Shelley watched as Megan Singlelaub stood and took her place beside the easel. His heart quickened. She was dressed in a trim silk dress festooned with vertical pink stripes of various shades blending in a heather pattern. Her light makeup had just a hint of coral. Shelley marveled at the sight of a woman in perfect balance—incredible beauty complementing sweeping intelligence.

"In my research," Megan Singlelaub began, "I constructed a number of scenarios for the future and then built computer models of the types of governing structures that would best fit those projections."

Underneath Megan Singlelaub's poised, confident demeanor lived a woman of growing frustration. Megan idolized a father who simply did not know how to return her love. She never married, having betrothed herself to her research. Her passion was to develop the political structures that would fit her father's visions for a new world order. Success in that, she thought subconsciously, would win his admiration and love. So far, it had not seemed to, hence her frustration.

James Shelley did not see that frustration, nor would it have mattered. He found Megan the most desirable of the many women he had known. He knew he must have her.

The notion that he might even consider marrying a woman like Megan Singlelaub teased at Shelley. He smirked as he considered the advantages of marriage to a woman of Megan's calibre. He could feel the leathery caress of power that would come with being Ernst Singlelaub's son-in-law. Shelley simply was not capable of love that wasn't based on self-interest.

"Ironically," Megan continued, "my computer models showed that there were elements of accuracy in the structure proposed by Plato's *Republic*." A faint smile touched her lips. "So, I would like to show you the system under which a new world order could be created and maintained."

With a delicate but dramatic gesture, she reached to her right and uncovered a set of posters resting on the easel.

"Why do we need a new political order?" Buck Prather inquired arrogantly. "Why can't we just adapt what we already have?"

"What we already have, Mr. Prather, is capitalism and Marxism. Capitalism overemphasizes consumption, creating the destabilizing economic disparity in the world. Marxism stresses the classless society—though it has never achieved one. We don't need a classless society. In fact, we need three clear classes within the new order," Megan replied.

"Just three?" asked Stelmetz.

"Yes, Doctor," Megan answered. She pointed to one of the charts on the easel. "The highest class would be the Primary Beings."

"The ruling elite?" asked Shelley, now hypnotized by her.

"Precisely, Dr. Shelley."

Shelley's heart raced as she spoke his name.

"The second class of beings would be termed the Producers," Megan continued. "They would be the workers."

Singlelaub's guests studied all the lines flowing on Megan's chart, indicating the positions of the various subgroups.

"Finally," she said, "we will have the Peacemakers, the people responsible for security—the warriors, if you will. Depending on the success of developing the posthuman species, this class could be temporary since the higher order of beings will be peaceable," she explained. "Through genetic engineering, persons could be assigned a class before birth and designed with the correct physical and mental structures for their roles. Questions?"

"Yes, I have one for your father," blurted Montgomery. "Producing this new order and its posthuman citizen would require much time. Maybe generations. What do you propose to do in the interim?"

"Ah, that's where you play an important part, Dr. Montgomery," replied Singlelaub.

"Me?" Montgomery looked startled.

"Yes," Singlelaub answered. "You could develop an instructional system, which would reeducate the masses to accept the new survival order. Don't you see, gentlemen? I'm inviting all of you to spend the rest of your lives in the most exciting mission anyone could envision—*creating a new world!*"

Singlelaub scanned the faces of his guests.

"Porteous and Stelmetz, your assignment would be to develop the biology and genetic structure of the posthuman," said Singlelaub. "Your challenge, Dr. Shelley, would be to extend the skills of brain surgery, so that we could actually alter the mental states of existing populations until we can create the posthuman."

"What about me?" interjected Prather. "I'm no scientist."

"You're as skilled at your craft as the others are at theirs," Singlelaub replied.

"You mean as a writer?" Prather inquired.

"No, I mean as a molder of public opinion," Singlelaub said. "Your task, Mr. Prather, would be to generate public acceptance of this plan."

"Dr. Singlelaub, each of us has a career that is financially rewarding," Stelmetz said slowly. "The research and development costs to do what you're proposing would be astronomical."

"Money is no problem," Singlelaub assured

him. "I'm prepared to double your highest yearly income to date. Just think: you'll have unlimited research and development funds! It's a scientist's dream."

"Where's the money coming from?" asked Montgomery.

"I'm not at liberty to answer that specifically," Singlelaub replied.

"What about time? This will all require so much time," Porteous fretted.

"Our sponsors understand that and are willing to measure our work in decades. My goal is to develop a prototype community within ten years," Singlelaub answered. He looked down at his watch. "It's getting late, gentlemen. I've given you much to think about. I do not expect an answer now. Let's get some rest, and we'll resume our discussion in the morning."

After the meeting, James Shelley managed to catch up with Megan Singlelaub and walked her to her car.

"Your father is a man of remarkable vision," Shelley said, patronizing her. "What produces a man like Ernst Singlelaub?"

"War, I suppose," answered Megan.

"War?"

"My father was a war orphan. He saw his own parents murdered by the Nazis in Austria."

"I'm sorry. I didn't know about that," said Shelley.

"My father and his parents lived in Austria at the time of the Anschluss," Megan continued.

"The Anschluss?"

Megan looked at him with impatience. "The Anschluss, Dr. Shelley, was the takeover of Austria by the Nazis. There was little bloodshed. Unfortunately, some of it belonged to my father's parents."

When the two reached Megan's car, they leaned against it, fanned by the breeze off Long Island Sound. A full moon rained droplets of light on the slightly cresting waves. It was the kind of night that evoked memory, conversation, and romance, for Shelley at least—romance with Megan and the power she represented.

"My grandfather was a minor government official in Austria back then," Megan explained. "He was determined that his family would never live under the Nazis. So, one night he attempted to escape. The Nazis caught my grandparents and gunned them down in the street. They made my father watch. Since he was only five years old, the murder of his parents is his earliest memory."

"He must have carried immense pain all his life," Shelley said.

"Yes. That's the reason for the plan he shared tonight. For as long as I can remember, my father has been driven by a dream to see a world where Hitler and his Nazis could never again exist."

"How did your father rise from an Austrian war orphan to be one of the most powerful men in the United States?" Shelley asked.

"The Nazis placed my father in an orphanage," Megan continued. "He stayed there four years. Then one horribly cold night in February, he and some other children escaped. They foraged their existence off the streets until the Allies liberated Austria. The Americans placed him in another orphanage, and he emigrated to the United States when he was eighteen."

"Was your mother Austrian?"

Megan glanced down uncomfortably. "No," she answered. "My father met her after he graduated from Harvard. They lived together only a year."

"Is she still alive?" Shelley inquired.

"Yes, but there's little contact," replied Megan.

"Megan, thank you for sharing so much with me," Shelley said, almost tipsy in her presence, surrounded by the breeze and the moondance on the water.

Megan turned to get into her car and Shelley placed his hand under her chin, lifting her lips toward his. Megan quickly grabbed his hand, removing it from her chin.

"You must understand right up front, Dr. Shelley. Our relationship is and will be purely professional. I have no interest, no time, no energy for involvement with a man." Megan slammed the door of her small sports car and sped up the road toward her motel before James Shelley could wipe the sweat from his blushing brow.

At that precise moment, in his suite, Ernst Singlelaub was consummating a marriage of sorts. His partner that evening was Anatoli Grigorevich Zotin. The Russian was a departure from the cliched appearance of his KGB colleagues. Zotin was tall and combed his heavy black hair back tightly over his head. His clothing belied a trace of western decadence. The suit he wore was obviously hand-tailored, expensive. Having heard of the late Leonid Brezhnev's taste for luxuriant western attire, Zotin reasoned that if the Secretary of the U.S.S.R.'s Communist Party could clothe himself that way, so could he. After all, Zotin was the top Washington resident of Directorate T of the KGB.

"And when will you tell your colleagues of our partnership?" Zotin asked, his English virtually unrippled by accent.

"In time, Dr. Zotin. In time."

Singlelaub's reference to Zotin as *doctor* always pleased the KGB officer. He preferred that to his title of *colonel*. Most officers in Directorate T were scientists with advanced degrees. Directorate *T*, the second largest office of the First Chief Directorate of the KGB, was charged with the collection of scientific data.

"Will they cooperate if they know the KGB is funding the project?" Zotin asked.

"I chose men of pure science. Their research comes before politics. Your government is being most generous, and when those men see the money you provide, they will work with gratitude."

"I sense, though, that you would have preferred financing from . . . other sources." Zotin felt he should test Singlelaub's own motives.

"I would wish that my adopted country, America, could have the sophisticated intelligence to appreciate what we shall achieve. But it does not. Thus, I admire the Soviet perception that could understand and respect my proposal. You need not worry. I am completely loyal to whoever provides the means to carry out my work."

Zotin had no worries about loyalty, but not because he trusted Singlelaub. Every day from this moment, Singlelaub would be under surveillance by the KGB.

"Then I must report back to Moscow that you are ready to commence operation."

"Are you returning to Washington?"

"Yes. I must communicate with Moscow through a secure channel. The safest line is at the Embassy. They've sent a plane for me."

Two hours later, in the lap of night, Zotin entered the basement of the Russian Embassy. In Russian, he ordered the communications officers on duty to establish a secure link with a certain Directorate T office in Moscow. Zotin wanted voice contact. The officer activated a scrambler telephone that garbled Zotin's voice as it bounced off a satellite twenty-three thousand miles above earth, then unraveled his words in the ear of his Moscow contact.

In Moscow it was 11:00 A.M. At a Directorate T research center near the Belyoruski railroad station in Moscow, a sharp buzz penetrated the tense silence of the facility's situation room. A duty officer answered the call and immediately summoned Yevgenni Sergeevich Poperechny, chief of the research center.

"Da!" Poperechny said into the phone.

"I have signed the contract," Zotin reported in Russian. "We are ready to begin."

"I have consulted with the State Committee on Science and Technology, and they have supported our request to the politburo. The secretary gives his permission." Poperechny almost sounded jubilant as he contemplated a massive KGB operation right under the Americans' noses.

That was the end of the conversation. Zotin smiled as he rose from the desk with the special telephone. He would go home now to his townhouse in Georgetown, and he would sleep well.

AT 4:00 P.M. on Friday, June 22, ten years after Singlelaub's meeting at the Glades of Bacchus, Mark Tilman's old car sped down the dry streets of Albuquerque.

Though he didn't fully understand, Tilman's probing spade had struck a portion of the roots that had sprouted a decade earlier at the Glades. He knew he must tell Trina immediately.

Tilman tugged the car into the parking lot of El Condor Mexican Restaurante. Trina had only been working an hour and wouldn't get off until midnight. Weekends at Albuquerque's favorite Mexican restaurant always meant extra hours.

Tilman's information couldn't wait.

Inside the restaurant, a curt college-age girl met him. "Table for one, sir?" she asked.

"Uh, no," answered Tilman. "I've got to see Trina Escobar."

"She's busy right now," the young woman replied.

"But it's urgent. It's about her brother."

Immediately the hostess summoned Trina.

"Mark, what is it? I don't have long," she said. "We're pretty busy."

Tilman pulled Trina into an alcove leading to the public phones and rest rooms. "Trina, tell me again what the authorities told you when your brother disappeared," he pleaded.

"You mean about his escape?"

"Yes."

"Well, they said that he was on a work detail from the county jail and just walked away."

"Who told you that?" asked Tilman.

"Sheriff Jeters."

"The sheriff told you that?" Tilman asked, surprised.

"That's right," Trina said. "Why should that be so amazing?"

"Because the sheriff lied to you. That's why."

"What are you talking about, Mark?"

"There was *no* work detail that day," Tilman answered.

"No work detail?"

"Absolutely none. I checked with a friend of mine at the county jail. There was a freak desert thunderstorm on the day the sheriff told you Manuel escaped. Rained all day. No work details went out at all."

"Mark, why would Sheriff Jeters not tell us the truth?"

"The word, Trina, is *lied*. Sheriff Jeters lied to us. I think he's trying to hide something."

"Trina!" the hostess shouted.

"Yes?" Trina turned.

"Look," the embattled hostess said, "you've got to make it quick. This place is filling up, and we can't keep up with your tables. Geraldo's asking where you are."

"Who's Geraldo?" Tilman asked Trina.

"Oh, he's the night manager. Stays mad. But I don't care. I've got to get to the bottom of this craziness."

"Look, Trina, I understand," Tilman said. "I've got two weeks of vacation coming. If you can take some time off, we'll go back to Alamogordo and start tracing Manuel's path. All we know is what he kept uttering about some city under the sands." A look of determination came over his face. "We'll keep at it until we find that city. Then maybe we'll know what happened to Manuel."

"Oh, Mark, thank you," said Trina. She reached an arm around his thick neck and kissed him lightly on the cheek, then turned quickly and ran back to her tables.

When Mark Tilman left El Condor Restaurante an almost-forgotten flow warmed the core of his emotions. He tried denying it came from the brief hug and kiss from Trina, but he knew he was lying to himself.

Carlos Mateos didn't like pretending. The sheriff of Lincoln County, New Mexico, held office by virtue of his reputation of being honest as a dry desert wind. Now Sheriff Mateos stared at the odd-looking couple seated across from him at his office at Carrizozo. The ponderous, tousled Anglo man and the slender, dark Mexican-American woman seemed too nice to deceive.

Mateos didn't have many high-level contacts, not even from the state capitol. He had been impressed, then, when an army colonel arrived at his office one day to ask his help in protecting a sensitive project at White Sands. The colonel said that the United States Government had contracted with a private firm to mine a cache of uranium located in the desert there. The magnitude of the site's uranium supply demanded absolute secrecy.

Colonel Billy Samuels had given Mateos code identifications in the event the sheriff had to reach him. The intrigue had delighted Mateos, especially when the army officer instructed the sheriff to refer to him as *"Darkhorse."* Mateos didn't know, however, that although Colonel Samuels really was in the United States Army, and was indeed based at White Sands, he was also a KGB agent. Mateos was simply being used as part of an elaborate wall of security the KGB was erecting around the White Sands project. That wall reached all the way to the KGB moles in the Pentagon.

"Yes, Mr. Tilman, I remember the report my deputies filed about you finding the strange man out in the desert," said Mateos. He turned to Trina. "I'm sorry about your brother's death."

"Sheriff Mateos, we're trying to retrace Manuel's steps," Tilman informed him.

"Well, there's a lot of hot, dry sand out there, Mr. Tilman," Mateos responded. "How do you know where to start?"

Trina answered. "We know my brother was in no condition to walk far. Whatever happened to him must have occurred near where Mark found him."

"Right," Tilman interrupted. "So we plan to start from that position and look until we find something."

"Just what do you expect to find?" Mateos asked.

"That's where we hope you can help us," Tilman said. "Manuel kept saying something about a city under the sands. Do you have any idea what he could have been talking about or what we should be looking for?"

"Uh, no, not really," Mateos answered, wanting the interview to be over so he could stop pretending. The disappointment he saw in Trina Escobar's face hurt him.

"Well, if you think of anything, Miss Escobar and I have rooms at the Hacienda Motel," said Tilman. "Please give me a call there if anything turns up."

As Mateos watched Tilman and Trina leave, he picked up the phone and dialed a closely guarded number.

"Code 38-Alpha," a male voice answered.

"Please state your code and the party you're calling."

"This is Code 9-Gamma," said Mateos. "I'm calling Darkhorse."

Mateos listened as the phone clicked, then sounded a high-pitched tone.

"Darkhorse," came the answer. "Report please."

"I've just been visited by a Mark Tilman and Trina Escobar. They were asking about Manuel Escobar."

"Tilman is the subject who found Escobar in the desert?"

"That's correct."

"Their intentions?"

"To retrace Escobar's steps until they find out what might have happened to him."

"I see," said Darkhorse. "Maintain surveillance of Mr. Tilman and Miss Escobar. If they seem close to any discoveries, please notify me immediately. Anything else?"

"That's all."

"Thank you," said Darkhorse, giving the only indication that the voice on the other end might be human.

"Who would have thought of finding a Chinese restaurant in Carrizozo, New Mexico?" Trina joked as she and Mark Tilman were escorted into the House of Wong.

"Refugees," Tilman answered.

"What do you mean?"

"Chinese refugees from Vietnam," said Tilman. "When the communists took over Vietnam, many of the Chinese there fled to America. They gave us platoons of Chinese restaurants. The country's drowning in egg rolls."

The light banter between Tilman and Trina thinly veiled the discouragement both of them felt. They had expected more help from Sheriff Mateos.

"Mark," Trina said softly, "I'm so grateful you are taking this time to help me. I know vacation time is valuable. And you're having to spend it away from Danny."

"Don't worry about Danny. My mother was delighted to have him visit her in Carlsbad. She's been terribly lonesome since my dad died."

Tilman winced a bit as he said that. His own pain at losing Donna had helped him understand his mother's grief, but it had been an awful price to pay. He didn't hurt as badly when he was with Trina though, and he ached to let her know that. As they sat silently at the table, sipping hot tea and waiting for their order, Tilman toyed with the idea of telling Trina that he cared for her. But he couldn't handle rejection. At forty-six, he was not handsome and lean. Still, he had to find courage to speak his mind.

"Besides," stammered Tilman.

"Besides?" Trina looked at him curiously.

"Yes, besides, taking this time off just gives me that much more time to spend with you." *There*, thought Tilman, *I got it out, and Trina didn't leave the table in disgust.*

"What exactly does that mean?" she asked.

"It means, Trina—" He gasped for words. "It means that I have more than a journalistic interest in your circumstances."

Cumbersome, awkward, he thought. It had been a long time since he had tried to be romantic. He could hurl words at a typewriter faster than the machine could keep pace. But he always had problems speaking his thoughts.

"I don't think I understand," Trina replied.

"What I'm trying to say, Trina, is that I really like you," Tilman stuttered.

"I like you, too, Mark. You're a very nice man to help me so much."

"No . . . I mean I care for you a lot deeper than that. I haven't felt like this about anyone since Donna died." *That was horrible,* Tilman told himself, expecting her to stab him with a chopstick.

Instead, a small tear fell from her eye.

Summoning incredible courage, Tilman reached for Trina's hand, and even found the strength to gaze steadily into her eyes. Just as he was about to admit that he was in love with her, a smiling Chinese waiter plopped down steaming dishes of pepper steak and sweet-and-sour chicken. The bright red sauce from the chicken dish spilled onto Trina's hand. Giving a slight squeal, she jerked her hand away and quickly wiped off the sauce with her napkin.

Tilman might have expected such a scene from his bumbling attempt to renew romance. His love affair with Trina Escobar had been drowned in sweet-and-sour sauce.

As they ate, conversation drifted again to Manuel.

"Mark, I hate to sound like Sheriff Mateos, but where *do* you plan to start looking for Manuel's tracks. What are we looking for?"

"I don't really know," Tilman answered between bites. "I keep hearing Manuel's tortured words. I can't get them out of my mind."

"You mean about the city under the sands?"

"That's it, Trina! Why didn't you just say city under the *sand*? Wouldn't that have been more natural?"

"I suppose," Trina said. "But I was just repeating what Manuel said."

"Exactly," replied Tilman, forgetting his food. "That was what was so consistent about Manuel's phrase. He used the plural for *sand* every time he said the word."

"What does that have to do with anything?"

"*Sand* could be anywhere," Tilman explained. "It's a general term. But *sands* is more specific. Trina, if I said I worked at the sands, where do you think I'd be referring to?"

Trina furrowed her brow, thinking for a moment. "I guess if you were talking about a place in New Mexico, I'd think of White Sands Missile Range." Suddenly she looked pale. "You're not thinking that whatever happened to Manuel had something to do with White Sands, are you Mark?"

"That's exactly what I'm thinking, and that's exactly where I'm heading first thing in the morning."

The rising sun set the horizon ablaze as Mark Tilman drove from Alamogordo to the Holloman Air Force Base headquarters within White Sands Missile Range. It was early Tuesday morning, June 26. Tilman wanted to gather all available information as early as possible. Then he and Trina would spend the rest of the day tracking it down.

They had decided that Tilman should make the journey alone. His press card would give him access to the base, but Trina's presence might complicate possible interviews.

Not long after motoring out of Alamogordo, Tilman approached the guard station at Holloman. A young sentry, looking as if he had spent the night pressed between two very stiff boards, walked out of the guard hut and waved Tilman to a stop.

"Good morning, sir. May I help you?" asked the guard.

"Yes. I'm Mark Tilman with the *Albuquerque Evening Star*. I'd like to see your public information officer."

"Identification, please."

Tilman, already holding his wallet in his hand, pulled out his press card.

The sentry examined it. "Do you have an appointment?" he asked.

"No. I need to see the PIO on a matter that came up rather urgently last night after the information office had closed."

"I see. One moment, please."

The sentry ducked back into his hut, carrying Tilman's press card. Tilman could see the guard was talking on a telephone. Within seconds, he hung up and returned to Tilman, who was still sitting in his car.

The soldier gave back Tilman's press card and handed him a visitor's clip-on badge. "Major Chisholm will see you in the information office, sir."

Inside the administration building, a reception-ist directed Tilman down a sterile corridor to the public information office. Dave Chisholm, the base information officer, was waiting for him. Chisholm was a slight man, dressed in Air Force blue.

"How may I assist you?" Chisholm asked briskly after the men had introduced themselves.

In his earlier years of reporting, Mark Tilman would have practiced some deception in respond-ing to such a question. He would have never re-vealed his true intentions in an interview.

But since he became serious about following the Bible, lies were hard to fashion. There were times when Tilman saw that as one disadvantage to being a Christian journalist. Nonetheless, he was serious about his commitment. He told Chisholm about Manuel Escobar.

"What do you think that has to do with Hol-loman Air Force Base?" Chisholm asked when Tilman finished.

"It has something to do with White Sands in general," answered Tilman.

"Then you need to be forty miles from here, over at White Sands headquarters."

"No, I don't think I should," Tilman replied. "When I found Manuel, he was wandering around near Carrizozo. He couldn't have walked far. Whatever happened to him happened up there somewhere."

"Mr. Tilman, there's *nothing* up there. It's what we call an impact area. It's a target zone. Closed to the public."

"What's *underneath* those sands up there?" Tilman probed.

"There are no underground installations in that part of the Missile Range." Chisholm answered, annoyed.

"The atomic bomb site is in that area, isn't it?" Tilman asked.

"That's right."

"Couldn't there have been some kind of underground monitoring facility in the region?"

"In 1945, when that bomb went off, Dr. Oppenheimer and his staff were in bunkers 5.7 miles from ground zero. But the bunkers were mostly above ground. No, I'm sorry, there's no city under the sands, as Mr. Escobar put it. I hate to break off our interview, but I've got some deadlines to meet."

The two men shook hands perfunctorily, and Tilman left feeling dejected.

When he was gone, Chisholm picked up his phone and placed a call. It was his duty to report all interviews to base intelligence.

"Colonel Ripley? This is Chisholm in the public information office. I just had a reporter in here asking about underground installations in the Trinity area."

Tilman's inquiry set off a verbal chain reaction at the White Sands Missile Range. As soon as Ripley hung up from talking to Chisholm, he placed a call to Colonel Billy Samuels in the National Range Operations Office, known at White Sands as NRO. Ripley had only been told that a secret uranium recovery project was underway in the Trinity area. All inquiries regarding that part of White Sands were to be referred to Colonel Samuels.

Samuels grabbed his jacket and hurriedly drove toward Alamogordo. Stopping at a farmhouse on the far side of the city, he picked up a secure phone and placed a call to a carefully guarded and often changed number in Washington.

"We have a new tracer on AB-2," he said to the party who answered and gave the proper identification code. "A Mark Tilman made inquiry this morning at Holloman about some phrase used by AB-2. The phrase was 'city under the sands.' Tilman asked the PIO at Holloman if he knew anything about underground installations."

"I understand," said the voice in Washington. "It sounds like Mr. Tilman is getting too close to Trinity II. We'll take over from here."

I've got to find a telephone, thought Tilman as he drove out of Holloman. Seven miles from the base's gates, Tilman pulled into a dusty service station and entered a battered phone booth with cracked and broken-out glass. Thumbing through the tattered phone list he carried in his shirt pocket, Tilman dialed the number of the only person in New Mexico who might be able to help him find some answers: Merritt Bonner.

"Why the big hurry to set up a meeting with this Mr. Bonner?" Trina felt rushed when Tilman returned to Alamogordo, instructing her to be ready to meet Bonner for lunch.

"Honey, I'm telling you, Merritt Bonner is New Mexico incarnate. He's been editor, publisher, and proprietor of the *Alamogordo Gazette* for at least thirty years. If anybody on earth knows what may or may not be at White Sands, it's Merritt Bonner."

"You sound like you've been friends with Mr. Bonner a long time," Trina said as she and Tilman drove to their noontime meeting.

Tilman smiled. "Yeah. I've known Merritt at least a dozen years. We used to work together on committees in the New Mexico Press Association. By the way, don't let his size fool you. He's a feisty little fellow."

When Tilman pointed out Bonner in the Holiday Inn lobby, Trina understood Tilman's comment about Bonner's size. Bonner may have been New Mexico incarnate, but the wispy, balding little man didn't look like a toughened range rider. He looked as if he would have been more at home in a New York gourmet restaurant eating quiche and drinking white wine than sampling the Holiday Inn lunch buffet.

All that signalled New Mexico in Bonner's appearance was his costume: a buff-colored western shirt, brown Levi's, and boots. At his neck, Bonner wore a string tie, encircled by a clasp of turquoise and silver. A cigarette dangled from his thin lips.

After they exchanged greetings and Tilman introduced Trina to Bonner, they headed for the buffet line. Tilman, waging his perpetual war between the guilt of gluttony and the temptation of food, heaped his plate with fried chicken, creamed potatoes, stewed tomatoes, and cole slaw.

"What are you going to drink?" Bonner asked when they were seated.

"I'll go with the iced tea," Tilman responded as Trina nodded her agreement.

"You ought to have a beer," Bonner added. "It's the only thing that'll put a dent in this heat."

"Uh, no. I guess I'll just put out my fire with the iced tea," Tilman responded.

"Oh, yeah, I forgot," Bonner said. "I heard you got religion. What a pity. One more master drinker down the tube. I remember some pretty wild times you and I shared at Press Association conventions. Come on, Tilman, why you can't have a beer?" he prompted. "The Bible is full of wine drinking."

"I guess my faith gives me a new perspective

on the responsibility I have for my body," Tilman answered.

"What does that mean?" Bonner asked, taking a long swig from the frosty glass of beer the waitress had set before him.

"It means my body is a gift from God, and I'm supposed to use it for his glory," Tilman explained. "Merritt, I was very close to being an alcoholic. I couldn't glorify God with the booze. Besides, I had to think about what I was teaching my son."

"Glorify God?" Bonner chuckled. "I guess you're going to take care of your body and glorify God with that mountain of creamed potatoes."

Tilman winced at the truth in Bonner's words. Gluttony was definitely one area over which he had not yet gained victory.

"What are you and this lovely lady doing down here, anyway?" Bonner asked.

Relieved to be off the hook, Tilman quickly recounted Manuel's story. Concluding, he told Bonner, "I've checked with the Lincoln County sheriff and the people at Holloman, and they all say there's no underground facility *anywhere* on the eastern side of White Sands. Yet that's where we found Manuel. And that city under the sands was all he could talk about."

"Well, somebody's lying to you," Bonner replied in his quick, terse way.

"What?" Tilman asked, glancing at Trina.

"I happen to know there are extensive underground areas along White Sands' eastern perimeter," Bonner explained. "You ought to know there are miles and miles of old mining shafts all over this region—silver, copper, gold."

"But I thought those old mines caved in when the bomb was set off in 1945," Tilman said.

"That's what they say, but it isn't true. Mark, you're from Carlsbad. You've been in the Big Room down in the Caverns."

"Sure."

"Remember the dimensions of the Big Room?"

"I've taken relatives and friends down there so many times I know the stats better than a professional guide," Tilman replied. "The Big Room is 4,000 feet long and more than 600 feet wide. The ceiling is as high as 285 feet."

"Excellent," Bonner said. "Mark, there's another Big Room, not fifteen miles from the Trinity site where the first atomic bomb was exploded. That chamber is three times the size of Carlsbad's Big Room.

Tilman looked again at Trina, then back at Bonner. "But didn't the bomb damage or destroy the room?" Tilman asked.

"No," Bonner said quickly. "In 1957, I interviewed some old-timers who'd worked at the Trinity site when the bomb was tested. They told me the government had completely reworked that huge cavern. They lined it with steel and lead. Built giant supports for the ceiling. According to those men, the roof was buttressed like a cathedral."

"But why?" Trina finally spoke. "That must have cost millions."

"One objective the government had, in addition to seeing if the bomb would work, was to see if life could survive in underground shelters less than twenty miles from ground zero," Bonner replied. "One of the men I interviewed had actually worked on the test room, as he called it. There were dozens of volunteers in there when the bomb went off, and they survived. Mark, that room is still down there somewhere."

For a long time, Mark Tilman ate in silence, pondering what he had heard. Finally, he spoke. "Merritt, somehow I've got to see that chamber."

"No way. It's in one of White Sands' most restricted areas. It's an impact zone for the missiles. They've pounded that chamber with missiles twenty-five times to see just how much it could take."

"But there's got to be a way in there," Tilman said.

Bonner stared intently at a bite of stewed tomatoes on his fork and shifted in his chair. He had to tell Tilman what he knew.

"Mark, there *is* a way in."

Tilman took a quick sip of iced tea, put down his glass, and looked at Bonner.

"My brother's a spelunker, and he found a cave passage that leads all the way back under White Sands, almost to the Trinity site. He found it by accident when he was exploring a small cave at the foot of Nogal Peak. It's near the western edge of Lincoln National Forest. Actually, the little cave is the entrance to a whole network of caverns. He's been more than ten miles up in there, all the way to White Sands by *his* calculations.

We never told anybody else about the cave at No-gal Peak . . . until today."

"Bonner, that's great! Can we get your brother to lead us into the cavern?"

"No, Mark, you can't. . . ."

"Why not?"

"Because the last time he went into that passage, he didn't come back."

MAJOR Vladimir Fedorovick Trek-
helebov cursed the day he was assigned to Line X
in Washington. Line X was the designation of
KGB officers working in the field for Directorate
T. Normally, KGB agents were pleased to draw
Washington duty. But not Trekhelebov. Mother
Russia clutched him to her bosom like a giant
babushka.

In Washington, creeping through rush hour
traffic on a hot summer morning was like riding
a snail. Trekhelebov tried to cool his tempes-
tuous mind with thoughts of cool June days in
Moscow and the absence of traffic jams. Americans could say what they wished about their
opulence, of which the automobile was the prime

symbol, but Trekhelebov preferred the wide, sparsely traveled lanes of Moscow.

This morning, the KGB officer headed north to the small village of Yellow Springs, Maryland, where the KGB had an estate. Trekhelebov always smirked as he thought of the grand house. To the neighbors, it was a rich horse farm. The couple who lived there, American employees of the KGB, carried out an ostentatious capitalist life-style. No one would have guessed the farm was the prime center for KGB activity in the eastern United States.

As he entered the mansion, Trekhelebov was ushered quickly into the library, then through a concealed door behind a bookcase to a room festooned with electronic gear. There, he greeted the special representative of the Soviet ambassador to the United States and an agent from the KGB's Directorate S, which controlled all KGB illegals working overseas. Hovering at the edge of the room like a sinister specter was the Directorate T's Anatoli Grigorevich Zotin. It had been Zotin who had negotiated the original agreements between Ernst Singlelaub and the KGB. Each person in the room knew that Zotin would monitor his every decision. He was determined nothing would go wrong with this project.

"We're going to establish contact with Dzhersinsky Square," said the special representative in his characteristic abrupt style. "We must solve the problem in New Mexico."

Trekhelebov knew the problem centered on

the nosy couple who were getting too close to Trinity II. He also knew that contact with Dzhersinsky Square KGB headquarters in Moscow meant that an assassination of American citizens would be proposed. Such action would never be undertaken without specific instructions from Moscow.

The communications center at the Yellow Springs mansion was cleared of all unnecessary personnel. Moscow was on the line on an amplifier.

"The simple fact is that the subjects are getting too close to Trinity II," said the special representative.

"How could this Tilman have become suspicious about an underground installation at White Sands?" asked the man from Directorate S.

"It doesn't matter!" the special representative shot back. "The fact is, he suspects something."

"If we remove Tilman, we must also eliminate the woman." The voice from Moscow sounded hollow over the loudspeaker.

"That's correct," answered the special representative.

"How can we kill two people without raising suspicion?" Directorate S inquired.

Trekhelebov smiled. "I wish all our Trinity problems were that simple. We have the subjects under constant surveillance. They're spending a great deal of time together. Any accident that affects one of them will of necessity affect the other."

"We agree they're too close," said Moscow.

"Then we're ready to vote?" asked the special representative.

Wry irony washed over Trekhelebov. Democracy was not the pattern of the KGB. But this operation was so delicate that the special representative wanted to be sure the blame was spread if anything went wrong. Their conversation was being recorded in Moscow. Dzhersinsky Square would always know who authorized the operation.

"Da," Moscow replied. "Let us vote."

The special representative sighed. "The proposal is that subjects Tilman and Escobar be eliminated. The ambassador votes da."

"Moscow says da."

"Directorate S agrees."

"Da," said Trekhelebov. As he cast his vote of assent, Trekhelebov saw Zotin standing in the shadows slowly nodding his head.

The Sierra Blanca Ski Area looked ruefully barren in the smoldering morning heat of Wednesday, June 27. As Merritt Bonner and his friends drove by it, Mark Tilman felt there was a sadness about the ski resort's deserted slopes.

The night before, Tilman, Trina, and Bonner had decided to explore the mouth of the cave at Nogal Peak. They left Alamogordo at dawn, drove the eighty-five miles up to Carrizozo, then turned eastward on Highway 380 for a short distance, and finally headed south through the little town of Nogal.

The trio stuffed into Bonner's Land Rover wasn't experienced in intelligence operations. Otherwise they might have noticed the blue Chrysler that had been following them all the way from Alamogordo.

Soon Nogal Peak came into sight. It loomed over Lincoln National Forest. Merritt Bonner drove straight to the cave at the foot of the mountain.

Because there was no traffic to hide behind, the blue Chrysler had fallen far behind, but its two occupants still had Bonner's Land Rover in sight.

"This hole's barely big enough for me to crawl through," Tilman said, as he walked briskly toward the cave entrance.

Tilman clutched Trina's hand tightly as they climbed over the rocky terrain to stand inside the cave.

"My brother was almost as big as you are, Mark," Bonner said. "But he found the cave got larger about a hundred yards inside. I'm afraid we'll have to bend and crawl a bit at first, though."

Trina almost tripped on a loose rock. "I wish I'd brought some hiking boots," she said.

Bonner moved to the front of the little group, a large lantern in his hand. "We'll go in just far enough to get the feel of the cave. It'll take some time to get equipment for a real exploration."

Once inside the dark passage, as the yellow

light bounced off the rough walls, Bonner battled a stifling fear of stumbling over his brother's body. Bonner squelched the fear before it locked his feet.

As the three eased deeper under the sands, the men following them crouched behind boulders, watching the mouth of the cave.

"Are we going in?" the tall one asked.

"No," answered his ally. "They're not going in far. They don't have any gear. They'll be out in a few minutes."

"Maybe we ought to go in and knock them off in the cave," the taller man suggested.

"No, that wouldn't be a good move. The lead guy seems to know where he's going. We don't. We'd be working in the dark." He wiped the perspiration from his forehead with the back of his hand. "Don't worry. In this wilderness, they'll give us a good opportunity to stage an accident."

When the three emerged from the cave, it was obvious they were continuing a conversation begun inside.

Tilman was speaking. "Merritt, I can understand your reluctance to go back in there but we really need you to guide us."

"That's right, Mr. Bonner," Trina Escobar agreed. "While we're searching for the answer to Manuel's death, we might get some idea about what happened to your brother."

Merritt Bonner turned away from them, looking straight at the boulder where the two spies hid.

"All right," Bonner said at last. "I'll go with

you. We'll have to go back to Alamogordo and put together some spelunking equipment."

"Great!" said Tilman.

"But before heading back," Bonner continued, "I know of a fire fighters' road that leads up to the peak. We can get a sighting of White Sands from up there, and a sense of direction. Later, we'll bring a compass and sight in the direction of Trinity. Then, if we have to choose between passages down in the cave, at least we'll have a better idea which direction to take."

The three jumped into Bonner's Land Rover and drove up the rutted dirt road on the mountain slope. Far behind, the spies followed in the Chrysler.

About 125 yards from the top of Nogal Peak, the road ended. Tilman, Trina, and Bonner got out and hiked toward an outcropping of rock that could serve as a viewing platform. As they disappeared into a thicket of trees, the spies quickly crept to Bonner's vehicle, lifted the hood, and drained brake fluid from the master cylinder. Dashing back into the forest, they were on the road toward the village of Nogal before the explorers returned to the Land Rover.

"Whew!" Tilman almost collapsed on the front seat. "I think I'm glad we're going to take that walk underground. The sun out here would parboil us."

"It's obvious you haven't spent much time underground," said Bonner. "After the first day, you'll be begging to see the sun."

Bonner started the vehicle. To turn around, he

had to pull forward, back up and turn several times before he could head back down the mountain road. Each time he hit the brakes, a little more of the remaining fluid drained away. Not long after Merritt Bonner started down the mountain, he tried to slow the vehicle. He had no brakes. Gathering speed, the Land Rover plummeted down the road raising a tide of dust. Bonner fought to maintain control. He watched the speedometer climb at a dizzying pace, forty miles per hour. Then forty-five. His heart pounded. The road ahead curved back to the left. On the right, a sheer precipice dropped to five hundred feet below.

"Hang on!" Bonner yelled. He had only one option. And there was no guarantee for that. To the left, the rocky mountainside rose up out of a deep drainage ditch. Bonner knew his only hope was to cut the speeding car into the gully.

Quickly, he whipped the wheel to the left. The car zipped off the road, crashed on the upper edge of the ditch, then careened downward. Trina screamed. The rear end of the Land Rover twisted into the rocky face of mountain. The vehicle flipped over, then came to a stop upside down in the ditch.

Tilman knew he was alive. Pain didn't exist in heaven, and he was enveloped in pain. His inner torment, however, became even greater than his physical pain. Trina Escobar and Merritt Bonner were silent.

Tilman couldn't see Trina. She had been sitting in the back. Bonner lay crumpled on his

SIX

shoulder. A massive head gash bathed the ceiling
in blood, but he was breathing.

"Trina?" Tilman gasped. It seemed to devour
his remaining energy. He collapsed in a heap of
nausea and pain.

"Trina? *Trina!*" Mark Tilman crawled up the
dark hole of his unconsciousness, still calling the
name of the woman who had relit his heart.

As Tilman groped toward the back seat, he became aware of two things: he felt as if a dragon
were trying to eat its way out of his head, and
there was no back seat!

Tilman's eyelids felt like lead slabs. Straining,
he got them open, but quickly he had to shut
them again. The Land Rover's shell was gone.
There was only piercing, devastating brightness.

He heard himself scream with the burning
pain. "Trina, *Trina!*"

Another sensation now curled into his brain.
Odor. Sharp. Pungent. Sterile.

And there were voices. Someone was speaking
to him. "Mr. Tilman? Can you understand me?"

Tilman fought to concentrate on the voice.
"Yes," he whispered.

"You're all right," the voice said.

Tilman tried again to open his eyes, to focus on
the face. He could barely make out the pleasant
features of a young man. As far as Mark Tilman
could tell, the man had no body, just a head float-
ing in space. Fleetingly, Tilman thought that perhaps the face was that of an angel. *Maybe I have
died,* thought Tilman.

"Easy, Mr. Tilman," the head said. "I'm Dr. Sanchez. You're in the emergency room at Alamogordo Hospital."

Tilman tried to raise up. "Trina Escobar—did you get Trina?"

"Yes, she's also here. And so is Mr. Bonner."

Oh, yes. Merritt Bonner, thought Tilman. In his desperation to find out about Trina, he had forgotten all about Bonner.

"You are three lucky people," said Dr. Sanchez. "The forest service patrol has increased its runs through Lincoln National Forest because of the drought. If they hadn't found you, you'd have all died in that heat. You and Mr. Bonner have mild concussions. Apart from some pretty bad cuts and bruises, Miss Escobar is fine. She was the luckiest of all three of you because she was sitting in the back seat."

"I ... I don't believe in luck," Tilman muttered. "God was with us."

Dr. Sanchez turned and grinned at the nurse in the emergency room cubicle with him. "Call it whatever you wish," he said. "But we'll have you and Mr. Bonner out of here in a few days."

"No," Tilman replied quickly, struggling to raise his voice above a whisper. "I've got to get out today. I only have one more week of vacation. That's not enough time to get spelunking equipment and find the city under the sands!"

"You're going to have to be calm, Mr. Tilman," said Dr. Sanchez, apparently assuming his patient was on the fringe of delirium. "Until I see how your brain is doing, I can't give you any sedation. So you've got to control yourself."

"But please help me," Tilman pled, still not opening his eyes. "I've got to help Trina."

"Mr. Tilman, *you're* going to have to help *us* get you back on your feet. Now just relax, and we'll transfer you to a room."

Mark Tilman couldn't answer. He found himself again slipping down into the pit of unconsciousness.

AT 11:00 A.M. Monday, July 2, six days after Merritt Bonner's Land Rover crashed at Nogal Peak, Mark Tilman and Merritt Bonner stood at the hospital door waiting for Trina to pick them up.

Trina stifled a laugh as she drove Tilman's old clunker up in front of them. The twosome looked like Laurel and Hardy after one of their chaotic comedy scenes. Both men wore bandages over cuts on their heads and faces.

"You look like two leftovers from a barroom brawl," Trina joked as they eased their sore bodies into the car.

Tilman noted the scratches and bruises on her arms and face. "You don't look too healthy yourself," he kidded.

"Where to?" she asked when the men had settled in.

"Let's go to my office to talk," Merritt Bonner answered.

About fifteen minutes later, they entered Bonner's office at the *Alamogordo Gazette*. Tilman had been to the office several times, but he never wearied of studying its decor. If Merritt Bonner was New Mexico incarnate, his office was the sanctuary of the state's mystical atmosphere. Indian relics were displayed in an antique glass case that might have adorned a frontier railroad office a century earlier. On one wall, photographs showed Bonner astride a silvery stallion, Bonner shaking hands with festooned Indian chiefs, even Bonner in an Indian war bonnet that seemed to gobble up the little man in its feathery teeth. The New Mexico flag, resplendent in its red sunburst on a yellow field, hung on another wall. Behind Bonner's desk hung a huge painting of the scenery along the Santa Fe trail.

Bonner sank into a crimson leather chair at his desk. "Mark, I'm more determined than ever to find out what's in that cave," he said.

Tilman sat down beside Trina on a sofa near Bonner's desk. "It's got to be something vitally important if somebody is desperate enough to kill us to keep us from going in there," Bonner continued.

"I really can't ask the two of you to risk your lives again to find out what happened to Manuel," said Trina. "Besides, he's dead—" She began to weep. "—and . . . and nothing we find will bring him back."

"We can't give up now," Bonner insisted. "Don't forget, I still don't know what happened to my brother, either, and I want to find out."

Tilman enveloped her small hand in his bear-size palm. "And I still think it's important to know what happened to Manuel," said Tilman.

The conversation turned to strategy for the next assault on the cave. Bonner estimated that the hike to the Trinity zone under White Sands would take several days. Using skills he'd acquired spelunking with his brother, Bonner would mark the passages they followed so they would be able to find their way out of the cave.

"That's going to take a good bit of equipment," said Tilman.

"Right," Bonner replied. "I figure it'll take me two days to get everything together. Since the July 4th holiday falls on Wednesday, it'll be Thursday before I get everything together. Friday's the earliest we can start into the cave. But that's just as well. It'll give us that much more time to get our strength back."

"But our vacations, Mark. . . . We only had two weeks. If we start Friday, and we've got to hike for three days into the cave and another three days out, that doesn't leave us enough time."

"You're right," said Tilman. "There's only one thing we can do. While Merritt gets our provisions, we'll have to go back to Albuquerque and try to arrange for more time off."

"Do you think your boss will agree?" Trina asked.

"I don't see why not. This may turn into one of the biggest stories I've ever covered. What about you?"

"I'm afraid they'll be hard on me. I just don't know, but it doesn't matter. I really do want to know what happened to my brother."

"I'll agree to your going back," interjected Bonner. "But don't start out this afternoon, Mark. If you're still as woozy as I am, you need to rest. You two can leave early tomorrow morning and still get there in time to talk to your bosses."

"You're right," answered Tilman. "In fact you won't believe this—I'm so tired, I'm not even hungry. I think I'll go back to the motel and rest this afternoon."

"OK," said Bonner. "I'm going to do some telephoning, then I'll take a cab home and get some rest myself."

Yancey Armstrong had been recruited by the KGB for the most precise intelligence missions because he wouldn't flinch even if a blowtorch were aimed at the soles of his feet.

But Armstrong was now flinching.

The husky, dark-haired man with a bushy moustache had emerged from Sterret's pharmacy in downtown Alamogordo just as Mark Tilman and Trina Escobar came out of Merritt Bonner's office. Since the pharmacy was directly across the street from the *Alamogordo Gazette,* Armstrong found himself staring straight into the eyes of Tilman.

Tilman, of course, did not recognize Armstrong. Armstrong had followed Tilman, Trina, and Bonner at a distance that day at Nogal. And Armstrong was certain the three hadn't seen him and his partner, Jed Phillips, tamper with Bonner's car.

But a chill shot through Armstrong's steely body as he saw Tilman. Yancey Armstrong's last glimpse of Mark Tilman was that of a corpse. Now he was looking at the man he had been certain was dead.

As quickly as possible without drawing suspicion, Armstrong drove to the house in a quiet Alamogordo neighborhood that he and Phillips had been using as a headquarters. Phillips, too, was appalled to learn that their mission had failed. Reluctantly, Phillips, the head of the team, placed a call to Washington.

"The mission will have to be undertaken again," said the man in Washington.

"Recommendation on timing?" queried Phillips.

"Don't try anything now. That will raise too many coincidences. They'll be going back inside the cave. Follow them in, and take care of them there."

"Yes, sir."

"And see to it that only you and Armstrong come out of that cave alive."

Mark Tilman could tell Cleve Stringer was unimpressed with the reasons he had asked for more time off. Stringer was city editor at the *Albuquerque Evening Star*. The dour man's brow furrowed. He was considering Tilman's request.

"I don't know, Mark," Stringer said. "This is summer. We still have to get out five editions every single day. And people are out on vacation."

"But Cleve, doesn't the fact that somebody tried to kill us suggest to you that there's something going on inside that cave, or somewhere under there?"

"Now, Mark, can you prove that somebody did a piece of work on that car?" Stringer asked.

"Merritt had just had his brakes relined."

"Mark, I can't make this decision. I really think you ought to talk to Tarver."

Tilman had hoped Stringer wouldn't say that.

Shortly after his conversion, Tilman, afire with new enthusiasm, had tried to preach his new faith to L. Richmond Tarver, the perpetually growling editor of the *Star*, and a devout disciple of H. L. Mencken. Tarver laughed when his reporter quoted the Bible, and he forbade Tilman to do any evangelizing in the newsroom. From that day forward, Tarver branded Mark Tilman a fanatic driven into religious madness by the death of his wife.

L. Richmond Tarver weighed less than 150 pounds, but the wiry, scraggly faced man could send tremors through Tilman's ample body. Tilman fought the tremors now as he knocked on Tarver's oak-paneled door.

"Yeah?" barked the cigarette-husky voice from inside.

Tilman cracked the door just wide enough to insert his face. "Uh, Mr. Tarver, may I see you a moment?" he asked.

"Make it quick, Tilman. I'm working on a deadline here."

Tilman stepped into Tarver's office. The cold room reflected Tarver's personality and his fascination with Medieval Europe. He had designed his office to look like a room in a Frankish castle. The floors were a dark slate. Mahogany paneling shrouded the walls leaving only narrow slits framed in black iron.

"You still on that religious kick?" Tarver stung Tilman with his words.

"Everybody's on a religious kick of some kind, Mr. Tarver." Tilman couldn't believe he had been so direct.

Tarver swore. "Don't be a fool. I agree with Mencken. Religion's like poetry—nothing but an attempt to deny reality."

"That may be true, Mr. Tarver, but everyone on earth has something that demands their absolute allegiance. That's their god," Tilman answered faintly.

"All right, Tilman, I didn't call you here to talk religion. In fact, I didn't call you here at all. What do you want?"

Mark Tilman detailed the whole story of Manuel Escobar, the cave at Nogal Peak, and the murder attempt.

"I really need some additional time off to pursue this," he concluded. "I believe there's a major story in this mess, but Cleve Stringer felt I should ask you for the time off."

"What?" bellowed Tarver. "That idiot Stringer is like all the rest of the deadheads I've got here. Can't make a decision on their own! As for you, Tilman, you're on one of your fanatical wild goose chases, in here ranting about someone trying to murder you. Man, you're paranoid. Your religious fanaticism has pushed you off the deep end."

Tilman bristled at Tarver's repeated use of the word *fanaticism*. "Mr. Tarver," he said, "something really did happen out there."

"Well, take the time!"

"Sir?"

"I said, take the time! In fact take all the time you want because you don't have to report back to work here at all. Now get out!"

Mark Tilman almost crawled from Tarver's office. Back at the city desk, Tilman looked at Cleve Stringer and said, "I've got the strangest feeling I've just been fired."

"I really thought it would be me that got fired, not you," said Trina as they sat across from each other at the Branding Iron Steak Emporium. Tilman nervously devoured his large, thick T-bone, while Trina could only pick at her small filet mignon.

"Frankly," Tilman answered, "I guess I was my

usual naive self. I thought Stringer would jump up and down over the possibilities of this story. And I thought the people at El Condor would understand about your brother and let you off."

"They did understand," Trina responded. "That's why they only asked me to take leave without pay." Her face clouded. "But Mark, how will you and Danny live if you don't have a job?"

Tilman put down his fork. A remote look came into his eyes. Trina had strummed a chord Tilman didn't want to sing to. "The newspaper carries small insurance policies on its employees. When Donna . . . uh . . . died, I got the money. I was gonna use it for Danny's college fund, but I can make do on it awhile."

Having stripped his steak to the bone, Tilman shoved the plate away and sipped on a cup of coffee.

"Mark, do you remember Noah's rainbow?" Trina asked.

"Sorry," he quipped, "I wasn't around back then."

"No, I'm serious. Do you remember *when* Noah saw the rainbow?"

"Sometime after Noah got out of the ark. After the storm," Tilman answered.

"To be exact, Mark, the rainbow appeared after Noah had built an altar and made a sacrifice, giving God thanks for delivering him and his family."

"What're you getting at?" Tilman asked.

"It takes rain to make a rainbow, Mark, and it

takes clouds to make rain. To get the kind of rainbow Noah saw, it took thanksgiving in spite of the flood."

"Trina, you're talking in riddles."

"What I'm saying is that we've got to apply the rainbow principle. The darker the clouds, the more brilliant the rainbow. The clouds are all the trouble we've been through—in your case, starting with the death of your wife."

"Well, I'm sure ready for the rainbow," Mark said in frustration.

"Maybe we need to erect our altar for giving thanks."

Tilman looked at her without comprehension.

"I've read in the Bible that we're to make a sacrifice of praise."

"What does that mean?" Tilman asked.

"I think it means that we're supposed to give up something. That's what sacrifice is."

"Trina, I'm depleted. I don't have anything else to give."

"That's it, Mark. That's what a sacrifice is. It's giving the last possession we have. What we've got to do is use the last measure of our spiritual and emotional strength to praise God."

"Right here in the restaurant?"

"No, let's go out to the car."

Moments after Tilman paid the bill, they were sitting in his old green flivver. Tilman listened in awe as Trina began thanking God as if there were no clouds in the sky at all. When she finished, Tilman sensed she was waiting for him to pray. At first, he could think of no specific reasons for

CITY UNDER THE

gratitude, so he began by praising God's perfect character. Suddenly, Tilman was enveloped in joy. He envisioned a clear river sparkling as it danced along banks adorned with multihued fruit trees. Tilman felt as though he were swimming in the river on a blistering day and eating the rich fruit simultaneously. He began to laugh as he praised, not worrying about how foolish he might appear to an outsider. But he didn't appear foolish to Trina. She was laughing with him.

Both Tilman and Trina had discovered the rainbow. The God of the universe had given them the strength of his Spirit to deal with what lay ahead.

WHEN Tilman took Trina to her apartment, she invited him in for a bowl of ice cream. As she went into the kitchen, Mark turned on the television. He spun the channels until he landed on a network newsmagazine program—the middle of a segment featuring the famous novelist, Buck Prather.

For years, Tilman had worshiped Prather's acerbic options. Prather kept one foot in the establishment while the other foot kicked the very establishment that lavished Prather with its adulation and royalties. It seemed the right mix of rebellion and obeisance.

But when Tilman became a Christian, he found himself in disagreement with Prather's conclusions. Still, Tilman admired Prather's style as a writer.

He listened intently now as Prather spoke.

"We've got to develop a new kind of society," Prather said to his host, expounding on the theme it seemed more and more opinion makers had taken up. The thesis was that world societies were getting too complex and insecure to have the luxury of worrying about anything but survival.

". . . We must move from the quest for the Affluent Society to a concept of the Survival Society," Prather explained.

"Do you mean," queried the host, "that there must be some values other than life, liberty, and the pursuit of happiness?"

"What is happiness?" Prather ducked the question. "Isn't survival the basic component for happiness?"

Though knowledgeable, the host clearly wasn't on Prather's intellectual level and could only drape an awkward silence on his professionally sculpted smile.

"Uh, Mr. Prather, what is the Survival Society?" the host managed to ask.

"It's a world in which all of us are willing to sacrifice some of our personal privileges for the sake of the survival of the human race," Prather answered.

Tilman suddenly became aware of the background for this TV interview. Prather and the television host sat under a big tree on a lavish horse farm. Tilman could see colts prancing in the background. He'd heard that Prather had a big farm in Virginia.

Tilman often wondered if the disciples on the Affluent Left really understood the implications of the socialism they flirted with. For a moment, Tilman considered how Prather would feel if he were suddenly required to share his hundreds of acres and three houses with several grubby, impoverished families.

"But how could you get people to give up their rights?" the interviewer asked.

"Rights?" Prather shot back. "The most important right of all is that of survival!"

The interviewer couldn't disagree with that.

"We must confront the fact that there is a need for coordination of world resources," Prather preached on. "There must be coordination of political and social aspirations. Otherwise, war and imbalances in world economies will deplete what little resources we have left."

Tilman was growing increasingly uncomfortable with the implications of Prather's remarks. And Tilman had heard these views too many times recently. The Survival Society thesis seemed to have permeated the intelligentsia, from the editorial writer for the *Albuquerque Evening Star* to several well-known preachers to influential academics.

"But how can you deal with the impulses of human nature that cause the imbalances, like greed?" the interviewer asked. "The problem of

Marxism has been its inability to change human nature to be willing to sacrifice personal desires for the collective good."

"Oh, but it's possible to develop a new kind of person—a posthuman, if you will. . . ."

At that moment Trina entered the living room, bearing a bowl of strawberry ice cream. Tilman lost the rest of the interview, but he had a chilling feeling that he might somehow be plunged into that posthuman world Buck Prather was talking about.

His concern soon evaporated, however, in the sudden rapturous awareness that he was alone with Trina in her apartment. He took the ice cream bowl and placed it on the coffee table as Trina sat beside him on the sofa.

"You're not going to eat your ice cream?" she asked, surprised.

"Later," he answered.

"It'll melt."

"Trina, you're melting me." Tilman almost blanched at the corny awkwardness of his pun.

"Mark, I—"

"Trina," he interrupted, "do you realize this is the first time we've ever been alone together in your apartment?"

"Yes . . ." Trina couldn't get the words out.

Tilman wrapped her in his giant arms and smothered her with kisses. "It's been so long since I loved a woman," he said.

Trina dropped her defenses and began returning his kisses. Suddenly she realized she was allowing Tilman's romantic temperature to get too hot.

She pulled away. "Mark, we've got to stop," she said, trying not to let him know that she ached for him as much as he did for her.

Tilman sputtered, struggling to regain control. "You're . . . you're right."

"I'm sorry, Mark," Trina said. "I think you'd better go before something happens that we'd both regret."

Tilman knew he must flee, but his feet were chunks of iron. "I know." He laughed nervously.

As he plodded out Trina's door, she gave him a light kiss.

"Mark, tomorrow's the Fourth of July. Let's stay apart—for our own good."

Reluctantly, Tilman agreed. "I'll pick you up at 5:30 Thursday morning for the trip back to Alamogordo," he said. "I hope Merritt will be ready so we can start out for the cave early Friday morning."

Tilman turned to walk away. Suddenly, Trina called his name. As he turned, she ran into his arms.

"Mark, I love you!" As quickly as she said it, she turned and ran back into the apartment, closing the door behind her.

Mark walked away experiencing the strangest mix of emotions of his entire life. The high spiritual experience in the car outside the restaurant mingled with the fleshly hunger he felt for Trina. And now the sweet tingling of her declaration of love added to the brew. All of it simmered in the big pot of fear and anticipation over what they would find inside the cave at Nogal Peak.

Man is an odd, complex being, Mark Tilman reflected, as he left Trina Escobar's apartment. *And I am very much a man.*

LATE Thursday afternoon July 5 the sun edged behind the horizon to the west of Alamogordo like the remnant of a Fourth of July rocket. Though it was late, Mark Tilman knew Merritt Bonner would be waiting for him and Trina at Bonner's office.

In addition to making him the target of many an acerbic joke or gibe, Mark Tilman's simple, open manner made him likable to many of his peers and lovable to people like Trina Escobar. While Tilman's emotions could be complex, his essential being was simplicity incarnate, almost to the point of naivete. Despite his years of writing about the deviousness of man, Tilman's character bore no traces of concealment, trickery, or manipulation. Soon, he would have to learn these wilier dimensions of the human personality. He would have to combine being harmless as a dove with being wise as a serpent—or he would die.

Had Tilman been a bit more crafty, he would have considered the likelihood that whoever was trying to murder him and his friends would have Merritt Bonner's Alamogordo office staked out. But Tilman didn't think of that.

As soon as he and Trina drove up to the *Alamogordo Gazette* in the hopelessly visible battered green car, Yancey Armstrong spotted them.

In contrast to Tilman, Bonner was innately suspicious. Thus, throughout Thursday afternoon and evening, while Tilman hooted at what he viewed as Bonner's paranoia, Bonner laid an elaborate plan for the three of them to get into the cave unseen.

It didn't work.

Yancey Armstrong and Jed Phillips had tracked Merritt Bonner all week. They knew he had bought enough survival equipment to last several days. A man didn't buy helmets with lights and a sack of batteries unless he planned to spend considerable time underground. When Mark and Trina returned to Alamogordo, the agents simply camped out in the woods near Nogal cave until their targets showed up. The possibilities of staging an accident inside the cavern were endless.

Armstrong and Phillips watched through binoculars from a distance of a hundred yards as Tilman, Trina, and Bonner arrived at the mouth of the cave, donned their helmets, and prepared to enter. And when the three descended into the tunnel, Armstrong and Phillips weren't far behind.

Not long after they had entered the passage, Trina looked around nervously. "Merritt, are you sure you know how to find directions down here?" she asked. She had seen a complex of smaller tunnels leading off the main cave in numerous directions.

"I've gone spelunking with my brother enough that I have a pretty good idea," answered Bonner. "That's why I took that sighting the other day of White Sands from the top of the peak. Of course, you've got to understand, no system's foolproof."

Bonner's last remark only raised Trina's anxiety level as they trudged over the rocky winding trail through the cave.

After forty-five minutes, Bonner announced that it was time for a rest period. Focusing their miner's lamps, they saw a small widened area where they could lean against the rock wall and stretch their legs across the path.

Far behind, Armstrong and Phillips walked in near darkness, following the lights of their targets. They also rested when the lights stopped moving, knowing they would have to strike soon before their subjects got too deep into the cave. Still, they wanted to be in far enough that no one would find the bodies.

Merritt Bonner's thirty years of writing editorials had conditioned him to begin philosophizing at the slightest provocation. Tilman, Trina, and Bonner had hardly nestled themselves on the ground before Bonner started.

"This is a bit like life," he said.

"Huh?" muttered Tilman, for the moment concerned only about his aching feet.

"What I mean is this: Life is like a walk through a dark tunnel," Bonner continued.

"Oh," said Tilman, still not focusing on Bonner's words.

Trina was also preoccupied, wondering if her brother had come through this cave.

"We stumble along in darkness, not knowing where life's trail is going to turn next," Bonner preached on. "For all we know, there might be a hidden treasure at the next turn—or a precipice plunging into a bottomless pit."

Hearing those words, Trina clutched Tilman's hand, grateful that he was sitting beside her.

"I don't think life's quite that grim and unpredictable," said Tilman, realizing Bonner's morbid comments were upsetting Trina.

"Mark, how can you, of all people, say such a thing?" Bonner asked. "If you'll excuse me, your life took a rather sudden tragic turn awhile back when Donna was killed."

Tilman glanced from Trina to Bonner. "Merritt, let me tell you how life differs from this walk through a dark cave," he said.

"You can try, friend," Bonner answered.

"You've been at least this far into the cave before, right?" Tilman queried.

"Yes, my brother and I have probably been several miles beyond this point. Why, one day—"

Tilman interrupted Bonner's new tangent. "Since you're leading us, Merritt, we're not walking totally into the unknown. You know there are no cliffs within the next few miles. So all we have to do is follow you."

"But remember, I haven't been all the way," Bonner said.

"That's why your analogy that hiking in this cave is like life doesn't quite hold up," Tilman said.

"What does that mean?" Bonner asked.

"Trina and I may be following *you* through this cave, but the guide we follow through life *has* been all the way."

"I don't understand," Bonner said.

"I'm talking about Jesus," Tilman explained.

Suddenly, Bonner regretted opening his mouth. "Come on, Mark," he said. "You can't compare Jesus to . . . well, to me as your guide in this cavern. I have something tangible you can see—a compass, my miner's lamp."

"Jesus has some tangible means of guiding us through life, Merritt."

"You're talking religious fantasy, old buddy."

"Not really. The Bible is like your miner's lamp, and the Holy Spirit is like our eyes which enable us to follow the Light."

"Are you honestly trying to tell me you don't have any fear or anxiety about the future turns your life may take?" Bonner asked sincerely. Beneath his crusty exterior, there was anxiety.

"I guess when you begin to look at the dark trail of life through God's light, with spiritual eyes, things take on different meaning," Tilman said.

Trina squeezed his hand.

"Huh?" It was Bonner's turn to appear ignorant.

"Merritt, when Donna died, I faced the worst fears I'd ever had, losing somebody close to me. But God used that very experience to let me hear the best news I ever heard."

"What's that?"

"That God knows every turn in the road and will use it as the route to the victory he's already won for us."

"What victory are you talking about?" Bonner asked.

"Victory over death."

"Donna *died*, Mark. Where's the victory in that?"

"I admit the pain of losing her was, sometimes still is, unbearable. But because she died, I found life in Christ. And I've been able to tell our son about that life. Besides, Merritt, Donna had received that life, too, and I know where she is right now."

"Now how can you know that?" Bonner asked.

"Because she followed Jesus as her guide. He went all the way to death itself. Merritt, there's no tunnel deeper than that one. But Jesus found the way out—into heaven. Because she followed him, Donna found the way out, too."

The conversation had gone further than Merritt Bonner intended. Quickly he turned his lamp toward his watch.

"This is all very interesting," he said, "but we

can't sit here forever talking religion. We need to get moving."

As they got up, Tilman turned to look back at the trail they had already covered. As his light beam scanned the tunnel, Tilman saw the glint of metal. Suddenly, he lost his naivete. He realized the metal was the crown of a miner's helmet. Someone was crouching behind a rock fifty yards behind them. Tilman knew he had to alert Bonner and Trina without getting the attention of whoever was following them.

"Merritt, I need a little help in putting on this backpack. The straps must be tangled," Tilman said.

As Bonner walked around Trina toward Tilman, Mark jerked out a notebook and pen from his pocket. Quickly he scribbled a note. It read:

> Someone's following us. Don't tell Trina. Just start walking. I'll try to jump him from behind.

"There, I think that's got it," Tilman said aloud.

"Good, let's get moving," answered Bonner.

Since they were following a ray of light from behind, Armstrong and Phillips couldn't tell how many lamps shone ahead. They didn't notice when Tilman hid behind a rock wall, waiting for them to pass.

When the tunnel took a slight curve to the left, Armstrong and Phillips hastened to remain in sight of their quarry. Within seconds they had passed the cleft where Mark Tilman hid.

Suddenly, with as much agility as he could muster, Tilman jumped out from his hiding place, flicking on the lamp of his miner's helmet as he did so.

"Stop right there!" he yelled.

The noise was Merritt Bonner's cue to spin around and run as fast as possible toward Tilman, dragging along a confused Trina Escobar.

Armstrong and Phillips turned to face Tilman. Just as Mark started to ask why they were following, Armstrong lunged at Tilman, knocking the big man into the rock wall behind him. Tilman thudded into the jagged granite. He slid back into the crevice where he had been hiding. Armstrong was going to pounce on Tilman, striking him with a small hammer, but for the moment, the cleft in the rock where Tilman had fallen protected him.

"Jed, come help me!" Armstrong hollered.

As Phillips turned toward his partner, Merritt Bonner came up from behind and slammed a hefty rock into Phillips's head.

Hearing the commotion, Armstrong spun around. Tilman dragged himself out of the cleft and leaped on Armstrong's back just as Armstrong was about to hit Bonner with the hammer.

Tilman drove Armstrong into the rock cleft. Lunging at him again, he stumbled against a big boulder. The boulder jarred a massive stone perched just above Armstrong. The big stone toppled downward. It struck Armstrong's face, crushed his skull, and killed him instantly. Tilman shrank back in terror, stumbling over Phillips, who lay fatally wounded from Bonner's blow.

Trina was hiding behind a rock. To her, the whole episode was a melange of light shards, curse words, groans, and falling bodies. She peeked out from behind her fortress as Tilman spoke.

"Thanks, Merritt," he said. "I guess you saved my life. If those guys had been able to get over here, they'd have killed me for sure."

"I guess that makes us even. If you hadn't jumped them from behind, I would've been finished, too."

"What are you going to do with them?" Trina asked from her hiding place.

"Oh, Trina," Tilman said, walking over to her. "Are you all right?"

"Just a little scared," she answered. "But really, you can't leave those guys in here. When they get their strength back, they'll come after us again."

"I don't believe these men are going anywhere," Bonner said. "They're both dead."

Trina gasped.

"Do you think these are the guys who sabotaged the Land Rover?" Tilman asked.

"I don't know about that, but there's little doubt in my mind that they followed us in here today to kill us," Bonner answered.

"But why—?" Trina began.

Bonner interrupted her. "I'm not sure, but I think we can find out."

"Let's search their gear," Tilman suggested.

As the two newspapermen began digging through the backpacks Phillips and Armstrong wore into the caves, Tilman suddenly struck cold metal. Slowly, he pulled out the object his hand had struck—a .22-caliber pistol equipped with a silencer.

Bonner took the gun and studied it.

"They could have shot us up close without making enough noise to bring the cave down on their heads," he said.

"We've got to find some identification," said Tilman.

The men continued rummaging. There was food, rope, extra lights, water, extra pairs of heavy hiking socks, but no identification.

Just as he was about to give up, Tilman's hand struck a small pocketknife lying in the bottom of the backpack. Tilman pulled out the small knife, examining it carefully. A few words were engraved in the metal casing. Rubbing the case, Tilman cleared the letters of dust and dirt. Under the beam of his miner's lamp, the words became clear.

"This looks like Russian," he said in disbelief.

"Russian?" Merritt Bonner almost yelled. "Now I *know* we've got to find out what's going on."

Four hours later, the three were plunging still deeper into the cave. At a small open area, they decided to stop to sleep for a few hours.

But sleep didn't come easy. All three shared a

common anxiety: whatever lay ahead was so sensitive that someone wanted to kill them.

Trina Escobar slumped on a flat ledge as the haggard threesome halted to rest for the tenth time in twenty hours. Merritt Bonner stretched out on another table of rock, and Mark Tilman lowered his body onto the cave floor, leaning wearily against the wall of rock.

Bonner scribbled calculations on a notepad. "According to my figuring, we ought to be just about underneath the Trinity site," he said. "If there really is a big room underneath the atomic bomb test area, we ought to be in the vicinity."

"How will we recognize it?" Trina asked.

"There should be some evidence of human engineering," Bonner answered. "A man-made passageway, a steel wall . . ."

"Or better yet, a door complete with a welcome mat," Tilman quipped.

"A door we may find," Bonner responded, "But don't count on that welcome mat. Seriously, I suggest we push on another six hours, and if we don't find something by then, we backtrack and try another tunnel."

It didn't take six hours.

Shortly after resuming their tedious hike through the narrow passage, they heard the rumble of engines and what sounded like the roar of a blast furnace.

As Bonner rounded a bend in the rocky corridor, he caught sight of an orange glow of firelight leaking through a chink in the cave wall a few yards ahead.

"Come here, Mark!" he said in a loud whisper.

"What in the world is that?" Tilman asked.

"I knew we were going deep underground, but I believe we've hiked all the way to hell," Bonner joked.

Trina didn't appreciate the attempt at humor. Easing over to Mark, she took his arm and peered toward the flickering light.

"I don't think they have gasoline engines in hell," said Tilman.

The roar of the motors grew louder. It sounded like large trucks stopping and starting.

"You two stay here," said Bonner. "I'll crawl over to that hole in the wall and try to get a sighting."

Within moments, Tilman and Trina could see Bonner's silhouette against the fiery chink.

When he returned, excitement danced on the edge of his voice. "I think we've found it," he announced above the pulsating engines.

"That's great," said Tilman. "What have we found?"

"It's a man-made passageway, big enough for three huge dump trucks and a giant incinerator."

"But how could anybody get three dump trucks down here?" Trina asked.

"Yeah," echoed Tilman. "And why would anybody want three dump trucks and an incinerator two thousand feet underground?"

"To haul garbage, what else?" replied Bonner.

"Garbage?" Tilman and Trina asked in unison.

"That's right," said Bonner. "Those trucks were loaded with giant garbage cans. There were workers tossing bags and cans into the incinerator. It looked like enough trash for a small city."

At Bonner's mention of the word *city*, Mark and Trina exchanged glances.

"Merritt, did you say city?" Tilman asked. "You don't suppose we've stumbled into Manuel's city under the sands, do you?"

"There's only one way to know that. We'll have to get to where those trucks are coming from."

Tediously, the three made their way through the narrowing passageway. Examining the walls around the chink, Bonner finally found what he was looking for.

"Mark! Trina!" he called. "Over here!"

Bonner showed them a large crack in the wall, leading into the man-made tunnel. Although Trina and Bonner had no problem squeezing through the crack, Tilman had to suck in his breath to pour his fat body through the opening. After the brief struggle, he stood beside his two friends inside. The three ducked behind a large rock.

"I've got an idea," said Bonner. "It might be a bit tricky."

"It couldn't be trickier than me squeezing through that crack in the wall," grunted Tilman.

"One of the dump trucks carries big metal containers," Bonner explained. "As soon as the workers empty them, the truck will ease away from the incinerator. As it passes by us, we'll jump on the truck and hide in the cans. I think we're far enough away the workers won't see us."

"We're going to hide in garbage cans?" Trina cringed.

"There's no other way," answered Bonner. "Unless, of course, you want to forget who killed your brother and just head back up the tunnel to Nogal Peak."

"No, I'll do it," Trina whispered. "I just wish there was another way."

Mark Tilman wished the same thing as he tried to lift his body onto the truck bed and into the container. When at last he was nestled inside the metal barrel, he wondered if the garbage odor was as nauseating in the containers bearing Trina and Bonner.

Since there were no lids on their hideaways, Tilman could see the top of the passageway high above as their truck lumbered forward. The tunnel was bathed in orange light, bright as day. Occasionally he could hear another truck pass by, going in the opposite direction.

After about a mile, their truck jolted to a stop, and Tilman heard voices.

"OK," said a voice from the truck, "I dumped that load. Where to next?"

"A/S Zone, Sector One," said a voice nearby. "There's a pile of building scrap at the corner of Elm and Duval. Oh, we got a report that some of the Peacemakers in that area have malfunctioned and have hidden in a building, so keep a watch. Those brutes are pretty mean."

"I keep wondering when Singlelaub and his bunch will get the bugs worked out in this system," the man in the truck answered. "They've only had ten years."

"That ain't my worry, friend," shouted the other man.

The driver laughed, then threw the truck into gear. It started forward. With the sound of a large motor, a massive door raised in front of the truck. As they crossed the threshold, Tilman caught his breath. The ceiling, which had been about fifty feet above him in the tunnel, seemed to disappear altogether. Tilman knew they were still underground, but there was no sign of the top of the cave. It was as if they had emerged on the surface at the brightest noon, yet he knew they were still far underground.

Ten minutes later, the truck halted again, and the driver got out of the truck. Tilman, Trina, and Bonner waited in their smelly hiding places.

"All right," the driver shouted with the tone someone would use in summoning a dog. "All you Producers wind up what you're doing and get those cans off the truck. Then load up this pile of trash."

There was no reply. Tilman and his friends could only hear the shuffle of feet. Suddenly, Tilman heard Bonner's low whisper.

"Mark, Trina, on the count of three, hop out of these barrels and jump off the truck. Follow me. Stay low!"

Bonner peered out of his barrel to make sure they wouldn't be seen. He gasped at what he saw. For a fleeting moment, he thought it might be safer to ride back to the incinerator. But Bonner knew that would be certain death. Catching a glimpse of a building ten feet away, Bonner hoped that would afford a hiding place.

As the truck driver supervised the strange people he had called the Producers, Bonner began counting. At three, he and his friends jumped from the barrel and dashed to the doorway of the building.

Shielded in an alcove, Tilman, Trina, and Bonner looked out at the world they had entered— the strangest world any of them had ever seen.

CHAPTER 1

DEEP in the bowels of the northeast corner of the huge cavern lay the Control Zone consisting of elaborate offices and a large conference room pulsating with electronic paraphernalia.

There, Ernst Singlelaub assembled the team he had brought together a decade earlier. Now they briefed him, as they did twice weekly, on the status of the projects they oversaw.

Singlelaub swiveled slowly to the right and left in a plush high-backed leather chair. His colleagues sat in lesser chairs around a massive oak table.

As Dr. P. T. Montgomery reported on his programs to reeducate the American public to accept advanced forms of behavior control, Singlelaub became frustrated at Montgomery's pompous verbosity.

"I remind you, Pete," Singlelaub interrupted him using the nickname Montgomery loathed, "that there are only two basic questions: 'Who will do what to whom?' And 'Who will decide?' "*

The others in the room gave Singlelaub a patronizing laugh. Montgomery, sensing his boss's displeasure, smiled tautly. "There is no question about who the subjects and masters are in this little enterprise," Montgomery answered.

"What I want to hear, Pete, is exactly how you will gain compliance with the reeducation projects you've detailed," Singlelaub demanded.

"Chemical control," Montgomery answered in uncharacteristic terseness. "In these last ten years, we've wrestled continually with the best means of rendering our subjects' minds as blank slates—the *tabula rasa.*"

"If you can't achieve that, you'll have revolution in every school in America once you set your programs in motion," Buck Prather inserted.

"We now have the means." P. T. Montgomery paused, allowing his breathless announcement to circle the little conclave at the table. "More than half of all U.S. residents now use mind-changing drugs occasionally. The reeducation system will mandate that every school faculty will include a biochemical therapist."

*Maya Pines, *The Brain Changers*, New York: Harcourt Brace Jovanovich, p. 225.

"What on earth for?" Singlelaub's frustration with Montgomery's tedious reporting was heightening.

Undaunted, Montgomery continued. "No less an expert than Dr. Kenneth Clark once suggested that biochemical intervention be employed to reduce man's aggressiveness. We shall take the proposal further than what Clark intended. We shall place all children on a biochemical program that will make their minds as open as an unwalled village."

"There's a hole in your scheme, Montgomery." The eyes of Singlelaub's team shifted to Dr. James Shelley, the neurosurgeon. "You're talking about children over whom the government can have some control—children in public schools. What are you going to do about private school children?"

Montgomery glanced at Singlelaub. "If the chairman will permit, I think Dr. Megan Singlelaub can best respond to that."

Shelley was pleased. Ten years before, Megan Singlelaub had rebuffed his advances. Throughout the decade, he had tried repeatedly to gain some small measure of attention from her, but it was clear she hated him. That fact, plus the grace and dignified beauty a decade had sculpted into Ernst Singlelaub's daughter, had made her even more desirable to Shelley.

But above all else, she *was* Ernst Singlelaub's daughter. A relationship with Megan Singlelaub would place James Shelley within touching distance of the throne of Trinity II. Shelley was almost intoxicated as he stared deeply into Megan's eyes.

She spoke confidently. "We are developing a legislative package, which our friends will soon introduce in Congress, that will effectively destroy private educational institutions," she said. "For most private schools, tax exempt status is like a government grant. If they lose that, they can't survive. We can ensure that they will lose that status."

"But what about those who are not exempted?" Shelley asked without blinking.

"Part of our legislation will focus on standards for teachers. Quite simply, the standards for state approval will be so exacting that no private school can continue to exist without impossible tuitions."

"You will force them to price themselves out of existence?"

For the first time in ten years, James Shelley brought a slight smile to Megan's lips. "That's correct," she answered.

"You'll never get it through Congress," spouted Archibald Porteous, who had long battled church-related private education.

"We have that covered, too."

Ernst Singlelaub struggled to hide the pride he felt. His daughter had obviously angled for every contingency.

"The National Federation of Educators," Megan continued, "has chapters in every state. We're arranging significant foundation grants to the NFE. There will be a private understanding that these grants are for distribution to their state chapters. In turn, the state chapters are to finance the campaigns of congressional incumbents—"

"Then the members of Congress will be obligated to the NFE." Porteous followed her line of thought.

"And the NFE will be obligated to us through our surrogates in the foundations," Megan said.

"Brilliant!" Shelley exclaimed. Megan Singlelaub's intellect and craftiness moved him to near ecstasy.

"Yes," pondered Ernst Singlelaub. "The NFE has long desired the elimination of the religious private schools. I believe this will work."

"It will, sir," Montgomery asserted. "And when it does, we shall have a free and open field in which to do our work. We now have several generations of Americans who've been educated correctly in our public institutions. It has been difficult, but through grounding them firmly in humanistic principles, we've been able to show most people that man is a mechanism who can be improved upon. There are millions of people who want to be improved."

Singlelaub glanced at his watch. "While we're on the subject of improving the human animal, I want to move on to the status of our genetic projects. Our time is limited. Stelmetz, give us your report."

A rivulet of excitement shot through Hyman Stelmetz. He sensed his report would be one more ingredient in fulfilling his destiny. The astrologer at Santa Fe had said he was in the era of his fulfillment—not that Stelmetz believed in astrologers and sorcerers, he reassured himself. But he had found the seer on a weekend trip to Santa Fe and felt obligated to visit her as part of his academic interest in the occult.

But the astrologer said that he was born to rule great empires. The only empire Stelmetz could see was that of Trinity II, and he wondered what strange confluence of events could depose Ernst Singlelaub and place him in power.

"We have finished with our IQC design." Hyman Stelmetz began. As always, his cockiness irritated Montgomery.

"I'm sorry, Mr. Chairman," interrupted Montgomery. He glanced at Singlelaub. "Dr. Stelmetz assumes we are all familiar with his designations. I wonder if he might tell us the meaning of IQC?"

"You've heard the term before, Pete. It means Infant Quality Control." Singlelaub's stinging retort silenced Montgomery for the rest of the meeting.

"Continue please, Dr. Stelmetz," commanded Singlelaub.

"Thank you, sir." Stelmetz glared momentarily at Montgomery. "In previous meetings, I've reported on our attempts to develop a comprehensive testing program for newborn infants."

"You're referring to the Crick Proposal?" asked Singlelaub.

Stelmetz showed slight irritation at being interrupted the second time.

"Refresh my memory on the Crick Proposal," Singlelaub ordered. Stelmetz restrained himself from signalling any displeasure at Singlelaub.

"Sir Francis Crick, the Nobel laureate who helped break the DNA code, suggested that no newborn infant should be declared human until tests had been made to determine its genetic quality." Stelmetz explained. "If the infant failed the test, Crick recommended that it be viewed as having forfeited its right to live."

"Of course," answered Singlelaub. "Proceed."

Hyman Stelmetz put on his reading glasses, glanced at a written report in front of him, and continued speaking. "For years, newborn infants have been measured by the Apgar Scale shortly after birth. This is a simple series of tests to check for the obvious, like reflexes. Our IQC program will actually investigate the genetic endowment of the newborn."

"And how will you use the results?" asked Buck Prather.

"One of our objectives will be to determine the class type into which the child should fit. By carefully investigating the baby's parentage, plus its own genetic qualities, we can determine whether or not significant alterations can make the child useful, and if so, toward which class we should direct the child's biological development."

Megan Singlelaub leaned forward. "We're constantly updating the computer projections of how many individuals we'll need in each of the three survival classes based on differing population levels," she interjected.

"The new dimension I wish to report on to-day," continued Stelmetz, looking toward Ernst Singlelaub, "is our monitoring program."

"Good, I've been eager to hear of your progress in that area," Singlelaub claimed, although his expression remained unaltered.

"With the help of Dr. Megan Singlelaub, we have completed the design for a comprehensive method of monitoring the gene pool," Stelmetz said. "The biotechnology is quite complicated, so I'll not burden you with the details. Perhaps Dr. Singlelaub would tell you how the program will be regulated."

Everyone sitting around the table gave Megan Singlelaub their attention.

"Thank you," she said. "My legislative team has developed a law requiring the U.S. Department of Health and Human Services to establish Genetic Control Clinics in every congressional district. Every male must report to the clinic no more than ten days after his seventeenth birthday. We'll require females to come to the clinic within ten days after the conclusion of their first menstrual cycle."

Stelmetz now resumed. "Certain body proteins will be analyzed in the subjects," he said. "After computer analysis, we'll grant a license to those who will be allowed to reproduce."

"And what about those who don't measure up?" Porteous asked.

Stelmetz laughed. "They'll get a one-month vacation in a sterilization sector."

"A sterilization sector?" asked Prather.

"Yes, Mr. Prather. We've developed such experimental reservoirs right here at Trinity II, in Sector Three of the Applied Science Zone."

"Do you surgically sterilize these subjects?" Prather queried.

"No, that's much too primitive. We've treated water supplies in the sterilization sectors with chemicals that will make those who drink the water infertile. During the month it takes the process to work, you and Montgomery can carry on some of your reeducation and behavior modification programs."

"I'm very pleased with this team progress," Singlelaub declared, not looking at all pleased. "We've spent enough time in discussion, however. We must get on with our work. All are dismissed except Stelmetz and Shelley, who will remain with me for a few moments."

Though they were accustomed to Singlelaub's abruptness, his team still struggled to keep from looking wounded when they were excluded from his private meetings with Stelmetz and Shelley. The closed sessions were becoming more frequent.

Ernst Singlelaub waited until the others had left before speaking. "Now we can come to the most important dimensions of our work. Give me your reports on Operation Gray Garden."

"You chose an apt title for this project," said Shelley. "We are very close to determining the type of device to plant in the gray soil of the human brain."

"Excellent," said Singlelaub in his taut, emotionless voice. "Give me your proposals. Spare no details."

"Your assignment to us," Stelmetz began, "was to develop an electrode that could be surgically implanted in the brain and that the subject would never detect."

"That actually is a minor problem," interrupted Shelley. "The interior of the brain does not experience pain. A person could wear such a device through an earthquake and never know it was there."

"The problem we faced," continued Stelmetz, "was in designing a stimoceiver that would be wireless, would be capable of receiving signals over thousands of miles, and would still be slender enough to penetrate the amygdala without injuring brain tissue in that region."

"What the devil is a stimoceiver?" asked Singlelaub.

"It's an electronic device we can plant in the brain," Shelley replied. "It can receive commands and respond by sending an electrical stimulus into the site of the brain where it's planted."

"And have you solved the problem of receiving signals over a long distance?"

"Yes, Dr. Singlelaub, we have," answered Stelmetz.

"I brought one of the devices we've created to show you." Shelley removed a thin stainless steel needle from a container. The slender, gleaming spike was no longer than four inches. A tiny plate was attached at the top.

Singlelaub picked up the stimoceiver and turned it around in his hand.

"The tip of the stimoceiver will be planted in the amygdala," Shelley explained. "The flat plate on the top will be near the brain's surface."

"That plate contains the receiver," Stelmetz said. "It has enough power to receive a concentrated signal from the moon."

Singlelaub was clearly fascinated with the device he was holding. "What can it accomplish?"

"A Spanish physiologist gave a graphic demonstration of the power of the stimoceiver," Shelley answered. "We've brought some film to show you what we can do."

Shelley briskly pushed a film cassette into a slot in the small projection chamber of the conference room. Stelmetz lowered the lights. As the film rolled, Singlelaub watched a massive black bull spinning through the dust of a bullring like a tornado.

Suddenly, a man walked into the arena, waving a red cape. The enormous bull spotted the cape and charged. In the dark, Singlelaub tensed as the bullfighter stood his ground. As the animal neared, rather than stepping aside, the man stood squarely in its path. Just as the bull was about to crash into the man, the beast slid to a stop, kicking up dust in front of him. The bull appeared frozen, unable to move.

"What on earth . . . ?" Singlelaub was stunned by what he saw.

"The man you saw," Stelmetz said, "was Dr.

José Delgado, the physiologist I mentioned. He put on that little demonstration years ago in a bullring in Cordova, Spain."

"How did he manage to stop that bull?" Singlelaub drove to the heart of the issue.

Shelley stepped out of the projection chamber. "Delgado placed a stimoceiver in the animal's caudate nucleus—an area of the brain that controls motor activity. When the bull approached, Delgado simply pushed the button of a tiny radio device he was wearing, and the transmitter sent the signal into the bull's brain."

"But, gentlemen—" Skepticism lay heavily on the edge of Singlelaub's voice. "There's a galactic distance between controlling the behavior of a bull and ordering a society."

"Perhaps the next portion of the film will answer that," said Shelley. Returning to the projection room, he started the film once more.

As the film rolled, Stelmetz talked. "Here we have a society of monkeys. Such societies are normally dominated by one of the animals."

Singlelaub saw what was apparently the chief of the monkey tribe flying into fury, chasing and biting other animals in the cage. But he always stopped as he approached a certain female monkey.

"The brain of the boss monkey was stimulated to aggravate aggressive behavior," Stelmetz continued. "As you can see, it strengthened his role as the master."

Suddenly, the scene changed. A different group of monkeys was again dominated by one fierce animal. The chief monkey was raging at a cowering group he had shoved into a corner of the cage when he suddenly lost his aggressiveness. Gradually, the other monkeys lost their fear of him and even came close enough to touch the creature that had been chasing and biting them minutes before.

"Stimulating the brain of that angry monkey altered all the relationships in the cage," Stelmetz noted.

"Will it work in human society?"

"Yes, Dr. Singlelaub, it will," Shelley responded.

"That's the rather exciting news we have for you today," Stelmetz said.

"We have something more to show you." Shelley grinned, pointing Singlelaub to two television monitors set up in the conference room.

Singlelaub watched as one of the screens showed the huge computer room located in the Research and Development Zone of Trinity II. Technicians wearing small headsets monitored the computers.

The other television monitor now came to life. It focused within a metallic room. Inside, there was one representative from each of the three survival classes being developed at Trinity II.

An enormous, beastly looking man dressed in a red experimental suit walked around the room. Stenciled across his back was the word *Peacemaker*.

Another hefty man, clad in yellow, bore the designation *Producer*.

Finally, a slight young woman with an enlarged cranium wore a blue uniform, labeled *Primary Being*.

"As you know," Shelley said to Singlelaub, "the computer room is located in the R-D Zone's northwest corner. The experimental subjects you see on the other monitor have received stimoceiver implants that are controlled by the computers."

"To simulate distance," Stelmetz interjected, "we've placed a metallic shield around the computers and located the subjects in a steel-lined room in Sector Three of the Applied Science Zone—almost a mile from the computers."

Shelley donned an electronic headset. "Begin the experiment," he said into the microphone.

Singlelaub could hardly control his breathing as he saw the technicians in the computer room respond to Shelley's command. The camera zoomed in on one of the technicians as Shelley adjusted a knob. On the other monitor, Singlelaub watched the Peacemaker in red growing more distraught. The gigantic creature's anger seemed to increase.

"The controller is sending a signal to the stimoceiver implanted in the Peacemaker's amygdala," explained Stelmetz.

Suddenly the Peacemaker exploded in fury and rushed toward the fragile woman. Just as quickly the big yellow-clad Producer changed from a docile lackey to raging beast. The Peacemaker now became a lamblike creature and didn't even fight back as the Producer began beating him.

"I thought you had developed the Producer class into mindless slaves," said Singlelaub. "That's the point," exclaimed Shelley. "We did, but we can alter the relationships within the society we've created. We can determine the behavior of an entire culture!"

"Never forget, Dr. Singlelaub, we can implant stimoceivers in the amygdala of any human brain and control aggressiveness," Stelmetz said. "It will no longer be necessary for human monitors to speak commands to their experimental subjects. The computer can control their actions through signals to the stimoceivers."

For the first time in years, Singlelaub laughed. "Yes . . . I see. Civilization stands or falls on the amygdala. We can forget all that religious tripe about the heart being the seat of human emotion. If we can control the amygdala, we can control the human race!"

"And we *can* control the amygdala!" Stelmetz picked up on Singlelaub's excitement.

"I want to stress the importance of maintaining the confidentiality of Operation Gray Garden," Singlelaub said. "My strategy, as you know, is for only the three of us to have the ability to maintain this kind of control. After we're gone, only the persons we have trained will be allowed to be the *master controllers of the human race.* Someday, of course, we'll be able to turn the process over to the biocomputer."

Shelley smiled broadly.

"Why are you grinning like a fool?" asked Singlelaub.

145

"I was just thinking," Shelley replied. "The miniaturization that made that computer-stimoceiver possible so that you can control the human brain came about through the American effort to reach the moon. Isn't there an irony about our having to go to the moon to discover how to reach the inner regions of the human brain?"

"Yes, it is an interesting relationship," said Singlelaub. "It's even more fascinating that in years to come, the great underground chamber housing our computers at Trinity II will be the *center of earth* from which all human beings will be monitored and controlled."

Stelmetz's face flushed as he remembered the prophecy of the astrologer. He was born to rule, she had said. If Trinity II was to be the center of earth, and he was destined to be its lord, would that make him lord of earth? The thought left him breathless, and he knew he must recover his scientific detachment lest he give himself away.

"I want to congratulate my colleague, Dr. Shelley, in coming up with a plan to motivate whole populations to receive the implant," said Stelmetz in uncharacteristic generosity.

"And how will that be accomplished?" asked Singlelaub.

"Quite simple, sir," Shelley answered. "We'll convince humanity that the implant will *prevent and cure cancer*. People will line up to get an implant like they did to get polio vaccine!"

A shrill tone cut into the conversation about Operation Gray Garden.

Singlelaub reached for the switch of the beeper he wore on his belt. He brought the device to his ear.

"Dr. Singlelaub, please call Central Control on the red phone," said the voice over the beeper.

Singlelaub looked up at Stelmetz and Shelley. "I've given instructions never to interrupt me in a briefing unless it is a matter of vital importance," he said. "So excuse me a moment while I call Central Control."

The two men got up as if to leave, but Singlelaub signaled them to remain. He picked up the red phone and dialed two digits.

"This is Singlelaub," he said. After listening a

few moments, he raised his heavy eyebrows almost imperceptibly. Ten years of association with Singlelaub had taught Stelmetz and Shelley that their leader never displayed emotional response, except for this tiny signal.

"I'll come to Central Control immediately," Singlelaub said into the phone. "Maintain current procedure until I get there."

Singlelaub placed the receiver back on the hook. "Gentlemen, I want you to accompany me to Central Control."

The three men left the briefing room and got into a small, open vehicle that took them the short distance to Central Control, at the core of the Control Zone. A passageway linked Ernst Singlelaub's office to Central Control, where he spent most of his time.

Stelmetz and Shelley were infrequent visitors to Central Control. Stelmetz, especially, was always fascinated with the technological cosmos Singlelaub had erected in the big room. Monitors constantly analyzed telemetry, reporting on everything from temperature readings in the many chambers of the three zones of Trinity II to the blood pressures of the hundreds of experimental subjects who populated Singlelaub's underground world.

A balcony room overlooking Central Control housed a Command Center, the exclusive domain of Ernst Singlelaub and those he chose to share it with. Singlelaub led Stelmetz and Shelley to the private room enclosed by glass. At its heart was an elaborate console of television screens and controls. A large swivel chair, like an aircraft carrier captain's, was clearly reserved for Dr. Singlelaub. Taking possession of his chair, Singlelaub motioned for Stelmetz and Shelley to occupy lesser seats nearby.

"Report!" Singlelaub seemed to speak into the air. Apparently a microphone somewhere in the console picked up his voice.

Another voice responded from equally invisible speakers. "As you have instructed, our surveillance team followed the subjects into Nogal Cave. The attempt to eliminate the subjects failed, and our team was killed in an accident. The subjects continued into the cave and have now entered Trinity II."

"Do you have a location on them?" Singlelaub lifted his eyebrows a fraction.

"Affirmative. They are presently in Sector One of the Applied Science Zone. We have them on a visual scanner."

"Display on my monitor," Singlelaub ordered.

"Coming up on your monitor three," squawked the invisible speaker.

Stelmetz and Shelley rose to peer over Singlelaub's shoulder at one of the television screens on his console. It leaped to life with a color picture of a pleasant-looking street in a small village. A street sign indicated the corner of Elm and Duval. Singlelaub, Shelley, and Stelmetz watched as the camera zoomed in slowly on two men and a woman who were partially hidden in the alcove entrance of a bookstore on Duval Street.

Clearly, they were strangers at Trinity II. Their

faces evidenced confusion and surprise. They had stumbled into an area of the village where Producers were repairing a street. Primary Beings, with their spindly bodies and large heads, walked past slowly, pausing and peering into the bookstore window. Peacemakers patrolled the street.

"Why don't the Peacemakers attack those intruders?" Stelmetz asked.

Ernst Singlelaub didn't move his eyes from the television monitor. "As you know, each of the three survival classes here at Trinity II has a separate control team positioned in Central Control. None of the subjects, not even Primary Beings, do anything unless the control team gives the command."

"You've apparently known about these intruders for some time," said Shelley.

"Yes, we've actually had them under surveillance for days—long before they entered Nogal Cave," Singlelaub responded.

"It's an unfortunate complication that they made it all the way in here," Stelmetz said.

"Perhaps not. Look at them!" There was an edge of excitement on Ernst Singlelaub's voice. "What do you see?"

"A Mexican-American woman, a big Anglo man, and a smaller guy," Shelley answered.

Singlelaub almost smiled. "The only subjects we've been able to supply for your experiments have been society's rejects—convicts, residents of mental institutions. But now, look at those three people."

Stelmetz studied the three subjects intensely. "Yes, I see what you're saying."

"They could fit into our three survival classes!" said Shelley.

"Is that what you're thinking, Dr. Singlelaub?"

"Yes, Stelmetz, it is. The big man is Mark Tilman, a newspaper reporter from Albuquerque."

"His bone structure and size would make him a good subject for the Peacemaker class," said Stelmetz.

"And the woman," Singlelaub continued, "would fit well into the Producer class. She's a waitress, also from Albuquerque. Her name is Trina Escobar."

"Escobar?" said Shelley. "I once operated on a subject here at Trinity II by that name."

"You did indeed," Singlelaub responded. "You ablated his amygdala, and he escaped."

"AB-2?" Shelley asked.

"Exactly. Miss Escobar's brother was Ablation Subject 2. That is why she is here." Singlelaub continued to focus on the three people on the screen.

"We've also had some contact with the family of the smaller man," Singlelaub continued. "He's Merritt Bonner, the editor of the Alamogordo newspaper. His brother stumbled into Nogal Cave some months back. We captured him and attempted a Producer transition, but he died."

"May I request the use of Bonner?" asked Shelley, studying Merritt Bonner's cranial structure.

"For what purpose?" Singlelaub asked.

"As you know, I've been experimenting with certain augmentation procedures in the hippocampus," Shelley said. "I've been able to expand the learning capacity of a rhesus monkey by 25 percent. Now I need to see if the procedure will work on a human."

"If you succeed, this Bonner could be the greatest of the Primary Beings," Stelmetz noted.

Singlelaub nodded. "You may use him."

Shelley smiled.

Dr. Singlelaub spoke again into the microphone on the console in front of him. "Peacemaker Control?"

"Peacemaker Control here," came the response.

"Instruct the Peacemakers in A/S Zone, Sector One, Elm and Duval to seize the intruders. Have them transported to the Analysis Sector of the Research and Development Zone. And instruct the Peacemakers not to harm the subjects. We have use for them."

"That's affirmative. Peacemaker Control, out."

Singlelaub pressed a switch and spoke into his microphone. "This is Singlelaub to Dr. Preston."

"Preston here." The response was almost immediate.

"Turn on your monitor to Sector One of the A/S Zone." Singlelaub glanced at computer-generated numbers flashing time, date, and camera number on the bottom of the screen. "That will be camera A/S-1-5."

"I have it," Preston reported.

"You will observe that our Peacemakers are taking some intruders into custody. They will be brought to you immediately. Hold them until I get there."

"Will do," Preston answered. "Additional instructions?"

"None. Singlelaub out." Ernst Singlelaub turned slowly in his chair to face Stelmetz and Shelley. "Gentlemen," he said, "it's always good to have fresh subjects to work with."

After Stelmetz and Shelley had left the conference room, Singlelaub sat for a moment, deep in thought. The words *fresh subjects* kept whispering through his brain like two unsettled ghosts.

Weariness suddenly slouched over Singlelaub like a familiar, sullen fog. It seemed always to follow these intense moments when he hovered between crisis and discovery. Despite crucial developments, Singlelaub knew that he must go to his apartment and rest.

In moments, he had traversed the short passageway between the conference room and the apartment. The room was as cold and uninviting as Singlelaub's personality. Every object, every piece of furniture in the small chamber was there because it had a function. There was no apparent need in Singlelaub's life for beauty, except that of his beloved Megan. Thus the appointments of the man's living quarters matched the bluntness of his spirit.

There was one object in the room that was an exception. It was the only concession to emotion Ernst Singlelaub allowed in the room. His eyes now fell on the solitary item, resting on his bed table. Feeling the weight of his physical and psychic fatigue, Singlelaub picked up the tattered book. He opened its age-worn cover gently, as if the thing would crumble in his hands, and read the inscription penned in elegant German classical script: The Diary of Maria Gruendel Singlelaub.

Instinctively, Singlelaub turned to the two pages he was always drawn to read when his cycles of soul-weariness swept over him. Singlelaub had concluded that this book must have been the second part of his mother's journal, for it began somewhere during Ernst's childhood. The account of her own childhood, courtship, and marriage to his father must have been in another diary, now lost as absolutely as his mother's gentle laughter and soft touch.

Singlelaub began reading at page one. It told of a happy day spent on a family picnic, deep in a brilliantly colored autumn forest near Vienna. Habitually, as if by ritual, Singlelaub would scold himself for the sentimentality he would feel when reading about that picnic he couldn't remember.

On this day, as on all others when he was lured in by his mother's delight, he cursed with the same German expletive and turned to the last page of the diary to balance his emotions.

"I am worried for our safety," his mother had written. "The Nazis seem to suspect anyone who works for the Austrian government."

There was nothing more written, but Singlelaub knew the rest of the story. His parents had tried to escape, were caught, and were shot right before his eyes. The event so wounded the five-year-old child that Singlelaub had erected a shell of lead around his emotions so that he would never feel such pain again.

That wounded child was still alive somewhere in Singlelaub's psyche, and it was the hurt of that child that caused Singlelaub's periodic emotional fatigue.

The words *fresh subjects* had stirred the child. Singlelaub knew what would happen to the three people who had blundered into Trinity II: they would be captured, imprisoned, and experimented with.

The pained child within Ernst Singlelaub now had new reason for torturing him with the accusation it held up to the adult constantly: *You and your experiments are no different from the beasts who destroyed my mother and father.*

For a brief moment, Singlelaub would feel trapped. The only way a man could save the human race from itself was to become a tyrant.

And the child would cry out, *Hitler excused his tyranny by arguing survival.*

Today, Singlelaub's weariness was so great that he screamed aloud at the child. "But it's different! I'm working for the survival of the human race. Hitler was working for its destruction. *There is a difference!"*

Singlelaub became suddenly aware that he was

shaking and talking to himself. Quickly, he closed the leaden shell of his psyche. No one must ever know of his inner turmoil.

Ernst Singlelaub downed two tranquilizers in one swallow, hoping they would still the pained voice crying within him, at least for a little while.

TILMAN, Trina, and Bonner peered
out of the bookstore's alcove entrance in silent,
incredulous shock. At first glance the town
looked like any small, pleasant village in America. Neat shops lined the streets, and smaller lanes
intersected the main thoroughfare. Yet heavy
army trucks lumbered down the roadway, and
the town was populated with strange-looking
beings.

At the corner of Elm and Duval stood three
frightening, hulking creatures towering well over
six feet. Each of the three man-beasts had mammoth arms dropping from shoulders as square
and seemingly as hard as steel beams.

The most horrid feature of the creatures was
their shrunken heads which were so flat on top

that they actually appeared to have been chopped off.

Mark Tilman gaped at the virtually expressionless faces of one of the beastly creatures. The eyes were as large as those of any human adult, but looked out of place in the small head. The eyeballs darted back and forth constantly as if surveying everything around. Two large nasal openings replaced the nose and electronic headsets covered their ears. Clearly, surmised Tilman, the heads of the beasts were made for eating and breathing functions, not for thought.

Each of the creatures wore a red coverall suit with the identification *Peacemaker Unit 5* stenciled across his back.

Tilman turned his attention to the scene immediately in front of him. There, another crew of human men clad in yellow overalls was making street repairs. The back of each worker's uniform bore the word *Producer* and a unit number.

The heads of the Producers seemed slightly larger than those of the Peacemakers—though they were still small for their gigantic bodies. The Producers' faces appeared more blank than did the Peacemakers'. In fact, the visage of the Producers seemed to have been frozen, the only movement in their faces the blinking of eyelids.

Like the Peacemakers, the Producers wore metallic headsets that seemed permanently installed on their ears.

With brittle movements, the Producers filled the potholes heavy army trucks had notched in the street.

Merritt Bonner nudged Tilman. "They look like robots," he whispered, "but look at their chests. They're breathing."

Trina gasped. "These people remind me of what Manuel looked like in the hospital," she said softly. "Remember how his limbs were swollen and his head seemed too small for his body? And that awful blank expression on his face!"

"Come to think of it," Mark said quietly, "he seemed to have been transformed into something between a human and these strange creatures."

Trina began pulling back into the alcove, unconsciously getting closer to the door of the bookstore behind her. Suddenly, she bumped into a small woman emerging from the shop and knocked her to the ground. Trina turned, emitting a tiny squeal.

Mark saw the frail woman fall and reached over to help her up. The female creature stood about five feet tall and weighed no more than ninety-five pounds. As the little woman got up, Trina stared directly into the widest, most intense blue eyes she had ever seen.

"Oh, I'm so sorry," said Trina.

Though the woman had struck the concrete hard, she had not uttered a sound. She seemed to experience no pain. Like the Peacemakers and Producers, she was clad in a jumpsuit and wore a headset over her ears. Her blue outfit bore the designation *Primary Being Unit 23*.

In contrast to the Peacemakers' and Producers' small head on a large body, she had a remarkably large head for such a tiny body. And although her facial features seemed to be frozen, her eyes were alive with thought. She studied the three humans momentarily and started to walk away.

Mark Tilman, seeing that the tiny woman had dropped a book she had apparently gotten in the bookstore, picked up the book. "Wait a minute!" he called without thinking. As he handed the book to the female creature, he glanced at the title: *Beyond Freedom and Dignity* by B. F. Skinner.

The woman looked at Tilman for a second as he handed her the book. Then she was gone.

Merritt Bonner grabbed Tilman's arm. "Mark, you've got to keep quiet," he whispered loudly. "You might alert those Goliaths over there on the street corner."

Ernst Singlelaub intentionally allowed Mark Tilman, Trina Escobar, and Merritt Bonner a few moments to observe the strange world into which they had stumbled. He wanted to study them. Singlelaub sat behind the control console in his Command Center and stared at the television monitor focused on the three intruders. He could detect their deepening desperation. The Escobar woman appeared close to panic. If Singlelaub allowed them to start running in fear, capture would be difficult.

"Seize the intruders," he ordered Master Control.

Immediately, Master Control relayed Singlelaub's command to Peacemaker Control for Sector One of the Applied Science Zone.

"Alert, Units Five, Seven, and Nine," said the technician in Peacemaker Control. "There are intruders at the bookstore. Bring them to Sector One of the R/D Zone. I am deactivating your electronic gatekeepers for zone crossing. Commence operation."

The three Peacemakers standing on the corner of Elm and Duval suddenly came alive. With the same ponderous movements of the Producers, they began moving unseen toward Tilman, Trina, and Bonner.

As the Peacemakers moved, the control technician's voice squawked into their headsets. "Do not harm intruders. Repeat. Do not harm intruders."

"Master Control to Peacemaker Control," called the technician to his superior. "We understand Unit Five isn't functioning properly. Should we remove it from pursuit?"

"Negative," answered Peacemaker Control. "There are no other Peacemaker units in the sector. Besides, the malfunction is just a short circuit in Five's headset. Apart from some static when we give the commands, there should be no problem."

But when they gave the commands, they got more than static. The short circuit resulted from a tiny exposed section of electrical wire that dug into Unit Five's ear. While the creature experienced no pain, the continual chatter from Peacemaker Control sent an electric shock into its body. The pulse of electricity probed deeply into what was left of the Peacemaker's brain, stimulating already heightened aggressiveness.

Mark Tilman heard the noise and turned around. What he saw sparked terror. He grabbed for Trina and Bonner. "We've got to get out of here!" Tilman cried.

In a berserk rage, Peacemaker Unit Five was flailing the other two units who were not programmed to respond to attack from one of their own. A tempest stirred within their small, angry brains.

Suddenly, all three creatures began lumbering toward the three human intruders at a surprisingly fast pace.

Clutching Trina's hand, Mark dashed out of the alcove and up the street, with Bonner close behind.

Glancing back, Tilman watched Peacemaker Unit Five gain speed. Apparently, the beasts had been equipped with enhanced muscular ability. The creatures would soon overtake them.

At that moment, Trina tripped on a wide crack in the sidewalk and fell, pulling Mark down with her. Bonner stopped to help his friends up.

"Run, Merritt. Get away!" Tilman yelled, scrambling to his feet.

Bonner waited until Tilman and Trina were standing, then all three began running again.

It was too late. Unit Five, pursued by Units Seven and Nine, was almost upon them. The fury of the other two Peacemakers, lit by Unit Five's assault on them, was now unfocused. Anything in their path became their target.

As Trina tried to run, she began sobbing. Her knees burned where they had scraped on the concrete sidewalk. She could now hear the lead Peacemaker's breathing, like the snorting of a galloping bull.

Bonner glanced over his shoulder as they ran. "Wait! Look!" he shouted.

Unit Five had halted suddenly. The other two Peacemakers also slowed and stopped. Unit Five appeared paralyzed for a moment and then instantly burst into flames. The other Peacemakers crouched in fear.

"What on earth . . . ?" Tilman left his question unfinished.

Ernst Singlelaub had watched the pursuit of the intruders on his television monitor from high in his Command Center. Because of the difficulty of getting experimental subjects, Singlelaub had issued rigid orders that no units were to be destroyed without his express command. Reluctantly, in this case he had ordered the deployment of the built-in destruct mechanism in Peacemaker Unit Five. He couldn't let a malfunctioning unit destroy the three human beings who would make even better experimental subjects. Within moments, Unit Five was a smoking pile of cinders.

"Now!" Bonner shouted. "We've got to get moving while they're distracted."

Mark grabbed Trina's hand, and the three dashed on through Ernst Singlelaub's strange world. Soon they found themselves on what appeared to be a quiet lane in a university village. They stopped to rest. Spires of ornate, dignified buildings reached up toward the ceiling of the awesome cave. A sign labeled one of the red brick buildings as The Ernst Singlelaub Behavioral Sciences Research Center.

For a moment, the name *Ernst Singlelaub* jogged Tilman's recollection of the past. All he could remember was that Singlelaub was the assistant to the long-vanished President Prentiss Pearson.

"Psst." Merritt Bonner broke into Tilman's thoughts. "Quick! Hide in here," he said, motioning toward some shrubs that somehow managed to grow underground in artificial light. "I don't like the way that looks up there," Bonner cautioned.

Tilman peered up the street. About fifty feet ahead, the little university town came to an abrupt end. A band of white had been painted on the floor, perhaps twenty feet across. Blue stripes were brushed diagonally on the white band spanning the concrete floor. A cable of cold blue-white light split the band precisely down the middle. The beam seemed to be at waist level on an average-size human being.

"It must be an alarm of some type," Tilman whispered to Bonner.

"It's strange they would make it high enough for someone to slip under," Bonner answered.

Trina glanced behind them. "That's what we better do, fast," she cried.

The two Peacemakers, having recovered from

their shock of seeing one of their number incinerated, were closing in on the human intruders.

"Get moving and stay low—under that beam!" Bonner ordered. He and his two friends scampered toward the slender thread of light.

Just as Tilman dived under the light, he realized that they were running into an industrial zone. There was heavy machinery to his right. Just ahead lay a long street of row houses similar to the old dwellings around America's eastern industrial cities. A large square sign announced Applied Science Zone, Sector Two.

In the lead, Merritt Bonner glanced back at Mark and Trina who were near collapse. Trina obviously had been hurt in the fall she had taken, and she needed to rest.

Suddenly, Bonner saw an alleyway and motioned Trina and Tilman to follow him in. The three hid behind a phalanx of used metal containers stacked in a corner of the alley. Still able to see the street, they hoped the Peacemakers would rush past.

As Tilman watched, he was struck by the oddity of the sight. Whole armies of yellow-clad Producers walked about with stiff gaits. While some of the Producers obviously had seen them hide behind the metal containers, they had not signaled the Peacemakers.

"Uh-oh," exclaimed Tilman in as loud a voice as he dared.

The two Peacemakers who had pursued them out of Sector One slowed down at the alley entrance. Joined by three other Peacemakers, all five now searched the alley. Trina shuddered as the Peacemakers approached the pile of metal containers.

Suddenly, Merritt Bonner shrieked like a mortally wounded dinosaur and dashed from behind the containers, running deeper into the alley. The Peacemakers, as stunned as Trina and Mark, chased him.

Tilman understood Bonner's sacrifice. As the Peacemakers went after Merritt Bonner, Tilman and Trina dashed in the opposite direction to the alleyway entrance. When the two reached the street, one of the Peacemakers chasing Bonner saw them and ran in their direction.

Tilman's heart thudded as he dragged Trina behind him through Sector Two. Everywhere he looked, Producers, like docile ants, performed heavy labor. Some factory doors stood open, and he could see the creatures working at lathes or repairing trucks.

"Mark . . . I can't . . . go any more . . ." Trina wept, pleading with him to stop.

"Just a little more." Tilman could see that they were nearing another border zone. "Let's try to get over into that other area. Maybe the Peacemakers can't follow us there."

Breathlessly, the two dove under the light beam into the area marked Applied Science Zone, Sector Three.

They scampered a hundred feet into the new zone before Tilman dared glancing behind him. Then he stopped so suddenly that Trina, who was hanging onto his arm, almost fell again.

Trina looked back. The pursuing Peacemakers halted at the light beam. For some reason, they wouldn't go through it.

Tilman and Trina tried to catch their breath. Trina groaned slightly from the pain of the cuts on her knees and hands. Tilman put his arm around her and looked about.

As they had crossed from sector to sector, the lighting had grown dimmer. They had moved from noonday brightness in Sector One to a late afternoon glow in Sector Two to a chilly dusklike darkness in Sector Three.

Adding to the sense of chill, the narrow street on which they stood bore nothing but row upon row of steel cubicles.

"Mark . . . I . . . don't want to go any farther." Trina clutched Tilman's hand tightly.

Mark stared down the street ahead of them. *The deepest dungeons of a medieval prison couldn't be more foreboding,* he thought. Then Tilman looked back toward the border. The Peacemakers still stood frustrated on the other side of the light beam.

"We have no choice, Trina. We have to go on. Those monsters will tear us to pieces."

Deeper into the cold darkness, Tilman led Trina. A half mile into Sector Three, the street angled to the right. The border's light beam and the Peacemakers were no longer in sight.

Again, Tilman and Trina halted. They were standing in the middle of a street bordering a huge lake. Because of the darkness, they couldn't make out its far shoreline. A stark white sign with red lettering warned Caution—Reproduction Control Experimental Reservoir.

Looking over his shoulder, Tilman could see more steel cubicles. Trina needed rest. Along the row of metal doors facing the lake, one of the doors stood slightly ajar.

"Come on, honey. Let's go inside there. Maybe we'll be safe."

Inside the metal room, Tilman noticed a cot and an entrance to an adjoining room. Slowly, he eased Trina onto the cot, then slid to the floor beside the small bed. Still grasping her hand, he rested his head on the side of the cot.

Suddenly, Trina screamed. Mark jumped and immediately felt a crushing pain in his right shoulder as a Peacemaker charged from the adjoining room and grabbed them.

Sector Three was the Peacemaker community, and the steel cubicles housed the strange creatures.

The Peacemaker clutching Tilman and Trina heard a command in his headset from Peacemaker Control.

"Do not harm the subjects. Bring them to the Access Area immediately."

A rivulet of blood, like a hot coil of molten steel, ran from Mark Tilman's shoulder and down his chest. Tilman knew his blood wasn't fiery. His body was just so cold that anything with warmth seemed ablaze.

Tilman hoped the Peacemaker wasn't gripping Trina's shoulder that tightly. If so, her bones would be crushed.

Tilman needn't have worried. Far away in Trinity II's Control Zone, a technician monitored the pressure exerted by Unit 37's handgrip, allowing a tighter grip for Peacemaker's right hand, which held Mark Tilman. The monitoring computer had assessed Tilman's potential for escaping the Peacemaker's grip and had given data to the technician on the precise amount of pressure needed.

Within moments, three other Peacemakers entered the cubicle where Unit 37 held Tilman and Trina. As soon as they arrived, Unit 37 released his prisoners, and the four Peacemakers encircled them. Any escape attempt would be futile.

Suddenly, Unit 37 nudged Tilman and Trina toward the door. Outside the cubicle, the four Peacemakers encircled the intruders, marching them back to the crossing point between Sectors Two and Three.

Trina shivered. The eerie atmosphere enveloped her like a cold swamp. The only sound coming from the Peacemakers was the tromp of their heavy feet and the thickness of their breathing. The dim, bluish-cold light of Sector Three remained unchanged.

Within moments, they arrived at the crossing point designated an Access Area in the Trinity II lingo. Just beyond the light beam stood four more Peacemakers accompanied by four soldiers in fatigues.

"Mr. Tilman, Miss Escobar, you are to come with us," ordered one of the soldiers with a thick, Slavic accent.

"Where are you taking us? What have you done with Merritt Bonner?" Tilman demanded.

The soldiers wouldn't answer.

The four Peacemakers from Sector Three didn't follow as Mark and Trina walked ahead. Tilman glanced back at the Sector Three Peacemakers.

"They can't follow you," the soldier said. "They are equipped with devices called electron-

170

ic gatekeepers. Unless these devices are deactivated, the light beam will set off a jamming signal, freezing the Peacemaker. They can only cross zones if we permit them. Peacemakers can be volatile creatures. We have to control them carefully."

Tilman stopped at the light beam and stared at the sentry on the other side.

"Oh, it's all right for you and the woman. The beam won't hurt you."

Tilman and Trina walked through the long spear of light, feeling nothing. Immediately, the soldiers and the Sector Two Peacemakers escorted them into a small open vehicle driven by a corporal.

"Analysis Sector, R/D Zone," the soldier ordered tersely.

The small electrically powered transporter emitted only a low hum as it traveled down the white roadway between Sectors Two and Three, the light beam to their right. In five minutes, they arrived at an intersection where the bright cable of light formed 90-degree angles to the right and left. Sectors Two and Three were neatly boxed in by the light that controlled access by the Peacemakers. The light shot in three directions from a slender metal tube about ten feet high, which stood in the middle of the road. The beam glowed from a focal point three-and-a-half feet up the pole. Five feet higher, a sign bore the warning Caution. Limit of Applied Zone. Service Road Ahead.

Tilman peered ahead. The service road was a

broad, four-lane highway stretching through the massive cavern to the right and left. On a median strip, bright lights gave off a brilliant orange glimmer, as at a highway interchange above ground. More big trucks sped back and forth on the service road. Immediately ahead, Tilman saw that a very high, stark metal wall bordered the service road on the other side.

A traffic light at the intersection turned green and the driver turned the electric car left, picking up speed as he moved down the wide service road. Tilman figured that they were traveling in the direction of Sector One, where they had first entered the Applied Science Zone. If that was the case, he thought, they would also be traveling toward the incinerator area they had stumbled into from Nogal Cave.

Suddenly, though, the driver headed the vehicle off the service road toward a guardhouse where a severe steel gate blocked the smaller roadway. The sign on the guardhouse read Restricted Area. Research and Development Zone. Only Security Clearance Alpha permitted entry.

Mark and Trina exchanged questioning glances.

The sentry on duty at the guardhouse quickly checked the identification badges of the soldiers escorting Tilman and Trina. Satisfied that the troopers had Alpha clearance, the guard motioned them through the gate. The guard hadn't even looked at Tilman and Trina. It was as if they had been expected and there was no question about their security clearance.

A quarter mile from the gate, the electric vehicle pulled to a stop before an austere building that seemed to grow out of the stone cavern wall. A sign labeled the structure as the Analysis Center and warned anyone of entering unless they had specific business there. A double door of hard steel forbade entry unless one knew the secret of how to make it part.

One of the soldiers moved to a microphone concealed behind a metal grid on the building's wall. "Sergeant Vasily. Serial A-75846. Clearance Alpha."

The microphone scooped up the soldier's words and funneled them into a computer somewhere inside the stone building. In microseconds, the computer checked the serial number and security clearance given by the sergeant and did a voice analysis. Satisfied that Vasily was who he said he was, the computer opened the steel doors.

Trina clung to Mark's arm as the soldier escorted them into a large, glass-enclosed reception area. The door leading out of the glass cubicle and deeper into the Analysis Center was marked by a sign which almost shouted Alpha-AA Clearance Only.

"These are the intruders we were ordered to bring here," Vasily said to a guard sitting at a desk in the middle of the reception cubicle.

"I have instructions regarding them," answered the man.

Turning in his chair, he spoke into a microphone on the console before him. "Double-A escort report to gate."

Evidently, concluded Tilman, the soldiers who had brought them here didn't have sufficient clearance to go beyond the reception area. He wondered what was so secret that even some of the people who guarded this strange world were kept out.

Five minutes later, deeper inside the Analysis Center, Tilman could feel Trina shivering beside him as they stood outside another ponderous door, waiting for it to open. His own uncertainty grew though he hid it well. *Perhaps inside this room we will find some clue to the mystery of this place,* he thought.

At that moment the door whooshed open, and the double-A escorts prodded him and Trina into the room. Tilman caught his breath.

Seated at a massive conference table in the center of the room was a man whom Tilman would recognize anywhere—Ernst Singlelaub. Tilman remembered the reams of newspaper copy he had read about Singlelaub. A decade earlier, news reports detailed Singlelaub's attempt to manipulate President Prentiss Pearson, and exposed his part in Pearson's downfall. Then the stories about Singlelaub had faded, and it seemed the man had crawled in a hole somewhere. Suddenly, Tilman realized Singlelaub had quite literally crawled into a hole—this massive cavern under White Sands.

Trina Escobar dug her fingers into Tilman's arm. On the side of the table nearest them on Singlelaub's right was Merritt Bonner. When

they entered, his back was to them, but he had
turned in his chair and now looked at them with
an expression of utter perplexity.

On Singlelaub's left sat three other men. One
of them Tilman recognized as Dr. Hyman Stelmetz, the famous geneticist and winner of the
Nobel Prize. But Tilman hadn't seen the other
man before.

"Please enter and sit by Mr. Bonner." Singlelaub's voice sounded like spitting electricity.

Taking his place beside Bonner, Tilman did a
quick visual check of his friend. There seemed no
harm.

"It is unfortunate that you have blundered into
this place," Singlelaub began.

"We came only because someone destroyed
Miss Escobar's brother," Tilman interrupted.

"A most distressing accident," Singlelaub answered, his voice emotionless. "But since you
will soon become a permanent part of this new
world, I want you to know all about it."

Hyman Stelmetz threw a brief, knowing glance
at James Shelley, the other man seated at the table. They knew why Singlelaub wanted to tell the
intruders about Trinity II. Singlelaub may have
appeared devoid of emotions, but they had been
with him ten years and knew there was a growing
frustration in Singlelaub, a man of no small ego.
With every accomplishment at Trinity II, Singlelaub grew increasingly edgy because there was no
one outside the Trinity II population before
whom he could flaunt his genius. Stelmetz and

Shelley knew their leader now had an audience.

"The two men seated with me here are a vital part of my effort to save humanity," Singlelaub continued. "Dr. Hyman Stelmetz is helping me design a new human being."

Trina's body began to tremble.

"Dr. James Shelley," Singlelaub went on, "is one of the world's most skilled neurosurgeons. He is the man who implements many of Dr. Stelmetz's discoveries."

"Does this place have a name?" Merritt Bonner's apparent anger gave way to his natural curiosity.

Singlelaub paused, as if savoring the words he would speak. "My world down here is called Trinity II," he said.

"Why Trinity II?" Tilman asked.

"To understand that, you must know something of history. You must grasp and appreciate where the human race stands in its perilous chronology." Ernst Singlelaub stared straight ahead, his voice as toneless as a computer's.

"In the last decade, mankind has passed into a new age, but because the passage occurred here at Trinity II, the race doesn't know it dwells in a new era."

"What kind of age is it?" Bonner asked.

Singlelaub looked at Bonner. A smile almost tugged at his thin lips. "We have moved from the Age of Pyrotechnology to the Age of Biotechnology," he said.

Trina's brow furrowed at the use of so much technical jargon.

"For countless eons," Singlelaub continued, "man built his world around fire. The technologies and skills developed all flowed from the energy of combustion. But man himself has not kept pace with his own technologies. His body is still subject to disease and death, his machines outlast him, and because of his psychological flaws, man has actually turned his machines on himself."

"I know," Tilman interrupted. "It's called sin."

Singlelaub shot Tilman an Arctic stare. "Trinity II is a world without sin, if you must call human error that," he said tersely. "What civilization needed was a period of advance in biotechnology that would equal and go beyond the accomplishments of pyrotechnology. What I understood more than ten years ago was that only then would the age of fire be more of a benefit to humanity than a peril. I was the first to grasp the fact that the Age of Pyrotechnology was controlling and destroying humanity, and I realized that without a new man, brought about by a new age, man was going to destroy himself by the works of his hands!" For the first time, Ernst Singlelaub showed enthusiasm.

"Uh, when did we enter this Age of Biotechnology?" Tilman asked.

"Nirenberg. Watson. Crick."

"Huh?"

Contempt crept into Singlelaub's voice when Tilman failed to recognize the names Singlelaub had mentioned. "Dr. Marshall Nirenberg brought us to the threshold of the Age of Biotechnology in 1961. Nirenberg managed to isolate a strand of DNA and found the protein it produced. DNA," he explained, "is the chemical that instructs the cells in a living organism how to arrange themselves."

The clarification did little to help Trina, whose face betrayed her growing frustration.

"Watson and Crick discovered the structure of DNA," Singlelaub continued. "But it was left to me—and my associates, of course—to take the work of these men to its logical extent, as you will see, and experience."

Trina again began to tremble and Mark slipped his arm around her protectively.

"The step that most immediately brought us to Trinity II was taken by two biologists, Stanley Cohen and Herman Boyer, in 1973." Singlelaub appeared thoroughly entranced by his own recital of history. "Those two men took DNA from two organisms that would never come together naturally, and they mated the chemicals. That literally produced a new form of life."

"Recombinant DNA," muttered Bonner, thinking aloud.

"Precisely," answered Singlelaub. The *combining* of two samples of DNA from disparate organisms meant the same for the Age of Biotechnology as Fermi's splitting of the atom meant for the Age of Pyrotechnology."

Singlelaub's taut control strained over the excitement of revealing his own greatness. "The most important step in the Age of Pyrotechnology happened hundreds of feet above where we sit right now."

"The atomic bomb?" Mark Tilman was beginning to piece together the information Singlelaub had been weaving.

"Yes, that's right!" Singlelaub stood and pointed upward. "Up there, at the surface Trinity site, mankind saw the crowning achievement of the Age of Pyrotechnology—the nuclear bomb. But here, in this underground cavern beneath the site, is Trinity II—the crowning achievement of the Age of Biotechnology!"

"That's a rather sweeping statement." Merritt Bonner momentarily forgot he was Ernst Singlelaub's prisoner. He wanted to debate him. "What happened up there at the Trinity site changed mankind. I'll grant that some strange things are happening here, but what's so special that you call it the second Trinity?"

"At Trinity I," Singlelaub answered, "all the existing knowledge of the atom combined to make that nuclear explosion. I have done the same thing here with biological knowledge. I have created a world where we have brought together all the advances and research in behavior control."

"But why?" asked Tilman, uncharacteristically shaken by the information they had uncovered.

"Because humanity will not survive without a change in *homo sapiens*," Singlelaub answered. "To stoke the fires of the Age of Pyrotechnology, man had to deplete earth's resources. This also increased greed. And that has been at the root of all the wars fought by mankind. The very achievements of the Age of Pyrotechnology are now the tools by which humanity may wipe itself off the planet. We must create an advanced species or earth will die."

"So, at Trinity II you've tried to create the new man?" Bonner queried.

"More than that! More than that!" Singlelaub shot back. "I have created a new society inhabited by a new man. For ten years, Trinity II has been a vast laboratory where we've been tediously developing that new man and working out flaws. Soon, we'll bring Trinity II above ground. We'll present our achievements to our benefactors, who will create a world just like what you see here at Trinity II."

"The American people will never accept it!" Tilman shouted at Singlelaub.

"You are correct," Singlelaub responded. "I've had to begin with a nation that appreciates our work and objectives—the Soviet Union!"

Bonner looked incredulous. "Then the accents of those guards . . ."

". . . Was Russian!" Singlelaub smirked at Bonner's discovery, but he would not reveal the totality of his plan to these intruders. Singlelaub knew that the citizens of the United States would not blithely accept control over their lives. But he knew that if the Soviet Union began to outstrip the United States, then the American government would be forced to do anything to keep up.

"I had to turn to someone who was willing to invest the billions of dollars necessary to carry out these projects," Singlelaub continued. He didn't mind sharing some of his secrets with the intruders, since they would soon disappear into the experimental chambers of Trinity II.

"The Russians financed all this?" asked Tilman in disbelief.

"To be precise, the KGB," replied Singlelaub. "The Soviet Union has an appreciation for secrecy that we have not yet cultivated in America. Our budget has been concealed for years in hidden KGB accounts."

Bonner frowned. "Then what you and the KGB have created here at Trinity II is a new order inhabited by a new being!" he exclaimed, horrified.

"Therefore if any man be in *Christ*, he is a *new creature:* old things are passed away; behold, all things are become new." The voice was that of Trina Escobar. The conversation had at last turned to something she knew about.

For a split second, Ernst Singlelaub was taken aback. Hyman Stelmetz glanced downward, studying his clenched hands, while James Shelley scratched his nose, looking up at the ceiling.

"Religion?" Singlelaub spat out the word.

"I think what Miss Escobar is saying," Tilman explained, "is that we agree there needs to be a change in man, even the creation of a new person. But we disagree with your methods."

"I suppose your method is religion?" Stelmetz entered the conversation.

"No, actually not," Tilman answered. "The

181

only method for creating a new person is the power of God."

Stelmetz laughed, and Merritt Bonner looked embarrassed.

"I believe that method was ruled out at the end of the Dark Ages," Stelmetz sneered.

"Religion is preposterous," Singlelaub sputtered. "Not even a worthy subject for scientific inquiry."

"Mr. Tilman," Stelmetz continued, "here at Trinity II we've even ruled out psychology as a means of producing a new person."

"Then what's left?" asked Bonner.

"Physiology," Singlelaub shot back. "All that matters at Trinity II is physiology!"

"There are really only three ways to alter the human brain, and, through it, the human psyche," interjected Dr. James Shelley.

All eyes in the room turned to the suave, tanned neurosurgeon.

"One way is to change the brain through surgery, what we call the ablation techniques."

"Is that what you did to my brother?" Trina's voice quivered as she spoke.

Shelley didn't even look at her. "Or we can alter brain patterns through electrical stimulation. Our third method is chemical intervention."

"At Trinity II, we have brought all these skills to the highest state of development," Stelmetz noted.

Anger simmered in Tilman's normally jovial spirit. "It's a shame Hitler didn't have you people."

Ernst Singlelaub shifted uncomfortably in his chair, the pained child within him prodded to attention by Tilman's words.

"Come now," Stelmetz sneered. "Must we endure a historical cliche?"

"It's true!" Tilman screamed. "It doesn't matter whether you're a Nazi or a Fascist or a left-wing Communist. You all treat people the same way in the name of your glorious cause!"

"That's right," Bonner joined the verbal assault. "The only difference between *your* attempt to build a super race and Hitler's is semantics."

Shelley, whose eyes had been darting between the jousters as if he were watching a boxing match, glanced at Ernst Singlelaub. Singlelaub's eyes were tightly closed. There was an almost imperceptible quiver on his tense lips though no one else could hear the wounded child shrieking its hurt deep within Singlelaub's psyche. The discussion of Hitler and the Nazis had been like driving a hot iron into that ever-present child.

Singlelaub struggled for control. At last he spoke in a taut, low voice. "We've been rude to our guests," he said. "We shouldn't limit their understanding to our conversation. Let's *show* them Trinity II, and later we'll let them *experience* our new world."

As Singlelaub watched the intruders being taken from the room, he knew that once more he had stilled the voice of the child. But he didn't know how much longer he could keep it from screaming out its agony in everyone's hearing.

SYLVIA Gladstone had the rich honor of being selected for Ernst Singlelaub's breeding program. For a prostitute, she was unusually intelligent. There was a time in what seemed like millennia ago when she was a slender, beguiling woman who commanded the highest prices for her favors. Only the elite of Albuquerque could patronize a woman of her caliber.

But something had gone wrong. It had begun with a little marijuana use. Life after that became a blur, a raucous, dizzying whirlwind madly tossing the debris of tranquilizers, alcohol, cocaine, heroin, and assorted other exotic drugs. The whirlwind finally plopped her in the Albuquerque jail. The elegant woman had been transformed into a skinny hag whose eyes rested like tiny corpses in casketlike pouches. Her once-silken skin became lined and scaly.

As she was coming off the drugs in the Albuquerque jail, Sylvia shriveled in agony.

Taking advantage of the merciless moment, the warden came with his offer. There was a man, he said, who could take away her pain. Whether it was by curing her or giving her more drugs, Sylvia didn't know. She only knew she wanted the torment to cease. The warden promised her help if she would cooperate with the man by assisting him in some scientific projects.

Sylvia had agreed without hesitation, and later that night she was whisked away to Trinity II. Within weeks, the chain of drugs had been snapped, Sylvia's physical and intellectual capacities had been measured, and she had been assigned a mission at Trinity II.

As a member of Singlelaub's breeding program, Sylvia never saw the fathers of her children. *In vitro* fertilization was Trinity II's method of reproduction. In fact, the whole process was so mechanical that Sylvia didn't even think about it when she was wheeled into the delivery room to bear her children before an audience of dozens seated in the operating theater.

On this day, Sylvia's normally cynical mind was sprinkled with an occasional flurry of optimism. The doctors at Trinity II had determined that she was good for three children, and then her task would be over. This was Sylvia's third trip into the delivery room. As she was transferred to the delivery table, Sylvia reflected on what her physician had promised. It was always hard to understand his thick accent, but she knew that he had promised that as soon as she had recovered from this birth, she would be free. Transportation would be provided to any place on the globe that she desired to go. Sylvia smiled as she thought of Tahiti.

The doctor, having indicated that she would be put to sleep for her third delivery, had crafted a fantasy. Sylvia Gladstone wouldn't wake up in Tahiti, but in the Processing Center of Trinity II. Surgery would have already been performed before she woke up, beginning her transformation into a sterling member of the Producer class at Trinity II.

Mark Tilman sat behind a glass wall in the spectator area of the operating theater. He glanced over at Trina Escobar, then at Ernst Singlelaub, who were with him in the audience. Tilman wondered if Singlelaub would use Trina this way. Hatred for Singlelaub pounded his soul like a turbulent thunderstorm. If Singlelaub did turn Trina into a breeding animal, Tilman knew he would kill Singlelaub given any chance at all. Tilman fought the rage, knowing it would rob him of any capacity to act rationally if the opportunity came to escape Trinity II.

"In another ten years," Singlelaub informed his guests, "it won't be necessary to surgically alter adults to fit their assigned survival classes. By then, some of the genetically engineered children born here in our birth clinic will be of breeding age. Their offspring will be just like their parents. Nature will have been employed as a full partner in developing the new man!"

Sylvia Gladstone, on the table below, drifted off into a deep sleep. Within a half hour, a child would emerge from her womb.

"Stelmetz, to what class will that organism be assigned?" A loudspeaker barked Singlelaub's query into the operating room where Stelmetz observed the delivery.

"We're very pleased with this specimen. This organism will be a Primary Being." Stelmetz seemed to be talking into the air, but a ceiling microphone scooped up his words and piped them into the glass viewing area.

"Splendid," said Singlelaub.

"How is the class determined?" Merritt Bonner asked.

"I'll show you." Singlelaub motioned for Bonner to follow. Tilman and Trina trailed behind, as did two meaty Russian soldiers. The little group walked a few feet to another area of the arena. A glass wall opposite that bordering the operating room looked out over a laboratory.

"You're looking at one of the most important areas of Trinity II—the genetic engineering lab."

As Singlelaub spoke, Tilman surveyed the room below. It also had the appearance of an operating room, but there was more instrumentation. A woman lay on the operating table.

"The woman you see is in her third month of pregnancy," Singlelaub explained. "Before the fertilized egg was replanted in her womb, we changed the DNA code in the organism to produce a specimen that would fit the assigned class."

Tilman noticed that the mother was a large stocky woman. He had seen enough of Trinity II to guess her child would be a Producer or Peacemaker.

"The next step," Singlelaub lectured on, "was to fuse cells from the developing organism with cells taken from subjects in the class toward which the fetus is being developed."

Merritt Bonner's brow furrowed. "Why are they operating on that woman? Is there some problem?"

"I assure you there is no problem," Singlelaub answered smugly. "At the third month of pregnancy, we take a chromosome sample from the fetus. Through a process known as chromatographic analysis, we can determine if the fetus has a genetic disease."

"What if there is a genetic disease? Do you try to correct it?" Tilman asked.

Singlelaub looked arrogant. "Mr. Tilman, the fetus is a disposable resource. It is much less time consuming to abort the organism and start all over again."

Trina Escobar could stand it no more. "Organism?" she shouted at Singlelaub. "Why don't you call it a *baby?* It's a *baby,* not an organism!"

Ernst Singlelaub paused and glanced down at the floor, maintaining his rigid self-control. "You must understand, we can no longer think of man as anything other than a resource to be developed for the good of survival. If we allow ourselves to think otherwise, we shall lose the courage to create the only kind of world where life will be possible."

Tilman's anger, sparked by Trina's outcry, now exploded. "If this is your version of life, Singlelaub, then it's not worth surviving! You could have given lessons to Mengele!"

Tilman's reference to the monstrous doctor who had experimented on human beings in Hitler's concentration camps once again poked at the child inside Singlelaub.

He closed his lips tightly so that no one would notice he was gritting his teeth. "I would expect such an archaic notion from you, Mr. Tilman," he said. "I won't waste time trying to explain our objectives. You're too outdated to understand them. Perhaps you'll get a better perception when you see other facets of our project."

Singlelaub steered his captives back to the area of the viewing room overlooking the delivery suite. They arrived just in time to see Sylvia Gladstone give birth to her third child—a boy.

Again Singlelaub spoke into a ceiling microphone to Dr. Stelmetz in the delivery room. "Stelmetz, explain to our guests your procedures."

"At this point," Stelmetz began, "we clean the neonate...."

"Neonate?" asked Trina.

"Newborn," Bonner translated.

"Now we proceed with Apgar." Stelmetz went on, unaware of the slightest interruption.

Tilman, Trina, and Bonner watched as the delivery team put the baby through a series of tests checking its reflexes and other health indications.

"Looks like the mother's habits have finally caught up with her offspring," Stelmetz muttered to his surgical team. The microphone in the delivery suite transmitted his conclusion into the observation area.

"What do you mean?" asked Singlelaub.

"The organism has every indication of acquired immune deficiency syndrome," answered Stelmetz.

"What?" Trina concentrated on the tiny baby she saw stretched on the examining table in the room below.

Stelmetz heard Trina and looked up. "AIDS. The gay disease," he shot back impatiently. "We see it occasionally in prostitutes who have had sex with bisexuals."

"What is your recommendation?" Singlelaub addressed his question to Hyman Stelmetz.

"ODU," came Stelmetz's icy response.

"What's ODU?" Mark Tilman asked.

"Organism Disposal Unit," answered Singlelaub. "When a neonate fails our tests, it has no further utility at Trinity II. We allow it to expire."

A tear seeped from the corner of Trina's eye as she pondered the destiny of the wiggly little infant lying in such loneliness on the small table. If the baby must die, she wished that she could clutch the child to her bosom and hold him there, lullabying him into the deep sleep of death. Trina was grateful the baby couldn't understand that he was rejected by his mother and discarded like trash by the medical team that should have been fighting for his life.

"Come with me," said Ernst Singlelaub, "and we can look into the ODU."

Again, he turned them around and walked a few steps to the left and rear of the viewing area. The glass wall looked down on a room adjacent to the genetic engineering lab. What they saw brought tears even to Merritt Bonner's eyes. A dozen cribs held infants who seemed to be in heavy sleep. Heart monitors revealed faint lines of fading heartbeats on each of the babies. Two nurses checked the infants' chests with stethoscopes.

"Are those babies . . . dying?" Trina Escobar could hardly get the words out.

"The organisms have no use and are being terminated," Singlelaub replied.

Tilman started to lunge at the wiry little man. Singlelaub's statement had been so sterile of compassion, so awash with evil that Tilman wanted to destroy him. Merritt Bonner sensed Tilman's anger and grabbed his friend's wrist. The guards in the room tensed. Tilman calmed slightly. "How do you kill them?" he asked, obviously controlling his rage.

"Terminate, Mr. Tilman," Singlelaub corrected. "The word is *terminate*. It's all quite painless. We give the organisms a very heavy anesthetic that slows their life functions. Either that eventually kills them, or, in the case of the healthier specimens, they starve to death. But they feel nothing."

"Singlelaub," Bonner screamed, still clutching Tilman's wrist. "How can you advocate such stark, cold cruelty?"

Singlelaub smirked. "Come now, Mr. Bonner. Surely you know that such termination procedures have long been practiced in your pristine, civilized world above."

"What are you talking about?" Bonner asked.

"The first public case I remember involved an infant called Baby Doe," Singlelaub answered. "The organism was born in Bloomington, Indiana, in 1982. Had a deficient esophagus, as I recall. That could have been surgically corrected, but Baby Doe also had Down's Syndrome. So the decision was made to not correct the esophagus and to simply let the organism expire." Singlelaub stared upward. "Quite the proper decision. I'm told the child, er, the organism died slowly and with some pain. We're actually more humane here at Trinity II. None of those organisms is suffering pain."

Suddenly, Trina began weeping uncontrollably. Her emotions disquieted Singlelaub, who had little experience in dealing with deep human feelings. Mark wrapped Trina in his big arms and glared at Singlelaub.

"Perhaps a tour of our computer center will give us a less emotional setting," Singlelaub said, grasping for some measure of control over the situation.

Moments later, Trina Escobar's volcanic grief

was chilled by the cool air in the computer center. The normal temperature at Trinity II was much cooler than that on the surface. But the heat generated by row upon row of grinding, pulsating computers necessitated the air conditioning.

As Ernst Singlelaub guided his captive guests into the computer center, a small, gnomish man wearing a white lab coat moved to greet them. A pair of wire-rimmed reading glasses perched on the edge of the man's nose as though they were a skier about to leap from a ski jump.

"I'd like you to meet Dr. Archibald Porteous." Singlelaub introduced Tilman, Trina, and Bonner as though they were a visiting delegation to a trade fair rather than captives. No one shook hands. There were only curt nods of greeting.

Tilman studied the room. It was similar to the control center at the National Aeronautics and Space Administration in Houston. There was, however, a shocking difference. Along one wall was a ward of hospital beds bearing some of Trinity II's strange human beings. Each creature was hooked up to a computer.

Singlelaub looked at Porteous. "Since these people will benefit from your advances in biotechnology, I'd like you to give them an overview of the work here in the computer center," he said.

Porteous, obviously pleased, motioned the group to follow him. Soon, they were looking over the shoulders of a technician seated before a large computer screen and keyboard. On the screen, the technician had typed a complex formula that seemed to have something to do with chemistry.

"What you're seeing," began Porteous, "is the code for the gene that will cause the enlargement of the cranium of Trinity II's Primary Being."

"Why an enlarged cranium?" Bonner asked.

"We have learned that the abilities of the human brain are enhanced when there is more matter," answered Porteous. "The Primary Beings will be the leaders and rulers of society. They must have enhanced intelligence."

"But how does the computer relate to the Primary Being?"

Porteous looked at Mark Tilman, who had posed the question, and smiled slightly. "Actually, the computer relates to the *production* of such a person. It will take a long time for evolution to begin naturally producing the beings we've engineered here, so we must produce them artificially until then."

At that moment, the technician pushed a key on the computer, and the formula on the screen seemed to jump as various numbers and letters changed into the graph of a molecule.

"The bioengineer has just created a new strain of DNA," said Porteous, proudly.

"How?" asked Bonner.

"The computer is capable of taking the engineer's command and producing the elements of genetic material that can be spliced together into the DNA strand. This DNA strand will carry the genetic code that we—we *men*—have called for," said Porteous. "Here at Trinity II, man is actually creating new species of man!"

"Are those people hooked up to the computers actually being created by the computer?" asked Mark Tilman.

Porteous chuckled and guided the captives over to one of the unconscious figures on a gurney.

"No, but we are improving these specimens," Porteous answered. "The computer is monitoring the metabolism, blood pressure, and other body functions of this organism, and it is fine tuning. . . ."

"Fine tuning?" Trina shuddered again at the cold, mechanical terms used in connection with human life.

"Nature leaves much to be desired," said Porteous. "We would all live much longer if our bodies were in a better state of harmony. This computer adjusts heartbeat, breathing, and metabolism rates to a higher rhythm. The body works as a whole rather than in different sequences. With periodic computer tune-ups these specimens live decades beyond the normal lifetime."

Singlelaub was obviously growing impatient. "I think our guests need to see our greatest success."

Porteous grimaced slightly. "But I thought we were going to keep that confidential."

"These people will soon be part of the world of Trinity II," said Singlelaub. "When we're finished with them, they will no longer remember. For the moment, I want the delight of showing them what we have done."

Shivering, Trina clung to Mark as they all followed Porteous into a chamber at the back of the computer center. The room was shielded by a heavy metallic door like that on a large vault. Two Peacemakers stood as sentries on either side of the door.

Singlelaub spoke to them. "I am Serial AA-6785, Clearance Double-Alpha. Open!"

One of the Peacemakers punched a series of buttons, and the huge door slid open. Singlelaub led his captives inside. As they entered the chamber, the door closed behind them.

Mark Tilman surveyed the surroundings. He and his friends followed Singlelaub and Porteous down a narrow corridor. Straight ahead, the corridor ran to right and left angles making a T shape. Along the front wall was a large glassed-in viewing area. As they approached the window, Tilman stared intensely at the strange form that lay on a table in the enclosed room on the other side. The object seemed to be a mass of flesh studded with electrodes. It was the size of an elephant, and resided under a giant glass globe.

Trina cringed at the monstrous sight.

"What in heaven's name is that?" asked Bonner.

"God." Ernst Singlelaub's answer was so terse, that Tilman wasn't sure he understood.

"Did you say *God?*"

"That's correct, Mr. Tilman. You're looking at

the entity that will ultimately control all life at Trinity II. Someday it will control all the life on this planet! Its official name is Sovereign, but you'll come to understand why we nickname it God."

"What is it?" Bonner asked again.

Porteous answered. " 'God' is a magnificent biocomputer unthinkable by even George Orwell. It is a combination of living tissue and the highest computer technology available."

"It has the capacity to think." Singlelaub picked up the explanation. "It is able to reproduce itself, and it is quite literally eternal."

"We have been growing this biocomputer for a decade," Porteous said. "Soon it will be ready to take over all functions at Trinity II."

"And as soon as we've had time to complete our testing of it, we shall introduce it to the world above," said Singlelaub, triumph teasing at the edge of his voice.

"We have programmed 'God' meticulously," Porteous went on. "It knows the precise balance between the various classes of the Survival Society we are creating, and it has the capability of converting other living tissue into the required organisms."

"The biocomputer will create life, determine its destiny, and, when organisms begin to deteriorate, they can report to a biotech center for a computerized checkup, spend a week in fine tuning, and come out with new zest," said Singlelaub. "All other computers will be controlled by this one."

"Now you see why we call the biocomputer Sovereign," said Porteous. "It is eternal, self-reproducing, and capable of controlling the destiny of an entire planet."

"Why is the biocomputer kept under that glass bubble?" Merritt Bonner directed his question to no one in particular, but kept staring at the mass of flesh and machinery that pulsated with life and electricity.

"The biocomputer must have a carefully controlled environment," Porteous answered. "The temperature in the glass is constantly maintained at just below freezing. It also requires an absolutely sterile environment. Even the slightest particle of dust will cause short circuits."

"Then your Sovereign is very fragile," said Mark Tilman.

"He may be fragile now, but there will be a time when he will control *your* life." Singlelaub's words had a sting to them.

"Appreciate what you're gazing at!" Porteous sounded like the high priest of the new religion of biotechnology.

Tilman bristled. "Do you suggest we bow down and worship your beast?"

"The day will come when you will," Singlelaub replied. "But Porteous is correct. Right now you are standing before the being that will ultimately guide the destiny of this planet."

"How are you and your thugs from the KGB going to force that on humanity? At gunpoint?" Merritt Bonner's anger was evident in his voice.

"Your question merely shows how archaic are

your perceptions," Singlelaub answered. "Your only concept of power is an army conquering geographical territory with guns. I'm not interested in controlling land. Through Sovereign we shall control something of infinitely greater importance—information systems that lead to creation of living organisms!"

Suddenly, Mark Tilman understood, and for a moment he felt the blood would stop in his veins. Tilman remembered the computers in the newsroom at the *Albuquerque Evening Star*. From across the country, the international news services could feed stories directly into the memories of the computers. The world was already linked through millions of computers, bouncing their voices off satellites, talking frenetically to one another day after day. The network for Singlelaub's cybernetic imperialism was already in place.

"Actually, what we're proposing is quite humane." Porteous picked up the argument again. "Every living organism is trying to move toward completing itself, guided by evolution. We are simply going to move life to its full potential by hurrying things along. Given man's warlike state, there's not much time!"

"This was the reason Francis Galton suggested eugenics," echoed Singlelaub.

"Galton?" asked Tilman.

"Yes, the cousin of Freud. Galton's idea was that human life be under a careful breeding program," Singlelaub continued. "Then evolution's goal would be reached much more quickly, and some of the painful aspects of slow development would be eliminated."

"But you're talking about human beings," said Tilman. "Man is created in the image of God. You have no right to toy with God's creation!"

"Absurd!" Meanness sharpened Singlelaub's voice like a spear. "Man is nothing more than an unraveling pattern of information!"

"Exactly," exclaimed Porteous. "And through Sovereign we shall control the way that information unfolds!"

"We've wasted enough time here," said Singlelaub. He looked at his three captives. "If it's religious jargon you want, Mr. Tilman, I'll give it to you. It's time for your *conversion!*"

Porteous chuckled at Singlelaub's sarcasm.

As Tilman and his friends were hustled away from the cold temple where Sovereign resided, he knew he must somehow escape and return to this *altar of Baal.* Mark Tilman would have to kill Sovereign.

DR. James Shelley was exultant. Ernst Singlelaub had presented the neurosurgeon with a sparkling new experimental subject for Shelley's endless quest to put more power in the human brain. Singlelaub had delivered Merritt Bonner to Shelley very much like Salome must have brought Herod the head of John the Baptist.

But even more exciting was the fact that Shelley had at last persuaded Megan Singlelaub to have lunch with him. They had even managed to find some seclusion in a small private dining room of the executive cafeteria.

For ten years, James Shelley had pursued Megan Singlelaub. At times there would seem to be a slight thaw in her feelings about him. Such seasons almost drove Shelley mad. Megan would tease him, taking him to the brink of conquest. Then she would again turn icy with the speed of the freeze that locked ancient mammoths in Siberian tundra.

Shelley thought he was once again in the season of thaw, and he intended to take full advantage of the balminess.

"Ever heard of the *Wormrunner's Journal?*"

Shelley's stark question broke through Megan Singlelaub's reserve, and she almost giggled.

"What an awful subject to bring up at lunch! Are you serious?"

"Absolutely. A group of scientists have been doing some fascinating experiments with worms and are publishing their findings in a periodical called the *Wormrunner's Journal.* The title may be tongue-in-cheek, but their findings are very serious."

Megan chewed slowly on a bite of ham that had suddenly become unappetizing. "What kind of findings?"

"The one I'm most interested in deals with the transference of knowledge through an exchange of RNA," answered Shelley.

"I'm a social scientist. You'd better explain." Megan was curious, but mildly chastised herself for suggesting that Shelley proceed.

"RNA is the chemical that carries the structural message of DNA from the nucleus of the cell to the surrounding tissue—the cytoplasm. There it manufactures enzymes, the building blocks."

"What does that have to do with the *Wormrunner's Journal?*" Megan asked.

"They have found that RNA seems to be the key chemical in the storage of long-term memory."

"Are you suggesting that the more RNA one has, the longer will be the retention of information?"

"Not only that," Shelley replied quickly, "but it also seems to have a correlation to the type and amount of memory one holds in storage!"

"What are you going to do with this notion?"

Shelley stopped eating, caught up in his visions.

"In one of the experiments," he began, "the scientists taught a worm to avoid electric shock. Then they ground up the animal—a flatworm—and fed it to another flatworm, which was untrained. The untrained flatworm now acquired the behavior of the animal it had just eaten. It learned to avoid the shock without ever being trained!"

Shelley's talk of cannibalistic flatworms totally destroyed Megan's appetite. She rested her fork on her plate and contemplated the strange conversation she was having with James Shelley.

"Are they saying that by transference of RNA you can give someone's intelligence and memory to another person?"

"That's what I want to find out," Shelley responded. "The experiments have never been tried on human beings. But now I can do it!"

"Surely you're not going to have this new experimental subject *eat* another person." Megan, normally as emotionless as her father, shivered.

"Of course not. We've been conditioning and programming Primary Beings for a long time now. Their intelligence is already 18 percent greater than any of us. I'm going to transplant cells from a Primary Being into the hippocampus of my experimental subject's brain."

"A clone?"

"Not exactly. The experimental subject won't take on all the characteristics of the donor. But if I succeed, we'll see a dramatic increase in the intellectual capabilities of the recipient."

For a moment, Megan Singlelaub disappeared into a deep world of thought. In her mind she saw her father, whose acceptance and admiration she sought constantly. She reflected on his jubilation and awe at seeing his daughter with 20 percent or perhaps even 25 percent more intellectual ability than she already possessed, which was considerable. Somehow, Megan would have to persuade James Shelley to allow her to be the experimental subject!

In a steel and glass chamber deep within Trinity II's Research and Development Zone, Merritt Bonner considered the small world in which he had been confined. His tiny cell provided minimum physical comfort and absolutely no emotional, intellectual, or spiritual stimuli. Bonner sat on a small cot with sterile sheets that could have easily blended into the empty walls. To Bonner's right was a stiff, steel chair. A metal table, overhung by a stark light bulb, occupied the center of the room. The cell, Bonner concluded, was strictly a chamber for eating and sleeping. He wondered if Mark Tilman and Trina Escobar had been dispatched to such rooms.

Suddenly, the heavy door to the cell swung open. A young man, an Oriental frocked in surgical dress, entered the room. Bonner couldn't sort out the various profiles of Asia, so he wasn't sure of the man's nationality.

"I'm Dr. Sul Park," the man said as he sat down in the chair across from Bonner.

Korea. Merritt Bonner recognized the Korean name. Bonner grew more irritated when Sul Park, one of his captors, flashed a patronizing smile.

"I've come to brief you on the procedures through which we shall take you." Sul Park's accent was quite heavy.

Bonner sat silently and glowered at Park, who talked as though he were preparing Bonner for a simple tonsillectomy.

"Since you have been designated for the Primary Being Class, we shall begin a drug treatment tomorrow morning to prepare you for the enlargement of your cranium."

"I don't believe it's legal or ethical for you to carry out medical procedures on a person without his consent." Bonner was more angry than afraid.

Park paused, his never-fading smile stirring Bonner's anger even more.

"I'm afraid you no longer live in a world that functions under such archaic notions as consent and permission," answered Park.

"That's obvious," Bonner shot back. "This place is a dictatorship!"

"That, too, is a dead concept."

"You can say that only because you can get up in a few minutes and leave this room."

"You will thank us for what we shall make of you." Park's smile sagged a fraction.

"Even if you made me the king of the world I wouldn't thank you because you'd do it against my will!"

"We know how to deal with the human will."

"I suppose you learned that in North Korea." Bonner had already concluded that Park had been brought to Trinity II as part of the KGB agreement with Singlelaub. Clearly, the Soviet Union was involving any of its allies that could supply the skilled technicians.

"North Korea is well on its way to being Utopia. That's why our Russian comrades needed us so badly to be part of this experiment."

"Utopia?" Bonner had heard of the brainwashed naivete of the committed Marxist. Now that he was seeing it firsthand, he couldn't believe it. "How can you call a world *utopian* that is based on tyranny?"

"Utopia is the realm of maximum function. It is a place in which all the machinery of survival operates at top efficiency."

"Including the human machine?"

Park paused and smiled for several seconds before he answered. Then, staring at Bonner with a coldness that contradicted his smile, he said, "Including the human machine."

They didn't wait until morning to start on Trina Escobar's conversion into the Producer Class. Not far from where Merritt Bonner was locked away in the R/D Zone, Trina was stretched out on a steel table in an operating theater. A tear ebbed out of the corner of her eye as she recalled the heavy treatment she had received at the hands of her captors. She had been humiliated as they stripped her naked and then strapped her onto the surgical table. Finally, someone had draped her with a sheet, but not before reducing her to the level of an animal on display.

A male nurse approached her now, wheeling an IV stand over to the table. There was a certain contempt for subjects to be processed into the Producer Class. No attempt was made to explain to them what was about to happen since it was assumed they wouldn't understand anyway. Thus Trina found herself strapped to an operating table with no idea what kind of procedure was about to be performed. When she felt herself slipping into terror, she quickly began to pray, regaining the balance she had trained herself to find through the years. She felt a measure of peace but still couldn't get rid of all the anxiety.

Finally, she had to speak. "What are you doing to me?"

"Quiet!" answered the nurse, exploring Trina's right arm for a good vein.

"I have a right to know!"

"You have a right to nothing," said the nurse, never looking up. Finding the vein, he jammed the IV needle into Trina's arm. The action was so sudden and so rough that she winced and began to weep.

Far above, in the glassed-in viewing gallery, Ernst Singlelaub watched Trina's torture. He always tried to observe the conversion of female patients. It somehow fulfilled a sexual need that Singlelaub didn't understand fully. It was his only emotional release.

"If you will be silent, I will instruct the physician to tell you what he's going to do." A voice seemed to come from all around her.

Trina couldn't tell the exact origin of the voice, but she knew it belonged to Ernst Singlelaub. She stared upward, but the bright operating lights blinded her. For a moment, she thought she could see the frightening little man looking down on her. She stopped sobbing.

"Tell her," the voice commanded.

A physician in a white surgical coat, wearing a stethoscope around his neck, moved to where the male nurse had stood at her side. He adjusted the drip mechanism on the IV. "I am about to inject you with a serum that will alter certain of your body features."

"You're going to change my body?" There was dread in Trina's voice.

"Your body type is ideal for our procedures. We can increase your muscle power by 28 percent. Your height will also increase. Later, with a surgical procedure, we'll remove a portion of your brain, and your head will be slightly smaller."

Trina remembered the strange being that had chased her and Mark through Trinity II. She suddenly realized she would soon look like them. She fought the urge to scream.

"My brain? Why are you going to remove part of my brain?"

"Because you won't need all of it anymore," the doctor answered. "Someone else will do much of your thinking for you."

"And we must remove those parts that cause aggressiveness." Singlelaub's voice entered the conversation.

"Ouch!" Trina winced as a burning sensation blasted through her arm. "What are you injecting into me?"

"This first treatment—which you will receive for a week—will plant hybrid cells in your body," the physician replied.

Confusion and pain furrowed Trina's brow.

"We have taken muscle tissue cells from a horse and fused them with human cells. The cells you are now receiving will begin to reproduce themselves in your body, and your muscular strength will be increased significantly after about three treatments."

"When will my body appearance start changing?" Trina wept openly now.

"That won't happen for another month," the doctor replied. "It'll take that long to complete the next phase, which is to inject you with giant cells."

"Giant cells?"

"Yes, we've been able to enlarge certain cells 750 times larger than normal. These will enhance your physical growth. You'll actually gain height."

"You are breaking God's law!" Trina screamed. "The Bible says God designed me in my mother's womb! You are not allowed to re-shape me!"

The physician and his medical team made no reply. They simply smiled at the hysterical woman's religious fanaticism and continued to pump her body full of their potion.

"This one's been chosen for the Man Farm."

Mark Tilman could hear the woman's voice just outside his cell in the R/D Zone. He pulled close to the small window in the steel door to hear more of the conversation.

A man's voice chuckled in response. "Then he's one of the lucky ones."

"I don't know if you can say that," the woman answered. "You must know nothing about the requirements of the Man Farm."

"It's a paradise of endless breeding—endless sex." There was a leering edge to the man's voice.

Tilman dared to look out the tiny window. A woman in a white lab coat conversed with one of the security men who helped monitor the hulking Peacemakers. Tilman could barely make out the profiles of the two Peacemakers standing guard at either side of his cell door.

"You must remember," the woman was saying, "this is a scientific environment—not a world of sexual fantasy."

"Come on, Doctor, all my friends in security say the Man Farm is the best place in Trinity II."

"That's only because they know nothing about our procedures there," the woman replied.

"Procedures? There's only one procedure to get a baby!" An evil, despicable laugh escaped from the man's twisted psyche like lava pouring out of hell.

"You are quite wrong." The woman tried to retain her scientific detachment. "The subject inside that cell will never see a woman, yet he'll father many children."

"What . . . ?"

"We'll use his sperm for *in vitro* fertilization."

The woman paused, apparently because her conversation partner was astounded or didn't understand.

"That just means we'll use his sperm to fertilize an egg from a female, but we'll do it in a glass container rather than inside a woman's body," the woman doctor explained.

"But how'll the baby be born?" the security man asked.

"We'll plant the embryo in a woman's uterus," the doctor answered. "But we don't have to. We could take the fetus through extra-corporeal gestation."

Again there was a pause, and the woman laughed softly.

"I'm sorry," she said. "Extra-corporeal gestation simply means that the baby develops outside a mother's womb. The result is what is commonly called a test-tube baby."

"Then that guy in the cell is just a baby maker and isn't going to be turned into a Peacemaker?" the security man asked.

"Oh, on the contrary," the woman replied. "The best farm is the one in which multiple use is made of farm animals. Sheep, for example, can provide wool, but they can also produce edible material—mutton."

"So that guy'll not only be a breeder, but he'll also help keep order by being a Peacemaker!" The security man delighted in his discovery.

"But that's not all," the doctor continued. "We've also selected him for cloning experiments. We begin gene therapy on him tomorrow morning."

"You'll have to explain again," said the security man.

"Oh, yes," the woman responded. "We'll introduce new DNA into his cells. Over a period of time, we'll monitor the changes. When we think we have the optimal result, we'll take some of his sperm, engineer it so it'll begin to reproduce until an embryo is formed, then we'll plant the organism in a human womb. The result will be an exact copy of the father."

The security man didn't ask for any more explanations.

Mark Tilman didn't need any. He shuddered. Escape was such an urgent priority that he would be willing to die trying.

Morning came for Merritt Bonner like an executioner's dawn. Before Mark Tilman or Trina Escobar awakened, Bonner was shaken from sleep, strapped to a gurney, and wheeled into an operating room. Bonner's first words of the day were, "Why are you shaving my head?"

"You should feel highly honored," said Dr. Sul Park, his words muffled behind a surgical mask. "You have been chosen for one of our first stimoceiver implants."

As Bonner drifted off into a chasm of unconsciousness, Dr. Sul Park moved toward his patient's skull with a sharp scalpel.

CHAPTER

16

MEGAN Singlelaub's personality was unsuited for seduction. She was smart enough to know that she lacked the guile, the subtlety to become a sensuous temptress. The best she could do was to present James Shelley with a stark proposition. The plan almost sickened her. But she had determined that she would pay any price to have Shelley work his surgical wonder of brain enhancement on her.

Thus, she had agreed to have dinner with Shelley on the outside. They sat now in Alamogordo's finest restaurant, sipping expensive white wine.

Shelley, very much the practitioner of seduction, considered himself a true artisan of the craft and planned one last attempt at seducing Megan Singlelaub.

"How is your new subject?" Megan asked.

"You mean the enhanced brain subject?"

Megan nodded.

"Very well. We performed . . . uh . . . a preliminary procedure on him, and he'll soon be well enough to undergo the experimental surgery."

Shelley was slightly unnerved that he had almost told Megan about implanting the stimoceiver in Merritt Bonner. Ernst Singlelaub had been adamant that one no one, including Megan, was to know about Operation Gray Garden.

"Do you really believe this subject has the inherent intellectual capacity?" Megan asked.

"We've tested his IQ, and it's quite sufficient," Shelley answered. "But you're right. Unless there's a good foundation, we won't get a good result. To enhance intellectual capability of a below-average subject by 25 percent would only bring him up to average."

Shelley was now working on his third glass of wine. He was melting into its warmth and enjoying the excitement of simply being with Megan and telling her about his accomplishments.

"Do you realize that with our knowledge of cloning, when we achieve the proper genetic mix in this subject, we can reproduce him as much as we want? And the man's a near genius!"

Megan stared intently into Shelley's eyes. "What would happen if you performed the brain enhancement surgery on a genius?"

"Why . . . why, I suppose we'd have a supergenius," Shelley answered. "But we tested the other two possible subjects, and this Bonner fellow produced the highest scores. We don't *have* a subject who'd score higher."

"Yes, you do."

"I beg your pardon?"

"I know of a subject at Trinity II whose IQ has been tested consistently at genius level."

For a moment, Shelley's wine-induced haze seemed to clear. "But it's not possible. I've tested every one of the potential subjects we've brought in. Only this new man qualifies."

"No," Megan replied. "There is one who measures higher."

"Who?"

"Me!"

Shelley suddenly understood what Megan was suggesting. "That's impossible, Megan. The procedure is experimental. It's never been done before."

"I'm willing to trust you, James. I've watched your work now for more than ten years. I know you wouldn't risk failure. You wouldn't have proposed the experiment to my father if you thought there was even the slightest chance of failure."

Shelley knew Megan could see right through him.

"All my life," she continued, "I've yearned to reach my potential and exceed it. Besides, without the best legal and social structures, the Survival Society my father dreams of will deteriorate into chaos. He's depending on me to construct the *social* order that will contain the new *biological* order you and your associates are producing. I must have greater creative ability!"

"It's out of the question," Shelley replied, appalled that Megan would even suggest the surgery being done on her. "The operation is extremely delicate. One slip and you could be a . . . a vegetable."

"How many times have you done brain surgery, James? A hundred times? Two hundred? I trust you!"

"The answer is no, Megan. Absolutely not!"

"My father wouldn't know until after it's been done."

"That's not my concern. *You* are my concern. I will not experiment on you."

Megan paused. Staring down at her half-full wine glass, she winced inwardly. Simple persuasion hadn't worked. She dreaded what she must now do.

"James, I'm willing to pay any price you demand if you will do that surgery on me."

Shelley shook his head. "There's no amount of money that could convince me to do that operation on you."

Megan gazed deeply into his eyes. "I'm not talking about money. I'm willing to give you what you've wanted for ten years."

"What's that?"

"Me."

Two weeks after Sul Park and his surgical team had opened Bonner's skull, the veteran newspaperman lay on the cot in his cell. A chill shot through his body as he once again saw the scrub-suited trio standing at his cell door. Bonner had no idea what they had done inside his head, but he could tell things were different. For one thing, he experienced cycles of anger bordering on rage, followed by periods of deep passivity. Now he could feel the rage stirring again as the people entered his cell.

"What do you want?" Bonner shouted.

Far away, in a secret chamber of the Trinity II Control Center, select technicians watched telemetry information on computer screens. The electronically generated lines told them what was happening in the most hidden regions of Merritt Bonner's brain. Looking behind the technicians, Ernst Singlelaub, Archibald Porteous, and Hyman Stelmetz gazed at the computer screen. A gleaming red line peaked with Merritt Bonner's mounting anger and fear.

"When the line peaks at plus-85 we know the subject will have reached the point of trying a violent act." The soft computer light bathed Stelmetz's face, giving him the appearance of a demon awash with the light of hellfire.

"Good," responded Singlelaub. "I wanted to implant the stimoceiver in this subject because he was the least aggressive of the lot. If we can stimulate and control aggression in him, then we'll know for certain the stimoceiver will work. If he doesn't reach plus-85, take him to that level. Then see if you can get an immediate reduction."

In his cell, Bonner was beginning to understand that he was being taken to surgery again. But it had only been two weeks. He knew he couldn't bear another penetration of his skull. Although

Bonner had always been fearful of violence, he wanted to strike at the three members of the surgical prep team. But his small size caused him to recoil.

Besides, in the background, he could see two Peacemakers who had accompanied the group from the operating room. Bonner began whimpering and retreated to his cot. Curling up in a fetal position, he pleaded with them not to take him.

In the Control Center, Singlelaub and his associates watched the computer line level off at plus-75.

"He's retreating," Stelmetz noted.

"All right," Singlelaub said, "take him to plus-85, and simultaneously freeze the Peacemakers, or else they'll tear him apart. Let's see the subject on a television monitor."

Technicians gave commands to computers. Far away, in Bonner's cell in the R/D Zone, the computer zipped the orders it had received.

Suddenly, Merritt Bonner felt strange. It was as if a flame thrower had blasted his interior with fire. His anger zoomed upward. Intense hatred took away all fear—even of the Peacemakers. Bonner shot off the cot like a rocket off the launching pad and rushed toward the surgical team. Despite the threat, the Peacemakers stood locked in place. They could do nothing.

"Bring him to minus-25!" Singlelaub commanded.

Bonner skidded to a halt. His body went limp. Again he began whimpering. The surgical prep team quickly scooped him up, strapped him in a wheelchair, and hurried to the operating theater. They knew nothing of Operation Gray Garden. They simply wanted to get this strange man strapped on the operating table before he had another of these outbursts.

In the Control Center, a satisfied Ernst Singlelaub spoke. "Gentlemen, the stimoceiver works."

For James Shelley to execute his charade, it had been necessary to go ahead with Merritt Bonner's surgery preparations. Because it had been only two weeks since his previous operation, not much hair had grown back. But once again, Bonner suffered the razor scraping the prickly saplings of hair from his skull. Though Bonner wouldn't be put to sleep for the surgery, Shelley had ordered him sedated heavily, using the possibility of another fit of rage as an excuse.

When the preparation was complete, Bonner was hustled off to the operating room and onto the surgical table. A male nurse started to catheterize Bonner.

"Wait!" The chief of the surgical support staff barked the command. "Dr. Shelley gave orders that we were to do nothing to this patient until he arrived."

The nurse who had begun the catheterization procedure quickly pulled back. The staff chief knocked twice on a door at the back of the operating room. Immediately, James Shelley stepped out.

As the staff chief moved out of Shelley's way, he tried to peek into the small room connected to the surgical suite. James Shelley's private lounge adjoining the operating room had become legendary among the Trinity II medical personnel. Entry into the room was forbidden to anyone but Shelley and his chosen guests. Shelley alone possessed the key.

Although none of them had ever observed the chamber, there were numerous rumors about what was enshrined there—a sauna, an exotic love nest.

Shelley walked into the operating room. "I want everyone out of the room except Nurse Curry," he commanded.

The staff obeyed quickly.

Elizabeth Curry stepped to Shelley's side. His appreciation for her could be detected even behind his surgical mask. For twenty years, Liz Curry had been his chief nurse and mistress. Two of James Shelley's conditions for signing on at Trinity II were the construction of the private lounge adjacent to the operating room and the employment of Liz Curry.

As soon as the staff vacated the room, Dr. Shelley and Liz Curry pulled Merritt Bonner off the operating table. The deeply sedated Bonner was like a big rag doll. An extra-heavy dose of the peaceful elixir would likely keep Bonner sleeping soundly for at least two days.

With Bonner's arms draped over Shelley's and Liz Curry's shoulders, Dr. Shelley rapped on the door of his private lounge. Megan Singlelaub opened the door. Shelley and Nurse Curry heaved Bonner's inert body onto the big bed at the back of Shelley's personal chamber. They shrouded Bonner until he seemed to be part of the bedcovers, then Shelley, Megan, and Liz Curry left the lounge. Shelley locked the door behind them.

"Since I have the only key, no one will find him there until we bring him out," Shelley said, partly to himself. Eventually, Shelley knew that Bonner would have to be taken to a recovery area. But he would give orders that no one inspect or treat Bonner's wounds except Dr. Shelley or Nurse Curry. No one else must discover that there was no fresh surgical scar.

Shelley knew it was a risk. But the moments he had held Megan in his arms were worth any price he might have to pay.

Quickly, Megan climbed onto the operating table, and Shelley and Nurse Curry began prepping her. While Shelley shaved her head, Liz inserted the catheter. Shelley, competent in anesthesiology, prepared Megan's arm for the IV.

When he was satisfied that Megan had been swathed sufficiently in green surgical sheets so that only the small surgical field of her skull was visible, he instructed Liz to reassemble the surgical team in an adjoining room.

"I'm sorry I had to ask you to leave," said Shelley, although explanations to Trinity II staff were unnecessary. Everyone had been conditioned to render near blind obedience. "This is a highly experimental form of surgery I'm performing, and there are some preparatory steps that must, for the moment, remain confidential."

James Shelley didn't like the feeling rushing through him as he sat on the stool positioned at the end of the operating table. In a window Nurse Curry had skillfully folded in the surgical sheets, Shelley could see the small square portion of Megan's skull that he would soon slice into. He understood why surgeons never operate on their loved ones. Shelley's hand trembled slightly. If anything happened to Megan . . .

He must regain control. He hadn't experienced such feelings since the years of his residency when he'd first begun prying into people's brains. Then it was nerves. Now it was love. But Shelley had conquered it then, and he could do so now. He steeled himself for a moment, looking down at the floor, readying himself to receive from Liz Curry the sharp scalpel by which he would open a flap of Megan's skin.

Before the surgical team had reentered the room, Shelley had sketched cutting lines on Megan's skull. For a moment, he studied the intersecting angles. It was time to start.

"I'm ready to turn the flap," he said. Shelley held out his hand, and Nurse Curry slapped a scalpel into his palm.

Shelley had opened flaps of skin hundreds of times before. Normally, he cut rapidly, precisely, barely penetrating the thin layer of skin. Shelley tried to be as dispassionate with this operation as with any. But he couldn't forget that this time the patient was Megan Singlelaub. He slid the knife along the marker lines a bit slower. "Hemostats."

Nurse Curry had them ready. She had assisted James Shelley with brain surgery hundreds of times.

"Raney clips."

When the clips were in place, Shelley paused a moment. Another nurse wiped his brow as he eased back to inspect his work.

"I'm ready for the craniotome," said Shelley, pulling in closer to Megan's skull.

Immediately there was the high-toned whir of the craniotome—the motorized saw with teeth that could easily zip through the bone of a human skull. As Shelley gently applied the instrument to Megan's head, the slight smell of singed bone rose in the room.

The motor stopped.

"Bone forceps—elevators." The section of bone gave way with a crack. Immediately, Shelley asked for damp gauze and applied it to the surgical site.

Again, he paused and considered his work. Shelley peered down on the dura—the semitransparent covering that sheathed Megan's brain.

Resuming his work, Shelley placed sutures in the dura, bedding them at the edge of the hole he had made in Megan's head. Taking a deep breath, Shelley prepared to snip through the dura and expose Megan's brain. Delicately, he cut the dura with small scissors, then placed small cotton strips between the dura and the brain.

Shelley stared at the gray lumpy tissue of Megan's brain, suddenly overcome with the emotions he felt for her. As he peered into her skull, he realized the depth of his love. Shelley had never been serious about any of the dozens of women who had been his lovers. But now he knew that he was carving into the brain of the only woman he had ever truly loved. He felt dizzy. The nurse at his left side dabbed away the new droplets of sweat pooled on his brow. Shelley wished it would be that easy to blot the emotions he was now feeling. Worse, he could detect a slight trembling in his right hand. Again, using emotional muscles he had exercised for years at the operating table, he calmed himself.

"Transplant tissue."

Liz Curry sensed the tension in his voice and quickly handed him a slender hypodermic needle.

Shelley held the instrument up to the light. He looked at the milky fluid inside the glass tube at the top of the needle. It contained cellular material from the most intelligent Primary Beings cultivated at Trinity II. The subjects who had supplied the transplant matter were the top specimens of a decade's worth of experimentation and development.

"Let me see the X ray."

Nurse Curry wheeled a portable X-ray viewing stand toward Shelley. She was worried. Shelley was out of sequence. He should have studied the X ray before asking for the transplant material. Its temperature was carefully controlled. If Shelley didn't implant it in the patient's brain soon, it could be infectious.

Shelley studied the X ray of Megan's brain that he and Liz had prepared two days earlier. Shelley had lied to the X-ray technician, telling him Megan Singlelaub was suffering from headaches and that he wanted to examine her brain.

Shelley measured the distance once more as he sought the precise depth within Megan's brain for the implant.

The hippocampus was nothing more than a bundle of pyramid-shaped cells in the temporal lobe toward the bottom of the brain. Endless experiments by Shelley and Porteous had confirmed what had long been suspected. The hippocampus was the center for the brain's learning activities.

Inspiration fired Shelley as he realized that if this experiment worked, Megan Singlelaub would be the most brilliant human being at Trinity II—perhaps in the world!

Dr. Shelley turned quickly and prepared to insert the needle. There was only a tiny tremor in his hand as he gently sank the needle into Megan's brain.

"Give me a check," Shelley said, pausing again. The syringe protruded from Megan's brain like a spike driven gruesomely into her skull.

One of Trinity II's most prized inventions was shoved beside the operating table. The X-ray machine, capable of taking a live television picture, was focused on Megan's head and turned on.

Shelley studied a monitor directly in front of him.

He was just short of entering the hippocampus at Megan's right temporal lobe. Watching the picture, he shoved the needle into the tiny organ and emptied the syringe's contents into Megan's brain. Then he withdrew the needle from her brain and handed it to Liz Curry.

"Congratulations, Doctor," she said.

"You'd better hold that until we see how the experiment turns out," answered Shelley.

A surgeon-assistant eased to Shelley's side. "Want me to close him up?" the assistant asked.

"No, I'll do it this time." James Shelley was determined that no one else would touch Megan.

It was a pity. Later, he might have been able to blame someone else.

MARK Tilman felt like a bull on a stud ranch.

Two weeks earlier, he had been brought to Trinity II's Man Farm, located in Sector Three of the Research and Development Zone. Tilman's small cell, characteristic of so many others in the horrid world he now inhabited, contained nothing more than a cot, a lavatory, and a toilet.

Tilman noticed that his cell was much cleaner than any other place he had seen at Trinity II. Twice each day, he was taken from his cell for exercise or testing, and when he returned, the chamber had been cleaned with pungent disinfectant. The Trinity II technicians obviously wanted no disease within the Man Farm.

The workers at Trinity II called the Man Farm

building *the barn,* and referred to the cells as *stables.*

In Tilman's two weeks at the Man Farm, he had been well fed. In fact, they almost fed him more than he could eat. In addition to his high protein diet, Tilman was given shots, which a nurse identified as a potent vitamin combination. Clearly, they were building him up for his mission of siring children.

Then, this morning it happened. After awakening Tilman and taking him to a laboratory, the Man Farm staff had extracted semen from him.

The process had been so humiliating as to be inhumane, reflected Tilman as he sat on his cot in the late afternoon, contemplating what had happened to him.

Tilman stared at his lunch tray. The meal had been brought to him not long after he had been returned to his stable. Normally, Tilman could eat anything at anytime. But now, as he looked at the untouched big steak and baked potato, the thought of his own circumstances—and more than that—of Trina's, killed his appetite. If the Trinity staff had subjected him to such indignity, what were they doing to Trina?

Like a bolt of lightning, Tilman jumped up off the cot. For a moment he lost control. He ran to the steel door of his cell and began beating it, screaming, "Let me out! Let me out!"

The small window in the door was covered with a sliding sheet of steel, which could only be opened from the outside. The door itself was four inches thick. Tilman's pounding and screaming were little more than slight, muffled sound to anyone outside the cell.

Within moments, he exhausted himself. And as Tilman thought of Trina, he began to weep. The tears, primed by sadness, were now pumped up from his deepest being by ground swells of anger.

Later the tears subsided, and a cold, calculating attitude settled over Tilman. He would escape the Man Farm. He would kill Ernst Singlelaub. He would destroy the biocomputer Singlelaub called Sovereign, or he, himself, would die.

The rattling of his cell door interrupted Tilman's plotting. Someone was entering. The door swung open, and a Man Farm technician, accompanied by two Peacemakers, entered the cell.

"Time for your exercise session," the technician said.

For a moment, Tilman thought of rushing the three intruders. Then he realized that could mean premature death. The Peacemakers would pummel him into submission. Tilman resolved to be alert for any chance of escape.

Every afternoon for the previous three days, Tilman had been hustled off to an exercise room, where he was put through a carefully planned regimen. Entering the exercise area now, his personal instructor met him. As the muscular coach studied Tilman's chart, Tilman surveyed the room, looking for instruments to expedite his escape.

There was another man in the room. Tilman had met him the first day and discovered that he was a volunteer for the Man Farm. A dedicated communist from Soviet Georgia and a member of an elite KGB military unit, he had volunteered for the Man Farm, hoping to one day be declared a hero of the Soviet Union.

That man would do nothing to help Tilman escape.

"Come over here!" Tilman's instructor motioned him to a weight-lifting machine. "Do your warm-ups, then we'll start on this routine."

Tilman began a series of stretching exercises he had been taught as a warm-up procedure. The technician who had escorted him to the exercise area had gone on to another task. The two Peacemakers stood at the entry of the exercise room. Tilman felt he had a chance of eluding the instructor and the Man Farm volunteer who now lay out on a bench, lifting heavy weights, but he didn't know how he would escape the two Peacemakers at the door.

Tilman completed the warm-up set and stood at the weight machine. With his back to the device, he began lifting the handle bars connected to the black weights on the sliding frame. Tilman pressed the weights and concentrated intensely on how he might escape. Despair ebbed over him. He prayed for a plan to break out.

Suddenly, Tilman heard a shriek from the volunteer doing bench presses. The man lay gurgling and choking on the bench with a 150-pound barbell across his neck. The man had obviously dropped the weight on his chest, and it had rolled down upon his throat.

When the volunteer cried out, the instructor, who had been readying Tilman's next exercise routine, spun around and ran past Tilman to help.

He turned quickly to the Peacemakers. "Come help me get this thing off of him," he ordered.

Tilman's moment had come. As the Peacemakers lifted the barbell off the man's throat and the instructor knelt down to examine the injured man, Tilman quietly headed for the door. Neither the instructor nor the two Peacemakers saw Tilman leave, and they did not miss him for several moments.

Tilman made his way to a storage closet off the corridor. Tilman's uniform marked him as a Sector Three experimental subject from the R/D Zone. He would have to get rid of that garb and disguise himself if he was going to be able to move through Trinity II. For a brief moment, he wondered how he would get through security to Ernst Singlelaub and to Sovereign. But for now he had to focus only on the problem at hand—how to complete his escape.

Cracking the door of the closet, he peered into the corridor. It was empty, except for a technician repairing a light fixture. Sneaking up behind him, Tilman jumped the man, knocked him unconscious, and stole his uniform. Changing in the storage closet, he stepped into the technician's jumpsuit and discovered what seemed to be standard equipment—a small gun tucked into a special holster sewn into the uniform. Although he felt uneasy carrying it, he knew he would probably have to use it.

Tying the technician securely, Tilman locked him in the storage closet and slipped out into the hallway.

Now Tilman could survive unnoticed at Trinity II—at least for a little while.

For fifteen minutes, Tilman walked the corridors of Sector Three, trying to look like he knew where he was going. As he passed workers, Producers, and Peacemakers, they paid no attention to him. At last, Tilman found his way to two big glass doors that marked the exit from the R/D Zone. Beyond them lay the big roadway that divided the Control Zone, the Applied Science Zone, and the Research and Development Zone.

Once outside the doors, Tilman's first mission was to get Ernst Singlelaub. Tilman studied a stark signpost in front of him. The Control Zone was to his left. Tilman remembered Singlelaub taking them into his viewing area above Central Control's computer rooms. That's where he would begin his search for Singlelaub.

After walking about a quarter of a mile, Tilman came to a Control Zone entrance. The color and design of his stolen uniform gave him the necessary clearances to enter. Tilman moved quickly through the reception-security area and into a passageway that he hoped would lead ultimately to Central Control.

Five minutes into the Control Zone, Tilman heard music, like that of a band in a bar. As he walked toward it, he was soon staring into a cocktail lounge, labeled a relaxation area for Central personnel. Tilman gazed inside and saw Archibald Porteous seated at the bar.

Porteous treasured his afternoon trips to the lounge. Years before, he had passed from sipping wine to guzzling drinks, right up to the edge of drunkenness. Porteous struggled to conceal his alcoholism from Ernst Singlelaub. Many afternoons it was agony to stop drinking, but Porteous couldn't allow himself to get totally drunk.

A voice behind Tilman made him jump.

"What's your business here?" the stern headwaiter asked.

Tilman turned to find the headwaiter glaring at him.

"You can't come into this lounge! What do you want?" he said indignantly.

Tilman's luck had run out. The uniform he wore had gotten him inside the Control Zone, but obviously the lounge was only for the top officers of Trinity II.

"Uh, Dr. Singlelaub wants to meet with Archibald Porteous. I was sent here to get Dr. Porteous." Tilman winced inside as he lied to the waiter.

"Just a minute," the waiter replied. "You wait right here. I'll get him."

Tilman watched nervously as the headwaiter talked to Porteous and motioned toward Tilman. As Porteous walked toward him, Tilman detected a little unsteadiness.

"Yes, what do you want?" asked Porteous, his wine slurring his voice slightly.

"Dr. Singlelaub wants to see you right away, sir. He's in the biocomputer chamber."

Porteous looked at Tilman for a moment. The lounge's lighting was dim, and Porteous's eyes were somewhat blurred, but still, he thought he recognized the man. He finally concluded that Tilman must be a technician he had seen frequently at Trinity II.

Tilman's chance encounter with Porteous suddenly rearranged his priorities. His first mission would not be the killing of Ernst Singlelaub, but the destruction of the biocomputer. Porteous would get him into the inner chamber where the computer-mass, Sovereign, pulsed ominously under its glass bubble.

It took ten minutes for Tilman and Porteous to reach the biocomputer's chamber.

At the entrance, Porteous turned to Tilman. "This is as far as your clearance will allow you to come," he said.

Almost by reflex, Tilman jerked the gun from the uniform's holster and shoved it into Porteous's ribs.

"I'm coming with you, or we both die," said Tilman, panic and anger in his voice.

Porteous gasped, realizing where he had seen this man before. Porteous had taken Tilman and the others to see the biocomputer.

"State your entry code!" barked Tilman, struggling for self-control. "And don't try anything, or you'll be dead."

Except for a trembling hand, Tilman hid his inner conflict well. Eons earlier, as a hippie, he had decried the violent world he saw around him. And his harsh threats to Porteous contradicted everything he had come to believe in as a Christian. But Mark Tilman was desperate.

He and Porteous approached the two Peacemakers guarding the doorway to the inner chamber of the biocomputer.

Tilman jabbed at Porteous's back with the nuzzle of the gun. "Go ahead. Give them your entry code."

"I am Serial AA-3947, Clearance Double-Alpha. Open."

The Peacemakers had been programmed like the computer they guarded. They had been instructed to respond to certain clearance codes. Upon hearing the proper combination, the Peacemakers punched a certain sequence into a numbered keyboard on the wall beside the door, and the door slid open. Tilman quickly shoved Porteous inside and followed.

Tilman had reached the end of his plan. He looked beyond the glass wall to the controlled inner chamber where the biocomputer pulsated under a huge glass globe. It would be easy to shoot the glass shields, then empty the gun into the biocomputer. But what would he do with Porteous while he destroyed Sovereign? Porteous wouldn't stand by while Tilman destroyed a decade of scientific research.

On impulse, Tilman brought the gun handle down on Porteous's skull as hard as he could, then recoiled at what he had done. He leaned over Porteous, now slumped on the floor. The scientist gurgled, struggling for air. Stunned momentarily by his own brutal action, Tilman suddenly remembered his mission.

Tilman raised the pistol at the thick glass window dividing the viewing room from the biocomputer chamber. He paused only a second, then fired.

Instantly an alarm sounded, but the heavy glass refused to collapse though Tilman had fired the bullet from only a few feet away. Instead, fault lines shot out from the point of impact. Tilman fired again, trying to hit the same place. More cracks zipped outward.

The screeching, high-pitched alarm inside the small room where Tilman stood seemed to have the decibels to tear his brain. The noise and refusal of the window to break threw Tilman out of control. For a confused moment, the screeches of the alarm became for Tilman the screams of Donna, burning to death in the downed helicopter. Then they shifted to imagined tortured wailings of Trina, undergoing gruesome experiments.

Tilman lost control. He charged the glass window and began pounding it with his arms and hands. Repeatedly, he beat it with the gun handle. At last the window began to open. Chunks of glass ripped at Tilman's hands and arms, but he was beyond pain. He had to get to Sovereign. He had to destroy the mechanical demon. Tilman realized that enough of the window was broken that he could climb through, but he hesitated. He stood for a moment, blood trickling down his arms from dozens of cuts all along his flesh.

The siren continued to screech. Waves of icy air raced out of the inner chamber through the broken window. The cold blast brought Tilman back to full awareness. Singlelaub had said it was essential to keep the temperature below freezing in the biocomputer's atmosphere.

The biocomputer—Sovereign. He must kill it. Tilman raised the pistol, aimed at the glass globe shielding the biocomputer and fired.

The door behind him opened. He turned just in time to see the Peacemakers charge at him. Tilman fired at them, striking both at close range. They collapsed, and Tilman dragged himself through the broken window. In a few moments all the security people at Trinity II would be on him.

Tilman rushed toward the mass of wires and what now appeared to be living flesh. The glass globe around the biocomputer hadn't been as strong as the window. The bullet did its work.

Mingled with the high pitch of the alarm came a terrifying sound, like that of a man whose fingernails were being ripped out. The biocomputer screamed. "Murder! *Murder!*"

Was the thing alive? Tilman paused. If it was alive, he would be a murderer if he destroyed it. But its life could be no more genuine than that of the Peacemakers he had killed.

Grabbing the slain Peacemakers' pistols, Tilman fired repeatedly into the biocomputer. The thing seemed to writhe. A yellowish liquid pulsed from every wound. Suddenly the horrible thing was silent. Everything was silent. The alarms had ceased. Then Ernst Singlelaub's voice echoed through every loudspeaker at Trinity II. "I want him alive! I want the subject kept alive!"

Tilman looked frantically for an escape route. The corridor leading into the viewing area wouldn't do. It would be full of security people by now.

Tilman spotted a door to the rear of the inner chamber. He rushed through it. This was the laboratory where the biocomputer had been developed and was maintained. The lab was empty. Inside, Tilman found another door. He tried it and found a small shower and dressing area for the scientists. Forcing open a locker, he found the white hooded coverall uniform of a Trinity II scientist. Quickly, Tilman washed and bound his wounds, then exchanged his technician's suit for the scientist's garb. Hoping he was adequately disguised, Tilman eased open a door leading from the lab into a corridor. People rushed to their security stations.

Suddenly, a guard stopped. Tilman tensed, fearing he had been caught.

"Get moving!" the guard commanded. "We're under full alert. One of the top secret experiments has been destroyed!"

Inwardly, Tilman applauded the effectiveness of his disguise and left the area, his mind filled with urgent priorities. He had to rescue Trina—if it wasn't too late—and then Merritt Bonner. He needed a place to hide until he could devise a plan.

Emerging from the Control Zone, Tilman stood at the edge of the main roadway. He remembered the village into which he and his friends had first stumbled. Now he knew it was the residence of Primary Beings, the most gentle people at Trinity II. He would hide there.

In pain, Tilman trotted across the road and headed off to his right. After a two-mile hike to the edge of Sector One of the Applied Science Zone, Tilman was stopped by a human guard.

"What's your business?" the guard snapped.

"I was sent here from the lab. Central Control is concerned about one of the Primary Beings."

The guard motioned him forward. Tilman ducked under the ribbon of laser light that bordered each area of the Applied Science Zone and headed toward the bookstore in the village. He could hide in its attic until he decided what to do.

Ernst Singlelaub looked around the long mahogany table at his associates. "I think I know how to find him," he said. Singlelaub had assembled his team in a private conference room in the Control Center.

Hyman Stelmetz, Archibald Porteous, and James Shelley waited for Singlelaub to detail his plan.

"Shelley, that subject you did the stimoceiver implant on . . ."

"Bonner?" Shelley tensed.

"Yes. The implant was a success?"

"Uh, you're right." Shelley wondered what Singlelaub was leading to.

"I think we can use Bonner as bait to lure Tilman." Singlelaub stared intensely at Shelley as he spoke.

"But have you forgotten, Dr. Singlelaub? I did a brain enhancement experiment on him just a week ago." Desperation threatened at the edge of Shelley's voice.

Singlelaub's brow furrowed. "Oh, yes, I suppose he'd still be recovering from that surgery."

"Yes, in fact he's quite weak." Shelley couldn't let Singlelaub discover that Merritt Bonner was being held prisoner in Shelley's private lounge off the surgery suite.

"But I'm sure you've had him up by now."

"Well . . . uh . . . of course, but the man is still very weak."

"That may be even better." Singlelaub's countenance showed that he was weaving an idea.

Shelley tried to divert Singlelaub from any use of Bonner. "It could distort the experiment if he injured himself," he reasoned.

"I'm sorry, Shelley," Singlelaub shouted. "Tilman destroyed the most important achievement of Trinity II. I'll pay any price to get him, including risking one of your experiments!"

The men around the table had never felt such fury from Ernst Singlelaub. Hyman Stelmetz thought of summoning Megan to see if she could calm her father. Then Stelmetz remembered that

James Shelley had told him Megan was in Albuquerque for a week.

Porteous leaned forward. "What is your plan, Dr. Singlelaub?"

"Simple. We shall let Bonner loose."

"What will that accomplish?" Shelley's desperation allowed a tone of disrespect in his voice.

Singlelaub glared at him before answering. "We'll let Bonner roam anywhere he wishes at Trinity II. When Tilman sees his friend staggering around in a weakened condition, he'll try to save him. And then we'll have him."

"Can we be certain Tilman will come to his friend's assistance?" Stelmetz asked.

Singlelaub smiled, but it was an expression of sarcasm, not humor. "Of course. He's a religious fanatic. Believes in the idiocy of being his brother's keeper. He'll respond."

Porteous nodded his head slowly. "How will you deal with Tilman once you have him?" he asked. A grim viciousness was in his voice.

"We'll let Mr. Bonner do that," Singlelaub answered. "We'll activate the stimoceiver, throw him into a rage, and allow him to kill Tilman."

"But Bonner is so weak, if we stimulate his muscle cells to that extent, it'll also kill him!" Shelley was almost screaming. If anyone found out that Bonner hadn't had any surgery the week before they might also discover that Megan Singlelaub had not yet regained consciousness after her secret surgery.

"Calm down, Shelley," Singlelaub scolded.

"I've never seen anyone so upset over a mere experimental subject. Besides, it will give us an excellent opportunity to see if the emotion of rage significantly increases physical strength. Confirming that will be worth the sacrifice of an experimental subject, don't you agree, Stelmetz?"

"Yes, yes of course." Stelmetz had no intention of disagreeing with the recognized creator and lord of Trinity II.

"Then it's settled," Singlelaub said. "Shelley, bring Bonner to us."

MARK Tilman, weak from loss of blood and his long trek, crouched in a corner of the small bookstore attic in Sector One of the Applied Science Zone. Packing boxes provided cover in case someone came investigating. If he had to run, the hooded uniform would conceal him from the television cameras scattered throughout Trinity II.

After dark, Tilman decided, he would begin his search for Trina. Once he found her, the two of them could try to locate Bonner.

Tilman recognized the flaw in his plan. *Dark?* Nightfall at Trinity was under human control. Ernst Singlelaub would never allow the lights to be dimmed as long as Tilman was loose. There would be no night at Trinity II until Mark Tilman was captured.

Pain crawled through Tilman's body like a gnawing rodent. There was no point in waiting long to find Trina if there would be no nightfall. Tilman decided to rest only an hour. Then he would begin his search.

The last thing he remembered as he slipped into unconsciousness was the throbbing pain in his arms and hands.

Ernst Singlelaub circled Merritt Bonner, inspecting him quickly from head to foot. He looked over to Dr. Shelley, who had obediently brought Bonner to the conference room in a wheelchair. "I must say, you've done a good job helping this fellow recuperate," he said, shaking his head.

"You're right, Dr. Singlelaub," said Archibald Porteous. "He doesn't look very weak."

Shelley, hoping to give Bonner the appearance of a man who'd had brain surgery a week earlier, had injected him with a sedative prior to bringing him to Singlelaub. Bonner sagged a bit in the wheelchair.

"Well, he has had a week of recovery," said Shelley, grateful that Bonner remembered nothing.

Bonner tried to focus on the people standing around him. They said he'd had another brain surgery. But all he could remember was occasionally waking up in the plush room where he had been kept for days. His only visitor had been Nurse Curry.

"Mr. Bonner, I believe you told me you lost a brother here at Trinity II," said Singlelaub. "To show you I am a man of mercy, I've decided to turn you loose. You're free to go."

Bonner, unable to think clearly, could only whimper his gratitude.

"There's only one catch," Singlelaub said. "You found your way in. You'll have to find your way out!"

The laughter seemed to echo all around Bonner. All he could see were sneering mouths chuckling at him. He fought dizziness, tried to restore logic. There was none.

Then heavy, crushing hands grabbed Bonner's arms and lifted him to his feet. He struggled for stability. His knees began to collapse. The hands clutched him even more tightly.

"I know you're weak," a voice said from somewhere behind him. Bonner tried to remember who it belonged to. A name rocketed through his tortured psyche: *Singlelaub*.

"But somehow you'll have to gather some strength if you want to escape," the voice continued.

Escape. The word was like a starter's pistol to Merritt Bonner. He tried to muster energy to run. The laughter started again.

"No, wait, Mr. Bonner. You will escape when we allow you to." As the same strident voice spoke, the big hands tightened their grip.

"Why are we waiting? Let's turn him loose," said Shelley, finally realizing that if Bonner were away from the inspecting eyes of Singlelaub and his associates, they might not discover his secret.

"Just a moment, Shelley." Singlelaub held up his hand with a sharp gesture. "I want to make sure we have adequate monitoring devices so we can keep up with his movements if we lose him on the TV monitors."

Technicians circled Bonner, hiding an electronic monitor under his shirt.

"Take him into the main roadway and set him free," Singlelaub ordered.

A sharp noise jolted Mark Tilman from his fitful sleep. His first sensation was the bite of the pain from his cuts. Numbness from the loss of blood hadn't shut down his nerves. He glanced down at the sleeves of the white coveralls he wore. Blood was soaking through the wrapping on his right arm, and a splotch of dark red was widening on the shirt sleeve.

But what was the noise? It had come from downstairs in the bookshop. Gingerly, he crawled out of the storeroom onto the narrow balcony and peered down at the room below. A lone Peacemaker was searching the shop and had knocked over a stack of books. Tilman's aching hands trembled with fear. If the Peacemaker found him, he would finish the task of mangling Mark Tilman.

In Tilman's weakened condition, he couldn't fight back. He also couldn't fire the pistol at the Peacemaker. The shot would be heard. Neither could Tilman simply wait for the Peacemaker to leave. If Tilman fled the shop, he might run into the Peacemaker in an alleyway. His only option was to kill the Peacemaker inside the shop, away from monitoring television cameras.

Tilman began to concentrate on a strategy to kill the Peacemaker. He crawled back into the storeroom and surveyed it for a potential weapon. In a corner, he saw several cans of paint and paint remover. He eased over to the cans and lifted one. The paint remover was heavy. He estimated the container was filled with five gallons of some type of cleaning liquid. It smelled like kerosene.

He could stand at the edge of the balcony and hurl the can down on the Peacemaker's small head.

Tilman's resolve faded. Killing the biocomputer was nothing more than battering a machine. But the Peacemakers? They were men—or had once been men. That was it, Tilman reasoned. The Peacemaker was no longer a human being, just a machine on two legs.

Renewing his determination, Tilman once again made his way to the edge of the balcony, moving the heavy can of paint remover inch by inch. When he reached the edge, Tilman stood to his feet. Daggers of agony ripped his hands and arms as he hoisted the big metal container over his head. Unconsciously, he screamed as he hurled the can down on the Peacemaker. The creature looked up. The container struck him in the face, forcing his tiny head back and snapping his neck.

As the can crashed to the floor with the falling Peacemaker, it burst open, spilling kerosene. Tilman, sickened by the sight of the Peacemaker who was in the throes of death, didn't notice a stream of kerosene rippling off into a small workroom where the books were rebound. There, a gas hot water heater provided steaming water for mixing glue. The stream of kerosene teased its way toward the water heater. Suddenly, Tilman heard a *whoomp*. A jet of flame dashed along the trail of spilled kerosene. The fire gobbled up the Peacemaker's body like a hungry serpent. Tilman fought panic.

The fire spat at the books, which sat on the shelves like arid logs awaiting a winter's fire. Exploring, the flames found the foot of the stairs. Tilman crouched on the balcony, almost in shock. Escape down the steps was impossible. He retreated into the storeroom.

He had to escape soon. Either he would be devoured by the flames, or the fire-fighting crews would capture him. Tilman ran to a small window in the back of the storeroom. Below, behind the store, was an alleyway. Soon all of Trinity II would bear down on him. He would have to risk a jump from the second floor window. He prayed he would land in the pile of boxes stacked against the wall.

Merritt Bonner was surprised. His head was clearing, and there was much more strength in his body than he would have thought. He stood at the edge of the big road near the Control Zone entrance. Crews of security people, fire-fighting personnel, Peacemakers, and Producers scurried past. No one seemed to notice him.

Gradually, it dawned on Bonner. He really did have the opportunity to escape. Should he try to find Mark Tilman and Trina Escobar? Bonner decided to free himself, then bring the authorities back to save his friends.

Slowly, Bonner remembered the route by which the three of them had penetrated Trinity II. Unfortunately, the way to freedom was in the direction of the fire. He could now see the tips of flames shooting above other buildings in Sector One of the Applied Science Zone. An orange glow reflected on the stone ceiling of the monstrous cavern.

Bonner started running. With everyone else hurrying along, he would be less conspicuous if he ran. Almost ten minutes later, he paused across the road from the Applied Science Zone. He wasn't far from the fire. Winded, he watched the flames licking at three buildings near the bookstore where he and his friends had first hidden.

Breathing hard, Bonner leaned up against the wall of a building to rest. As he did, a hand shot out, covered his mouth, and yanked him back. Bonner spun around. He gasped as he looked into a pale, pained face.

"Tilman!" Bonner cried.

In Central Control, Ernst Singlelaub gritted his teeth. His monitor screen showed fire fighters trying to douse the flames that threatened much of Sector One in the Applied Science Zone. And the television cameras had temporarily lost Merritt Bonner!

"Location on Bonner." Singlelaub spoke tersely to the surveillance technician.

"He's just crossed in front of Sector Two of the R/D Zone, sir. He seems to have stopped just inside Sector One," the technician replied.

"As soon as he's visible again on a scanner, let me know!"

Hyman Stelmetz and James Shelley, who had been watching the fire on another screen, now hovered around Singlelaub.

"There he is, sir!"

The technician's alert took precedence over the fire. Suddenly, Singlelaub's monitor revealed Merritt Bonner, walking rapidly along the walkway. A large man dressed in a white lab suit leaned on Bonner as they walked. Bonner was almost dragging the large man with a limp.

Merritt Bonner struggled to hold up Mark Tilman. Tilman's thick body had been too much for his left ankle when he leaped from the bookstore window. Though Tilman had hit the pile of boxes, he'd sprained his ankle. Swollen, its pain vied with that of his cut arms and hands. Tilman could hardly move.

"Drop me, Merritt! You'll never make it dragging me," he yelled.

"No way, man. *Both* of us have to get out of here."

"But I can't leave Trina."

"We can come back for her, Tilman. But if we don't get out of here, none of us have a chance!"

Ernst Singlelaub slammed his fist down on the monitor. "That's Tilman!" he screamed in an untypical frenzy.

Stelmetz gazed into the monitor. "I believe you're right."

It was hard to tell. The man with Bonner wore the protective hood of a technician who worked in a sterile lab.

But certainty settled over Singlelaub. He forgot the fire that was destroying more and more of his precious underground kingdom. He now had his eyes on the man who had killed his Sovereign.

Stelmetz took over the controls of the stimoceiver implanted in Merritt Bonner.

Singlelaub didn't look at Stelmetz. He simply spoke the command. "Bring him to plus-85."

Mark Tilman felt Bonner's gait slowing. "Why . . . why are you slowing down?" Tilman was slipping from Bonner's grip. They stopped. Tilman looked at Bonner in horror. He was looking into the face of a snarling demon!

Singlelaub and his friends saw the vicious look on Merritt Bonner's face.

"It's working," said Stelmetz.

Porteous looked at Singlelaub in awe. "Doctor, this proves we can control human behavior over distances," he said.

"Take him to plus-100." Singlelaub's command was emotionless.

James Shelley jumped forward. "You can't do that! His blood pressure will go too high. He'll have a stroke."

"Then we'll destroy them both. Tilman is much bigger than Bonner, but he's so weak he won't be able to resist Bonner's attack." The cruelty in Ernst Singlelaub's voice chilled the entire room.

Merritt Bonner felt as if he were in a microwave oven, cooking from the inside out. Heat forged a splitting channel of fury somewhere deep within him.

As Tilman watched, dazed, Bonner began moving his head from side to side as if to find a focal point for his rage. Weakening, Tilman collapsed on the walkway, dropping his pistol.

Bonner stared at Tilman. Only a fleck of sanity remained to fight with his growing fury. Ninety percent of his emotions screamed to kill Mark Tilman. Bonner breathed heavily. His pulse sounded in his ears like a timpani.

Then he spotted the pistol. Frantically, Bonner picked it up. His tiny army of sanity called to him. Tilman was his friend. He must not harm him. But it was too late. Bonner brought the handle of the pistol thudding down into Tilman's face. Tilman, weakened from loss of blood, pulled himself into a fetal position, trying to ward off Bonner's blows.

Then Bonner's sanity reasserted itself. Burning

with pain from the stimoceiver, he remembered who Tilman was. He looked into his friend's bleeding face. It was little more than a scarred blur.

Then, like an army of sand, Bonner's reason began crumbling. *No!* Bonner cried within himself. *Cannot . . . cannot destroy Tilman.*

Agonizingly, the little army of reason regrouped one last time. Forcing his arms to move, Bonner turned the gun toward his own face and hooked his finger around the trigger. The blast blew away his face.

Singlelaub's self-control had collapsed. "Tilman must not escape! Alert all Peacemaker units."

"Do you want him killed?" Porteous asked.

"No! I was going to give that pleasure to his friend. But since that opportunity has been lost, I want to deal with Mr. Tilman personally. He has destroyed too much of my labor!"

THE sign taped to the hospital door was as foreboding a sentry as a fire-breathing dragon. The words hand-lettered with a thick felt-tip marker on a piece of cardboard read Extreme Contamination Hazard: Entry only by authorization of Dr. James Shelley.

Personnel working that area of the hospital shuddered as they hurried past the sign. Another of Trinity II's experiments had gone awry, they assumed. Most workers at the hospital, which was buried deep within the steely heart of Sector Five of the Research and Development Zone, had seen the abominable results of a failed experiment.

In fact, there was a wry joke among the Trinity II hospital staff: if one had to choose between being locked in a nuclear bomb and suffering through a Trinity II experiment, it would be better to pay for the first class section inside the bomb.

Those who saw the sign assumed that another subject had been overdosed with radiation or had contracted one of the new diseases unleashed by the genetic engineering lab.

Regardless of whether it was a radiation threat or a biohazard, no one at the Trinity II hospital wanted to enter the room. Everyone was quite happy that Dr. James Shelley and his nurse, Liz Curry, would care for the isolated patient. What a sacrificial gesture that was.

But the person inside the room was not contagious. Swaddled in the hospital sheets lay Megan Singlelaub, her eyes riveted shut. She slept in some deep abyss from which James Shelley was unable to summon her.

As the smoke from the fire in Sector One of the Applied Science Zone settled over Trinity II, Shelley and Nurse Curry hovered over Megan.

"I must try to walk through each step of the operation one more time." Shelley didn't look up as he said the words.

Elizabeth Curry, standing on the other side of the bed, felt as if Jim Shelley had forgotten that she was in the room. She yearned for him to look at her just once. She wanted to share this experience with him, to carry a portion of his pain. But the only person he seemed to think about was Megan.

"Could it have been too much pressure on the craniotome?" she asked.

"Ummh?" Shelley seemed to barely hear Liz's voice.

"I said, could you have pressed down too hard on the craniotome when you cut through her skull?"

"Oh . . . why, no. . . . No, of course not!"

Actually Shelley wasn't certain about anything. If she were awake, he could tell if a speech area was destroyed or a key motor center damaged. "But she just won't wake up!"

Liz Curry blanched slightly. She thought she could detect a trace of crying in Shelley's voice. His emotion over Megan suggested weakness, unprofessionalism. She couldn't stand it.

"All I know to do is study the X rays one more time." He shook his head as though he knew another look wouldn't reveal anything.

"Why don't you watch the videotape of the operation?" Curry suggested.

"Yes! That's what I'll do." Shelley still looked at Megan as though he felt Megan had made the suggestion, not Nurse Curry. "I'll be back to relieve you in a little while," he said, glancing at Liz as he rushed from the room. The emptiness of the glance shrouded her heart in cold darkness.

Ernst Singlelaub burned with anger as he sat at his console in the Command Center of Central Control. "Status report!" he shouted. The video monitors around him flicked from scene to scene throughout various sectors and zones of Trinity II. Singlelaub focused on a television screen showing the fire's devastation in Sector One of the Applied Science Zone. Within seconds of his command, a ragged fire fighter appeared on Singlelaub's monitor.

"The fire is under control, sir," the man said. "But we've lost five buildings down here."

"Casualties?"

"Uh, so far, three Peacemakers, five Producers and two men, sir."

"What do you mean *so far?*" Singlelaub hated imprecision.

"There are two other Producers and a Peacemaker damaged seriously. And we've got three men with pretty bad burns."

"Anything else?"

"No, sir."

"Return to your duties!"

Ernst Singlelaub slowly shifted from the computer console. The digital clock's bright green numbers declared that the time was twenty hours, three minutes. *It's 8:03,* thought Singlelaub. He hadn't eaten but wasn't hungry.

Suddenly he wanted a drink. And Megan. If he could just talk with Megan, she would calm him. Surely she would be back from Albuquerque by now. Singlelaub left the Command Center and walked to his apartment nearby.

At 8:15, Singlelaub dialed Megan's number on his secure phone. Though her apartment at Trinity II was near his, Singlelaub preferred telephone. He wanted no one to see him seeking out anyone else, not even his own daughter. Singlelaub let the phone ring seven times before conceding that Megan wasn't in her apartment.

He cursed himself as worry drifted over him like a tiny rain shower. *That's why it's better not to get involved emotionally with anyone, not even one's own family*, he reflected. Emotional involvement meant having one's mind diverted from truly important things by the very kind of anxiety he was suffering now.

The anxiety stirred the tortured child within Singlelaub. Again, the inner voice was whimpering. It suggested that Megan was in trouble, and that she was being punished for the sins of her father. Singlelaub spat out his favorite German expletive in the hope of shocking the child into silence.

He picked up the phone receiver again. Scanning an internal telephone directory, he found and dialed the number of Rebecca Townley, Megan's assistant.

"This is Rebecca Townley." She answered on the second ring, pert, efficient. Singlelaub detected a slight remnant of a southern accent in the black woman's voice.

"Yes, Dr. Townley? This is Dr. Singlelaub. I . . . I have some business to discuss with my daughter, but I can't seem to locate her. Do you know where she might be?"

"Why, no," she answered, the tension of talking with the master of Trinity II evident in her tones. "All I know is that she went to Albuquerque on personal business."

"Yes, and I understood she was due back today. It's getting rather late."

Singlelaub caught himself. He couldn't allow Rebecca Townley to know of his growing concern. "But I'm sure she'll be in soon," he said, trying to restore a businesslike atmosphere to the conversation.

"I'll be happy to alert you if I hear from her," Townley offered.

"Yes, do. Thank you. You may call the switchboard, and they'll give me the message." No one besides his immediate associates had Ernst Singlelaub's personal number. And he didn't intend to give it to Rebecca Townley.

Singlelaub turned to the small cabinet where he kept his liquors and caught a glimpse of himself in the mirror over the cabinet. His eyes were drawn. Wrinkles surrounded them like tiny crevices snaking out from moon craters. His thin face looked more gaunt and sallow than ever.

Singlelaub thought of Solzhenitsyn's description of the aging Stalin, penned in Solzhenitsyn's book *The First Circle*. He had depicted the Soviet leader alone in his apartment, like Singlelaub now. Solzhenitsyn wrote of Stalin: "Death had made its nest in him and he didn't know it."

For a second, Ernst Singlelaub contemplated his finitude. He was fifty-three but looked ten years older. The burdens of the Roman Solution, the pressures of attempting an alliance with the KGB without becoming its slave, the cycles of exhilaration and stress over creating Trinity II, had all worn him down. Now there was the added concern over Megan's absence, the ceaseless voice of the child within Singlelaub's psyche, always pulling him back to that hellish moment when the Nazis shot his parents and suggesting that Singlelaub was no different from Hitler's goons. And the fire. *The fire!* The thought hit him like cold water. Tilman must be dealt with. Somehow the big newspaperman would have to pay for the damage he had brought upon Ernst Singlelaub!

Resentment was building to volcanic proportions in Elizabeth Curry.

Megan Singlelaub had begun sweating profusely. Dr. Shelley had insisted on staying nights with Megan, sleeping on a cot in her hospital room. But he had also ordered Liz to change Megan's sheets every evening before turning the shift over to him.

Liz Curry rolled Megan onto her left side while she straightened the fresh sheet on which Megan was lying. The nurse was working in a tight corner between the bed and wall. On Megan's tray table at the foot of the bed, Curry had placed a strong antibiotic to hook up to the IV as soon as she finished the bed. Liz Curry's supper tray of scraps also rested on the table. Liz had been unable to eat much because of her growing jealousy over Megan's grip on Shelley.

As she tucked the sheet at the foot of the bed, she bumped the tray table, and the bottle of antibiotic shattered on the floor. The supper tray fell on top of the spilled medication, the scraps mingling sickeningly with the antibiotic.

Liz swore, grabbed a rag, and crouched on her knees. As she tried to clean the disgusting assortment, she became increasingly revolted. She had been James Shelley's lover periodically for twenty years. She had waited on him as he had trysts with other women. And now, her reward for all her loyalty was to be on her knees in the hospital room of another woman James Shelley loved. And she had to clean up spillage like a chamber maid!

Liz Curry threw the rag on the floor. She wouldn't be reduced to such a level. There would be nothing wrong with calling in an orderly to clean up, if she made sure Megan Singlelaub was well hidden.

Within a few moments, an orderly came into the room, mop in hand. As he cleaned the floor, the telephone rang.

Nurse Curry answered it. "Isolation room." "Liz," came James Shelley's voice. "I just wanted to see if everything is OK."

"Yes, of course." Her response was almost too terse.

"Fine. I'll be there in a half hour. Be sure to have the sheets changed." Shelley hung up without even saying good-bye.

A tear trickled down Liz's face. Not wanting the orderly to see her grieving, she went into the small bathroom in the isolation unit.

The orderly moved to the narrow space between Megan's bed and the wall. As he knelt to wipe up the spillage underneath, he bumped the bed. Megan's head slipped slightly. The orderly rose and found himself staring into the face of Megan Singlelaub.

The orderly said nothing as he left the room. Nurse Curry was still in the bathroom, and he felt awkward. Silently, he walked out of the room, happy to be out of the isolation area.

In the staff locker room, he stripped down and took a scalding shower. As he redressed, one of the orderly's friends came in for a cigarette. For a few moments, the two made small talk. Then the orderly said, "I sure hope there's nothing serious wrong with Miss Singlelaub."

Midnight seemed to have raced to its position on the clocks at Trinity II. Ernst Singlelaub was still up, walking a tension-compelled gauntlet around his rooms. Every ten minutes he rang Megan's phone. No answer.

Singlelaub had worked out a strategy. At midnight, he would take action. When the shrill little tone on his watch announced midnight, Singlelaub went to his telephone.

"Colonel Arnov?" he said to the voice that answered.

"Yes."

"This is Dr. Singlelaub. I need your assistance in my apartment."

Singlelaub hung up the phone. The KGB officer who was chief of security at Trinity II would be at his door in a moment.

Frantic, Singlelaub dialed Albuquerque information, securing the number of the Hilton, where Megan normally stayed when she visited Albuquerque. A sleepy reservations clerk told him there was no Megan Singlelaub registered there, nor had there been in the last five days.

By the time Singlelaub hung up, Arnov was at his door. Singlelaub invited the Russian in, quickly telling him of Megan's disappearance. Arnov immediately knew his assignment: find Megan Singlelaub, even if it meant tearing New Mexico apart.

"I've already checked the Albuquerque Hilton. Now I want you to screen every decent hotel in the city." Singlelaub's orders came so fast, Arnov couldn't remember whether to respond with a da or a yes, sir!

"May I make a suggestion, sir?" Arnov said when Singlelaub ceased giving commands.

"Yes, of course."

"We could start in the garage where Miss Singlelaub keeps her sports car. If the car is there, we know your daughter is perhaps nearby," he said with only a slight accent.

"All right, good idea," Singlelaub replied.

The smell of vodka was so strong on Arnov's breath that Singlelaub was glad when the KGB colonel scooted out through the door.

Within minutes Singlelaub's phone rang again.

"Dr. Singlelaub, your daughter's car—"

"What? Slow down, Arnov!" Singlelaub commanded.

Arnov, in his frenzy, was mixing English and Russian, but Singlelaub determined that Megan's car was in the garage. Arnov said something about ordering a soldier to touch the vehicle's radiator, then lapsed into his native tongue. To Singlelaub, the jumble of words sounded like *goryachee lee ohn eelee khonlodhnee.*

"Speak English, man, speak English!" Singlelaub screamed into the receiver.

"Sorry, sir. I asked my man if the radiator was hot or cold."

"And?"

"It's cold, sir!"

Singlelaub pondered the revelation. Not only was Megan's car in the garage, it hadn't been driven in a while. She was either kidnapped or . . . *Shelley!* Perhaps the rogue had seduced his daughter, and she was at this moment lying in his arms.

"Thank you, Colonel Arnov," Singlelaub said, his anger evident. "Tell your men to search Trinity II thoroughly. Report back to me in an hour or sooner if you find anything."

As soon as he ended the conversation with Arnov, Singlelaub dialed Shelley's room. There was no answer.

Singlelaub stayed awake through the night getting periodic reports from Arnov. All the KGB officer could tell him was that there was no trace of Megan Singlelaub.

Basor Semichastny cursed with weariness as he dragged himself into the staff cafeteria. When he had been selected for this American assignment, his KGB superiors had promised him it would be plush duty. The promise had turned out like nearly all others he had heard in the Soviet Union—as void as Novaya Zemlya, the Arctic island where he had once been posted as part of a forward radar unit. Sometimes the underground world of Trinity II seemed as cold as Novaya Zemlya. This was one of those moments.

He had been up all night, searching every quarter of the Applied Science Zone, his assigned area, looking for Megan Singlelaub. He was allowed only twenty minutes to gobble down some breakfast. Colonel Arnov had commanded that no one on the security force could rest until Megan was found.

Semichastny was grateful for the good Russian cooks on the kitchen's staff. At least he could warm himself with a bowl of heavy porridge. The hot, thick soup had made mornings bearable at Novaya Zemlya. It would do the same at Trinity II.

Semichastny emerged from the food line, carrying his tray of porridge, black bread, and hot tea. He scanned the cafeteria for a place to sit. He wanted to find some other KGB officers, but the only places available were with Americans.

Semichastny hated Americans. This antipathy had deepened when he found out the meaning of the joke they made about his name. "Hey, Russian," they would yell, "is it true you're only semi chaste?" Then the Americans would explode with laughter.

At last Semichastny found a table. The only person there was an American named Mick Causey. Causey seemed different from the others. He was quiet and never joined in the kidding about Semichastny's name.

"Hello, Basor, sit down," Causey said as the Russian approached the table.

"Whew!" Semichastny almost collapsed into the chair. "What time is it?" he asked in a heavy accent.

Causey looked at his watch. "It's, uh, 0600 hours."

"That is why I am so tired," Semichastny said. "I not sleep all night."

"Were you sick or something?"

"No. I worked all night."

"Now what kind of crisis has the security been digging into this time?"

Semichastny glanced around the room. He wasn't sure he should reveal what the KGB had been doing, but Causey *had* been kind to him.

"We search for Dr. Singlelaub's daughter. She is missing!"

Causey looked at him, puzzled.

"You are sad that Miss Singlelaub is missing?" asked the Russian.

"No, I could care less about that," Causey replied. "It's just that I don't understand what all the fuss is about. I know exactly where she is!"

Basor Semichastny didn't expect to be named a hero of the Soviet Union, but he might earn plaudits from his superiors. He had happened to sit down for breakfast with Mick Causey, the orderly who had cleaned the floor in Megan Singlelaub's hospital room the night before.

MARK Tilman couldn't fight. When the security team of humans and Peacemakers caught up with him, he was lying on the ground, too weak to move. Tilman lost consciousness as the Trinity II security people plopped him onto a stretcher. When he awoke, he had no idea where he was.

The bed on which he had been placed was a mechanical contraption that could only belong to a hospital. He tried to raise up, but his arms and ankles wouldn't obey. They were tied to the bed.

He fell back, expelling his breath loudly. All he could do was lie there and gaze at the ceiling.

The tiles above him seemed to become a movie screen. The first face to come into focus was that of Trina. In Tilman's mind, the vision was so real that he tried to reach out and caress her face. But the stern cords that bound him to the bed jerked him down again.

He kept studying Trina's face. She smiled at him lovingly. "Trina," he cried, "Trina, where are you?"

A slow transition began. Trina's features changed. Now Tilman was staring into the face of Donna. His heart raced. Again he lunged forward but was yanked back by the ties.

Suddenly, Merritt Bonner's horrible countenance, seconds before his rage-driven suicide, blasted into Tilman's vision. Bonner was dead. Tilman could no longer contain the ocean of tears backed up behind the eroded dike of his self-control.

He began to weep and pray. "God! Oh, God, where are you?" Mark Tilman asked with the desperation of a man headed for a monstrous death.

"Please, God, let me feel your presence!"

With only a slight stirring of awareness, the words he had memorized from Psalm 139 drifted into Tilman's consciousness. "*If I take the wings of the morning, and dwell in the uttermost parts of the sea; even there shall thy hand lead me, and thy right hand shall hold me.*"

Still, his heart raced. If only he could calm his emotions. Then Tilman recalled a counseling session with his pastor when Tilman was trying to rise from the pit of Donna's loss.

"Mark," the pastor had said, "God doesn't require you to *feel* something you can't. He asks for your will. The emotions will follow."

Tilman learned that the pastor's counsel was sound. Many mornings when he wanted to crawl into the bosom of night and forget existence, he would force his will to thank God for the new day. Eventually, his emotions did indeed catch up with his will.

In his mind, Tilman could hear the pastor's voice. "The answer to your prayers doesn't hinge on your emotional perceptions but on the *fact* of God's presence and promise."

Mark Tilman still *felt* alone, but now he knew he wasn't. And he began to wonder how God would deliver him from these bonds.

A constricting cord woven of fear and frantic plotting wrapped around James Shelley's chest, crushing him and bringing his breath in short desperate gasps. The tightening began with the call from Ernst Singlelaub.

"Something very strange is happening," Singlelaub said. "My men have found Megan in an isolation room in the hospital sector." Singlelaub instructed Shelley to meet him there.

Shelley hung up the phone realizing that Dr. Singlelaub had already begun to probe. When Singlelaub discovered that Shelley had destroyed the great doctor's most treasured possession, Dr. James Shelley was a dead man.

Shelley couldn't go to that hospital room. He would sneak away from Trinity II. Already, a strategy was shaping in his head. He knew enough information to topple Ernst Singlelaub's kingdom and send the man to prison for life. Once above ground, Shelley would put his plan into action.

The surgeon began gathering the things he wanted to take with him. He couldn't walk away from Trinity II with a suitcase, so he placed a few valuables in a medical bag.

Suddenly, Shelley thought about Elizabeth Curry. No more than an hour earlier, she had taken up the vigil in Megan's room. Perhaps, Shelley thought, Liz should be warned. But suppose he called as Singlelaub entered the room? It was too risky. Liz Curry would have to survive on her own. With chilling ease, Shelley erased from his emotions the woman who had been his lover for twenty years.

Finally, Shelley was all ready to run. He paused at the apartment door, surveying the rooms that had been his home for a decade. Then, without regret, he was gone.

Elizabeth Curry had just settled into a large leather chair in Megan's room and had begun scanning a magazine. She had read the magazine numerous times, but was trying to squeeze some small respite from boredom out of its pages. Suddenly, Liz felt someone was in the room with her. Looking up, she gasped. She was staring into the angry face of Ernst Singlelaub!

Behind him, in the shadows of the entrance to

the room, she could see the frightening profiles of two Peacemakers and two security men.

"Where's Shelley?" Singlelaub demanded.

"I, uh, I suppose he returned to his lab." Liz Curry determined not to tell him that Shelley had returned to his room. In spite of his unfaithfulness, she loved him. She would cover for him even if it cost her life.

Singlelaub swept suddenly to the bed. He bent over Megan's face. "Megan! Are you all right?"

The unconscious form on the bed didn't stir.

"Where's Shelley? What has he done to my daughter?"

Liz glanced down at the floor and remained silent.

"Megan. Megan, please answer me!"

Ernst Singlelaub's stony exterior began to crack. He reached out, holding his precious daughter's face. It was a gesture of profound love he had never before extended to Megan. Suddenly, inexplicably, Megan became to his troubled spirit the wounded child who lived within his psyche. The child no longer tortured him. He was filled with sympathy for the little one who had been in agony so long.

"Megan, my child, what have they done to you?"

Seeing the father weep for his child crumbled the rock wall Curry had erected around herself. She forgot her fear. Before she knew what was happening, she was telling Singlelaub everything that had been done to his daughter. Anger returned and spite mingled with sympathy as she told of Megan's sexual bargain with James Shelley to persuade him to do the surgery on her. It had hurt Liz Curry when Shelley had boasted of his conquest of Megan. Now, in some measure, she had paid him back.

When she was done, Ernst Singlelaub placed both hands on the side of Megan's bed and gazed intently at the sheet.

His brilliant daughter had suffered perhaps irreparable brain damage. His most trusted surgeon had violated his daughter.

Ernst Singlelaub had carried the weight of seeing his parents murdered by the Nazis and his own escape from the same beastly troops. Somehow he had shouldered the load of the collapse of the Roman Solution and the bitter conclusion of Prentiss Pearson's presidency. Singlelaub had managed the continual stress of living in a partnership with the KGB. He had endured for decades the voice of the pained child always whimpering in the background of his inner man. But Megan's destruction was the final tragedy.

Ernst Singlelaub sagged to the floor beside Megan's bed and began to weep.

Liz Curry was almost dragged to a cell inside the Processing sector of the Research and Development Zone. Ernst Singlelaub had paused long enough in his grieving over Megan to order Nurse Curry to be transitioned into the Producer Class. And now a rough Peacemaker virtually threw her

inside the cell. As Liz thudded to the floor, she
suddenly felt another pair of hands reaching out
to help her. At first she recoiled, fearing she
would again be manhandled. But these hands
were more gentle, even compassionate.

"Don't be afraid. I'll help you." Trina Escobar's
soft Latin accent comforted Elizabeth Curry.

"Who are you?" Curry asked.

"I'm a prisoner here," Trina answered, telling
the woman her name.

"What are they going to do to us?"

Trina paused and looked down before answering. She felt the stiffness in her joints from the
injections she had received and wondered if this
new woman would undergo the same treatment.

"I . . . I really don't know what they'll do to
you," Trina replied.

Liz Curry began to cry. "They said I'd be made
into a Producer."

"Oh, I see."

"Does it hurt?"

"They've already started on me," Trina responded. "Just some injections." She didn't want
to tell the woman everything. She tried to divert
the conversation. "How did you get here?" she
asked.

Liz Curry talked for a half hour, leaving nothing out. She told Trina about the excitement she
had seen in James Shelley ten years earlier when
he had returned from Singlelaub's meetings at
the Glades of Bacchus, of her own joy in the move
to Trinity II with Shelley, and of the experiments

she had helped Shelley perform there. She concluded by describing the crisis with Megan Singlelaub.

When Liz Curry paused for breath, Trina attempted the question she had feared asking, but to which she knew she must have an answer.

"Did you hear Dr. Singlelaub say anything about another prisoner, a big man named Mark Tilman?"

"I didn't hear any names. But Jim told me Singlelaub was very upset because an experimental subject escaped and started a fire."

"There were actually two men . . . ," Trina ventured.

"Yes, I remember now." Liz concentrated, trying to recall what Shelley had told her in casual conversation. "There *were* two of them. But one of them is dead. I don't know which."

Cold fear gripped Trina as she realized Mark Tilman might be dead. She turned away from Liz, weeping softly. Amidst her sobs Trina prayed intensely, trying to squelch the anxiety threatening to erupt as panic.

James Shelley drove like a madman. He scurried across the barren New Mexico terrain as if the KGB were already in pursuit. He knew it would only be a matter of time until they were. Perhaps, he thought, the chase had already begun.

Shelley headed for Alamogordo. Not long after arriving at Trinity II ten years earlier, Shelley's insatiable sexual appetite had led him into a relationship with Marla Dorsett. While her looks matched the vigorous beauty of Elizabeth Curry, Marla had something Liz didn't even know she lacked—sophistication.

Marla Dorsett and James Shelley had met by chance one evening at an Alamogordo lounge. He bought her two drinks, discovered she was a female stockbroker, laughed as she made urbane little jokes about being the token female at her firm, and happily accepted a key to her apartment. He had seen her rather frequently over the past ten years.

Now he glanced at the digital clock on the dash of his sports car. It was 11:18 A.M. Marla wouldn't be home, but Shelley had the key. He could find refuge at her apartment until he devised a plan.

By the time Shelley pulled into the garage at Marla's plush condo, he knew what he would do. He watched with relief as the garage door gradually descended, hiding his presence from anyone who might see him. Shelley bolted through the door leading into the condo.

Once inside Marla's apartment, his racing heart eased. The surroundings were comfortable and reassuring. As the tension softened, Shelley realized he was hungry. Searching the refrigerator, he found a plate of spaghetti. Shelley warmed it in the microwave oven, then sat down and ate. As he mixed a drink for dessert, he phoned Marla.

"Honey?" he said when her voice came on the line.

"Jim! Where are you?" There was hunger in her voice.

"I'm at your condo. Look, I need to see you badly. Can you drop whatever you're doing and get over here?"

"Lover, for you I'd cancel a date with the King of Siam!"

Shelley winced. Her statement told him two things: it revealed the depth of Marla's feelings for him, and it told him that she misunderstood the purpose of his summons.

"Great. I'll be waiting right here," he said, concluding the conversation. He heard her growl teasingly into the phone as he lowered it to its cradle.

Thirty minutes later, Marla entered the condo. He rose from the desk where he'd been writing, and the vivacious woman charged into his arms kissing him incessantly.

"Wait a minute, wait a minute," Shelley said, untwining himself from her. "I, uh, need to talk to you before we—"

"Talk?" Marla looked at him in mock surprise. "Who wants to talk when there're such better things to do?"

Shelley feigned a small laugh. "Really, sweetheart, I've got a problem, and I need your help."

Marla grew serious. "Darling, you know there's nothing I wouldn't do for you."

As they sat at the table in Marla's dinette, Shelley told her the entire story of Trinity II. At first, Marla was incredulous. Then fear shrouded her as she realized Shelley was telling the truth.

"Marla, I've written out everything I've just told you." He handed her a large brown envelope into which he had stuffed the story he had written while waiting for her.

"What do I do with it?"

"I have to get away from here. Eventually, when I've found a safe place to settle down, I want you to join me," he lied. "Marla, I want you to spend the rest of your life with me!"

Marla gasped her delight.

"Until then," he continued, "I'll call you every morning at eight, no matter where I am. But Marla, here's my insurance. The first morning I don't call you at eight, I want you to mail that package to the address I've written on the envelope."

Marla glanced down at the package she held. The envelope was addressed to the editor of the *Albuquerque Evening Star*, New Mexico's largest newspaper.

A tear pooled in Marla's eye. "How long before I see you again?"

"I don't know, sweetheart."

"Then you must not leave me without some kind of memory."

"I'm a master at making memories," Shelley said as he encircled the woman in his arms.

A half hour later, Shelley was once again in the garage, watching the door open. He and Marla agreed it would be safer to take her car since anyone tracking him would know his vehicle. Marla would hide his car in her garage and rent an automobile for her transportation. If anyone asked, she would tell them her car was undergoing repairs.

As Shelley backed out of the garage, he considered the chance that someone might eventually find his car in Marla's garage. *That,* he thought, *will be her problem.* Even if the KGB tortured her, she wouldn't be able to tell them where James Shelley was. He would never tell her.

Shelley turned Marla's blue Buick Riviera northward up Highway 54. Meticulously, he had plotted his escape. He would head toward Colorado, taking back roads as much as possible. He would cross into Colorado at Chromo in the Carson National Forest, drive to Durango, then find a place in the wilderness to lose himself for a few weeks. He knew there would be days of boredom. But in a month or so, when he knew that no one would find him, Shelley would reward himself for his brilliant escape.

But when Shelley had driven away from Marla's condo, a gray car pulled out behind him, unnoticed. The same car, bearing two KGB agents, had been on his trail since he left Trinity II.

The grieving, angered Ernst Singlelaub had told the KGB agents precisely how to reward Shelley for the surgery he had performed on his precious Megan.

"The man has lost his mind!" Hyman Stelmetz almost yelled the words. P. T. Montgomery, Archibald Porteous, Buck Prather, and Vadim Arnov gazed intently at Stelmetz, who sat at the head of the conference table around which they were gathered. Normally, that was Ernst Singlelaub's position. That Stelmetz now sat there without being challenged was a clear sign that Stelmetz was in charge of the meeting.

As far as Stelmetz was concerned, the moment foreseen by the Santa Fe astrologer had now arrived. He must seize the leadership of Trinity II now or the opportunity would be lost.

Montgomery voiced his concern. "I agree that Ernst is deeply troubled by his grief over Megan, but I hardly think he's insane," he said.

"Oh, but Hyman is right," Porteous said. "Singlelaub's mind has certainly been lost to the projects here at Trinity II—and to us."

"I have asked you to meet me here because I have come to a regrettable conclusion," Stelmetz talked slowly. There was almost a sinister tone to his voice.

Buck Prather lit a cigarette.

As always, the smoke irritated Stelmetz, but there was a greater target for his passion now—the peril of the collapse of Trinity II. "Ernst Singlelaub must be removed from the leadership of Trinity II," he said with cold finality.

"Oh, come now," Montgomery protested. "That's a bit extreme. Allow him time to recoup from his grief."

"There is no time." Vadim Arnov, the chief KGB officer at Trinity II spoke in a near monotone, but his face belied the determination behind his words. "I have been in continual contact with my superiors at the embassy in Washington. We have spent billions of dollars here, and we will not permit it to rest in the hands of a man who is mad."

"But Singlelaub is *not* mad."

"Enough, Montgomery!" Stelmetz glared.

"But we've been together here for a decade!" Montgomery shot back. "All of us have a stake in Trinity II. Any changes in leadership should be put to a vote."

"There is only one vote, Dr. Montgomery," declared Arnov. "That vote belongs to the person who, as you Americans say, pays the bill. *I* vote that Ernst Singlelaub be replaced by Hyman Stelmetz!"

THE cabin was precisely what James Shelley had been looking for. After driving all night, he arrived in Durango, found a rental agency, and booked a remote cabin in the Granite Peaks camping area for a month.

Following the map the rental agent had supplied, Shelley pulled into the yard of the chalet-style cabin. He cut the engine and sat in the car a few moments, resting, and surveying his refuge. Couched in a bed of tall fir trees, the chalet sat at the edge of a slope trailing gently into a forested valley. Shelley sighed his relief and went into the cabin.

An hour later, refreshed from a shower and fruit he had purchased in Durango, Shelley sat on the deck attached to the rear of the cabin. The vista from the deck revealed the distant glory of the fourteen-thousand-foot Sunlight Peak, a few miles to the northwest. He planned to nap briefly after enjoying the view.

With little effort, Shelley had placed Trinity II behind him. He suppressed any thoughts of Elizabeth Curry or of Marla Dorsett. Women, after all, existed for the gratification and service of James Shelley. Both of them had performed their functions well. He smirked as he thought of Curry and Dorsett, both of whom expected James Shelley to return to them someday.

Shelley had heard it in Marla's voice earlier that morning, when he had made the prearranged eight o'clock call. He smiled again as he remembered his lie to her. He told her that he was hiding out in the Guadalupe Mountains in southeastern New Mexico.

Shelley rose and moved into the bedroom, which had sliding glass doors opening onto the deck. He prepared to climb into bed and sleep. He had driven all night, and even a small measure of sleep would be welcome.

Suddenly, there was a knock at the door. Shelley tensed, then eased slightly, presuming the person at the door was a forest ranger making sure he had indeed rented the cabin.

Shelley opened the door and froze. Two ugly men stared at him. Their crumpled, somber suits and outdated ties betrayed them as Russian agents. Shelley ran toward the deck. He would leap off, even if it was a twelve-foot drop, and escape into the woods.

One of the Russians lunged after him, bringing Shelley down with a flying tackle. Quickly, the other agent helped his colleague bind Shelley's hands tightly. Then they jerked him to his feet. The agents muzzled him before he bargained with them. He didn't have a chance to tell them that if they harmed him, the whole story of Trinity II would be mailed to the *Albuquerque Evening Star*.

The men jabbered to one another in Russian as they hustled Shelley out the door of the cabin. They pushed him down a path behind the house into the small valley behind. After walking for about fifteen minutes, they stopped. With a few words in Russian, one of the men gave Shelley a sharp push. Shelley staggered, caught his foot on a rock, and tumbled into the ravine. The pain was intolerable. Mercifully, by dusk, he was dead.

At ten o'clock the next morning, Marla Dorsett knew what she must do. There had been no call from James Shelley.

Unlocking her desk drawer, Marla removed the brown envelope, walked to a mailbox outside her office building and dropped the envelope inside.

As Ernst Singlelaub sat in Megan's darkened hospital room, gazing at the silent profile of his daughter, he traced the silken thread that unraveled deep within his soul.

The thread was a melody. Somewhere, in another eon of his life, the faint strand had been woven into the fabric of his psyche. In times of crisis, when he sought solace, the thread would spin itself into his brain, and he would hear its soothing melody.

For a moment, Singlelaub dangled his voice in a whispery song upon the thread of melody. His one lyric: "Megan . . . Megan."

Suddenly, a shard of the past broke through into his consciousness like light through a break in the cloud, then was quickly covered again. Singlelaub could see the face of the cantor. The cantor had been the singer who wove the silken thread into Singlelaub's life!

Singlelaub forced his mind to remember. Pain heaped upon his sting of sorrow over Megan. Ernst Singlelaub avoided thoughts of his parents. He feared that the heaviness of that memory would shatter his tough facade. But those memories were the gateway to the cantor. Singlelaub sensed that somehow the cantor might be the gateway to peace. He had to confront his murdered parents once more.

As Singlelaub contemplated the faraway thought of his mother and father, he could see them entering a synagogue in Vienna. His father clutched the hand of a small child. Like his father, the boy's head was covered with a *yarmulke*. The child's face was alive with awe. Strangely, as Singlelaub studied his memory-vision, he saw the face of the boy was his own. This was the same child whose awe soon turned to terror, and whose voice now tortured Singlelaub with its burning memories!

Singlelaub forced his memory to continue. He

saw the three people take seats on hard wooden benches. Before them in the synagogue burned a great sparkling menorah. But the center of focus was a brilliantly decorated scroll.

An awesome voice floated into Singlelaub's ears. To the child, it sounded like the voice of God. "Hear, O Israel, the Lord our God is one Lord. . . ."

Emotion flooded Ernst Singlelaub as the voice of the ancient rabbi thunderously spoke the *Shema*.

Then came the cantor. The thread of melody glimmered across Singlelaub's mind. Its smoothness stroked his troubled soul. He remembered the peace and warmth he always felt, even as a small child, when his parents took him to synagogue.

Then another thought threatened the web of peace being woven around him: perhaps Singlelaub hated God because God had allowed Singlelaub's parents to be cut down by the Nazis. Now, not only were their lives lost to him, but so was their religion.

God. Singlelaub hadn't thought seriously about God since he was a university student more than thirty years ago. The only time he used the word was in cursing. He had named the biocomputer Sovereign in mockery.

But he couldn't deny the peace he felt as he recalled his childhood attendance at synagogue. Was it possible God really did exist? To even raise the question took an immense step for Singlelaub. If God did exist, would he help Megan? Apparently God hadn't helped his parents. *Still* . . .

Singlelaub couldn't turn the possibility loose. He would do anything to help Megan, even try prayer. But Singlelaub realized he knew nothing of prayer, not even how to begin.

For a moment, he reflected on the irony: Ernst Singlelaub was a master of the university, and had some knowledge of virtually every human field of endeavor, but he knew nothing of prayer. If God really did exist and prayer was the means of contacting him, then, prayer was the only subject worth knowing about, Singlelaub deduced.

The last thought was too much. He shook himself from the religious reverie. He cursed. *My desperation is driving me into fanaticism*, he thought.

Still, he couldn't let go of the notion that prayer might help Megan. He must find someone who could teach him about prayer.

Cleve Stringer picked up the big brown envelope addressed to the *Albuquerque Evening Star*. It was marked *Personal and Confidential*. Heavy swatches of tape sealed the package, and Stringer had to tear at the envelope with his letter opener to get it open.

The papers inside bore the letterhead of a Marla Dorsett, Financial Analyst, Alamogordo, New Mexico. But as Stringer's eyes trailed down the first sheet, he saw that the document had not been written by Marla Dorsett. The article began, "I am Dr. James Shelley, a neurosurgeon attached to the secret project at White Sands, which I shall describe herein. . . ."

The words *secret* and *White Sands* were enough to alert the overworked editor that this was not just another press release. Cleve Stringer read the document, refusing phone calls and other interruptions.

Ten minutes later, he slowly put down the papers and stared off into space, heavy thought furrowing his brow.

"Cleve. *Cleve* . . ."

Stringer hardly noticed the voice of Benny Forstman, the assistant city editor.

"Cleve, the news desk wants to know if you have anything else for the two star."

"Uh, no. I don't think so."

Stringer was preoccupied, trying to recall his conversation with Mark Tilman weeks earlier. Although Tilman's name was nowhere in this document, Stringer remembered that Tilman had wanted time off to investigate the death of some fellow he had found wandering in the desert.

"Benny, cover the desk." Stringer hopped up from his position in the slot of the city desk.

Forstman moved from his chair to Stringer's as Stringer headed for the "morgue," where the *Star*'s files were kept.

A librarian sitting at a computer terminal helped him sort through recent pieces by Mark Tilman. Surveying a list of Tilman's stories displayed on the computer screen, Stringer finally found one titled "Encounter in the Desert." He instructed the librarian to call up the story and print it for him. Soon Stringer was reading the printout of the piece Tilman had written in June.

Cleve Stringer swore. He and Richmond Tarver, publisher of the *Star,* had not taken Tilman seriously enough when he requested time to investigate. Stringer wouldn't make the same mistake again. With determination, Stringer strode back into the city room to take over his desk.

As he passed the desk of Phyllis Benetti, he pointed at her. "Drop what you're doing and come here," he barked in typical Stringer style.

The heavy, tough woman, who looked every bit of her forty-five years plus some, followed the editor.

"Read through this, then come back and talk to me." Stringer thrust the brown envelope into Benetti's hands. She returned to her desk to read.

In a few minutes, she was again standing before Stringer at the city desk. "Sounds pretty wild," she said.

"I want you to find out how wild. Head up there and see if you can find out what's going on."

Hyman Stelmetz dreaded entering the room. As he cracked the door, he could already hear Ernst Singlelaub speaking his daughter's name. Stelmetz turned, giving a disgusted look to Archibald Porteous and Vadim Arnov, who accompanied him on the visit to Megan's hospital room.

Singlelaub didn't hear them enter.

Finally, Stelmetz shook Singlelaub's shoulder.

"Doctor, we've come to talk with you," he said.

"Oh?" answered Singlelaub, obviously distant. "They told me to keep saying Megan's name. Maybe she will recognize my voice and wake up."

"Well, we all hope your daughter will regain consciousness," said Porteous with rare, but yet genuine sympathy.

Vadim Arnov cleared his throat.

"However, there are more important matters we must consider." Singlelaub stared incredulously at him. How could anything be more important than Megan?

"What Colonel Arnov means, Dr. Singlelaub, is that whether Megan wakes up or not, we must focus on the important work you've told us to do here at Trinity II," explained Stelmetz. "This must not be lost!"

Singlelaub's eyes darted to Hyman Stelmetz. "I must pray that Megan will wake up! But I don't know how. Stelmetz, you went to synagogue as a boy, do you remember how to pray? Perhaps we can find a rabbi. . . ."

Arnov almost spat out his disgust. Porteous looked down at the floor in an attempt to conceal his embarrassment. Stelmetz stood stunned by the brazen fanaticism into which Singlelaub had plummeted.

"Doctor, we must deal with this as reasonable men." Porteous was almost pleading.

Singlelaub said nothing. He merely held out his hand to Porteous. Porteous could only turn away. Singlelaub's gaze moved back to the sleeping form of Megan as if she were a magnet tugging at his soul.

Stelmetz looked at Arnov, signaling him to follow Stelmetz out of the room. Arnov nudged Porteous's arm, and he, too, followed.

"You know we must do something, don't you?" Stelmetz hated sounding like a zealot plotting a palace coup.

"Of course," Arnov answered quickly. "In the Soviet Union, we know how to deal with religious fools. I've broken up many religious cells and sent the maniacs to Siberia."

An element of anger flashed in Porteous's eyes. "Yes, there is no country as wasteful of human resources as the Soviet Union," he said.

"What?" Arnov bristled at hearing anyone challenge the virtues of Soviet methods.

"Your only strategy for dealing with anyone is to lock them up in the Lubyanka, or send them to Siberia, or melt their brains in an asylum," Porteous continued. "Why don't you try to reeducate people, to recover them for usefulness in society?"

"That's what we try to accomplish in the asylums!"

"Absurd!" Porteous retorted. "You destroy people's minds in those places!"

Stelmetz feared a verbal brawl. "Gentlemen! What does all this have to do with solving our problem with Dr. Singlelaub?"

"The point I'm trying to make," Porteous said, "is that it would be tragic for us to lose the benefit of the eminent doctor's brilliance. I agree we must depose him as Trinity II's leader, but let's not be wasteful. Let's use him."

"And how do you propose to do that?" Arnov taunted.

"By turning Ernst Singlelaub into a Primary Being!" Porteous looked triumphant.

"Of course!" Stelmetz wished he had thought of the idea.

Arnov appeared irritated that Porteous had hatched the strategy, but he had to admire the notion.

"Ernst would readily go along with our approach if he were sane," Porteous continued. "He'd want to contribute his best to Trinity II, even if it meant the sacrifice of his personality."

On that, all three men had to agree.

Phyllis Benetti once cracked that she had written enough obituaries in her twenty-three years at the *Star* to fill an entire set of *The Encyclopedia Britannica*. Now one of those obituaries was about to open a door for her.

She remembered the scene six months back. A grieving United States Army colonel had come into the news room, bearing a picture of his recently deceased wife. Stringer, in his perpetual cynicism, had told the man there was no way the photo could run in the obituary column, but that Miss Benetti would write the death report.

Benetti had listened as Colonel Lynn Cofield told her his wife's story. The woman, a victim of multiple sclerosis, had refused to allow the disease to paralyze her activity. Even after it had progressed to an advanced stage, Mrs. Cofield would spend each day on her couch, telephoning potential contributors for a fund to preserve a section of Alamogordo as a historic site.

Benetti promised to write the story as a human interest feature and persuade Stringer to treat it as such.

The next day, the story had run on the front page of the *Star*'s feature section. As he read it, Colonel Cofield called Phyllis Benetti, offering an insider's tour of White Sands, where he was an officer. Benetti had only half meant it when she assured him the day would come when she would accept his invitation.

The day had indeed come. Benetti sat now in a waiting area of the White Sands administration building, waiting to see Colonel Cofield.

Cofield greeted Benetti with genuine warmth and escorted her into his office. At first, they made small talk. Benetti decided to approach slowly the reason for her visit. For all she knew, the subject she had come to explore might be so sensitive that Cofield would refuse to talk about it, even under torture.

"What exactly is your job here, Colonel?"

"I'm the ARMTE officer."

"I beg your pardon?"

"White Sands has several major directorates." he explained. "There's National Range Operations, or NRO; Instrumentation, ID; Army Air Operations, which we refer to as AA; and Army Missile Test and Evaluation, or ARMTE."

"So you spend a good bit of time on the testing range?"

"Yes. Inspecting the test and evaluation facilities is a major part of my responsibility."

Benetti knew she must be careful now. In her briefcase she carried a copy of the Shelley document, but she didn't want to show that to Cofield unless it was essential to win his assistance.

"What goes on up at Trinity?" she asked. "I hear there's a good bit of activity up there."

Cofield tensed. All he had been told was that the army was cooperating with a private contractor's secret uranium recovery operation. Obviously, the reporter had uncovered some information about the project. If she knew anything at all, Cofield reflected briefly, it was likely more than he knew. His reluctance to talk, however, made him appear coy.

After several more attempts to break through Cofield's determination not to tell her anything, Benetti decided to shock him.

"Colonel, if you're not going to tell me what's happening at Trinity, let me tell you."

As she summarized for Cofield the story in the Shelley document, adding information involving Tilman that Dr. Shelley didn't know about, it was clear that Cofield knew nothing. "Miss Benetti, I don't mean to be rude to someone who's done a favor for me, but I just have to tell you: that's the most absurd tale I've heard in a long time," said Cofield.

Benetti had no other recourse but to show him the document itself. "Colonel, that information came from a highly reliable source—a man who's one of America's top neurosurgeons."

"I'm sorry, Miss Benetti, but I haven't talked to him."

"Then read this." Benetti yanked the Shelley document from her briefcase and tossed it on Cofield's desk.

The colonel picked up the sheath of papers and thumbed through them. "I, uh, don't know what this proves."

"It proves, Colonel Cofield, that the KGB has for ten years been operating under your nose, and you haven't even suspected it!"

Cofield hesitated. If Washington discovered that a KGB operation was underway at White Sands, and the White Sands command had been oblivious to it, and he had information about it and told no one, he would be hoisted to the highest gallows at the Pentagon.

"All right, Miss Benetti, I'll bring the matter to General Prosch, the commanding officer here at White Sands."

"Fine, I'll wait," she said, exhibiting the tenacity of an octopus.

"But I probably can't even see the general until tomorrow."

"You're going to wait a day while the KGB sits up there at Trinity?"

"Well, no, of course not. But even if I can get to see the general today, it won't do you any good. We can't let you go up there."

"Oh, then you'd prefer me to go ahead and file

the story for tomorrow's editions with the information I have?"

Cofield swore. "You people in the media are all alike. OK, I'll go see the general. You can wait outside, and I'll let you know what we decide. But you have to promise to keep your mouth shut."

"I'll promise that," Phyllis Benetti answered with a slight smile. "For now, anyway."

ERNST Singlelaub, master of Trinity II, sat in a big chair in the corner of his daughter's room speaking Megan's name again and again. He didn't even stop when the nurse came in to change Megan's bed. He just kept repeating the name, hoping Megan might recognize the continual repetition of her name and wake up. The thin, sallow man with the stubble of beard on his face appeared more as a derelict than the sinister genius who had inspired this dark underworld.

At the core of Singlelaub's turbulent psyche, he was thinking about prayer as he spoke Megan's name. At times, Singlelaub thought he was actually praying to Megan. But that would do no good. She could not heal herself. *If only I could think of someone who could teach me how to pray,* Singlelaub mused.

His thoughts were like pebbles tumbling down a slope. At the bottom, someone seemed to shovel them up and toss them back to the top of the incline. Then they would roll down again.

At last the thought-pebbles stopped. Singlelaub's mind traced back to his first conversations with Mark Tilman and Trina Escobar when they were captured. Both of them had spoken of God. They would know how to pray.

Desperately, Singlelaub leaped from the chair, grabbed the telephone, and called one of his assistants.

"I want those two people brought here, now!"

"Er, yes, sir," the surprised assistant replied, recognizing Singlelaub's voice. "But sir, whom do you wish to be brought where?"

"Those two religious people—the ones we captured, you idiot. Bring them to my daughter's hospital room."

"Certainly, sir. Right away!"

Singlelaub hung up the receiver and returned to his chair. Once again, he began speaking Megan's name.

In less than twenty minutes, Mark Tilman stood between two guards outside a room in the hospital sector of Trinity II. Still tightly bound, he glanced around, looking for an escape route. Suddenly he noticed three people approaching, farther down the corridor. The corridor was dark, and they were fifty yards away, but Tilman could make out their profiles. One was a Peacemaker.

Another, a human security guard. The third person, walking beside the human guard, was a woman.

Tilman's heart raced. The woman was Trina! He sobbed in relief. She wasn't dead or transformed into a horrid Trinity II creature. Tilman's arms were bound, but he lurched away from the guards, screaming her name.

Trina ran toward him. Though her hands were also tied, they met in a passionate kiss.

Instantly the guards tried to separate them. Just as quickly, Ernst Singlelaub emerged from the hospital room and saw Tilman and Trina.

"Bring them in here. Then leave us!" he commanded.

"Sir, they might harm you," a guard protested.

"Leave, I said!"

Trina watched the guards and Peacemakers leave. "What do you want with us?" she asked.

Singlelaub didn't answer.

Tilman nodded toward the young woman in the hospital bed. "Who is that?" he asked.

"My daughter," Singlelaub answered. "She's been injured in a brain experiment."

"Those who live by the sword shall die by the sword," Trina quoted softly.

"What?" Singlelaub looked puzzled.

"It's from the Bible," Tilman answered. "It simply means that God allows people to suffer the consequences of their choices."

"I did not choose for my daughter to end up this way."

"No, Dr. Singlelaub, but you chose to create a

system that excluded God and his way," Trina said. "Now you must harvest the seeds you've sown."

"I just want her back." The wiry man began to weep.

Mark and Trina looked at each other in disbelief.

"I spend hours sitting here, repeating her name just as the doctors instructed, but she never responds."

"That makes sense," Tilman said.

"What? What makes sense?"

"Your speaking your daughter's name."

"Why do you say that?"

"Your child is lost to you, so you are seeking her. It's quite logical."

Trina followed in Mark's train of thought. "Dr. Singlelaub, if God were your Father, and you were lost to him, don't you think he'd do something to try to get you back?"

"If God exists at all, it's only as an impersonal intelligence," Singlelaub argued weakly, dredging up weary cliches he had used amply in the past. "But I don't want to debate religion." He turned and walked to Megan's side. "Megan. Megan, my child."

"I think God must have acted just like that when he lost Adam," Tilman said.

Singlelaub looked up.

"What are you talking about?"

"When Adam rebelled against God, it was like he died to his Father, just as Megan has died to you," Tilman explained. "The Bible says God came to the garden asking, 'Where are you, Adam?' Isn't that what you're asking of your daughter?"

Singlelaub stared intently at Megan. "Yes, I suppose so."

"If Megan were lost in a cavern somewhere here at Trinity, what would you do?" Trina asked.

Tears blurred Singlelaub's vision as he stared at his beloved daughter. "I'd try to find her."

"That's what God did," Trina said softly. "He came to earth in the form of Jesus of Nazareth to seek us and win us back."

Ernst Singlelaub stared now at the pretty Mexican-American woman, whose words suddenly made sense. He was just about to agree with her logic when a terrible thought stabbed at the embryo of faith forming in him.

"No . . . no," he said like a man who wanted it to be true. "You weren't there when the Nazis gunned down my parents. If God is my Father, how could he let his child hurt like that?"

Tilman carefully chose his words. "It's because God created us for love," he said.

"That's preposterous!" Singlelaub stared at Tilman with genuine anger, the tortured child within him shrieking *help me!*

"No, Dr. Singlelaub, think about it! To have love, you must have *choice*, and to have choice, you must have *freedom*."

"Freedom." Singlelaub savored the word as he spoke it softly, almost in meditation. Again, he stared down at Megan.

"That's right," continued Tilman. "God opened the window of freedom in this universe so that we could choose to love. A great deal of good came in through that open window, but so did accident and tragedy, and evil—like the Nazis."

"Does God love?" Singlelaub asked.

"Yes," answered Trina quickly.

"Then why isn't there some way to him, some approach?"

"There is, Dr. Singlelaub," Trina continued. "The approach is through Jesus, who has removed every barrier between us and the Father."

Singlelaub was close. For the first time, faith was making some sense to him. The screaming child even seemed to become quieter. Still, he pulled back.

"But if I talk to God now, it'll only be because I want my daughter healed. Would he take me on that basis?"

"He'll take you however you're able to come, Dr. Singlelaub."

"He'll work with you where you are," Trina echoed. "In fact, the greater your need, the more God can help you. Jesus said that to know God, you must become like a child. Sometimes it takes real desperation to make us as open and trusting as a child is."

As soon as Trina spoke the word *child*, Ernst Singlelaub turned and looked at Trina and Tilman. There was profound longing in his eyes. For a moment, his lips quivered and he seemed about to speak. Then, the agonizing child shrieking inside, Singlelaub closed his eyes and mouth tightly, battling for control. Attitudes of trust and openness were foreign to Singlelaub. It was too great a step. With immense pain, he pulled back. The child in his psyche cried on.

It was ninety miles from White Sands Headquarters up to the Trinity site. But when Colonel Lynn Cofield relayed James Shelley's information to Major General Erwin Prosch, Prosch ordered Cofield to waste no time finding out what was happening at Trinity. Over ninety miles of desert, Cofield moved an attack force that might have stormed one of the Normandy beaches on D day.

Phyllis Benetti had managed to stay close to Cofield and heard the summons squawk over Cofield's walkie-talkie.

"Colonel Cofield, I think you need to see this."

"Colonel Cofield," he spoke into the radio. "What have you got, sergeant?"

"I think we've found the entrance to the underground cavern, sir," came the response.

"Give me your position, and I'll be right there. Do nothing until I get there. Oh, by the way, is there any evidence of uranium mining?"

"Sir?"

"Thank you, sergeant. That's what I was afraid of."

Ten minutes later, Cofield, Phyllis Benetti, a *Star* photographer, and a battalion of soldiers arrived at the location given by the sergeant.

"It's right over here, sir," said the soldier.

Looming over the Trinity site was a rocky hill Cofield estimated to be fifty feet high. The sergeant and his patrol had moved some large boulders from the face of the hill. A monstrous metal door lay behind the boulders, which were obviously intended to disguise the door's location. The soldiers were almost finished removing the rock.

"Any ideas on how to get past that door?" Cofield asked the sergeant.

"I just talked with my ordinance man, sir. He believes he can rig a blast strong enough to open those doors."

"Very well, sergeant. Proceed when ready."

In a half hour, the rest of the huge stones had been heaved away, and explosive charges had been planted at key points along the big doorway. The sergeant made sure everyone took cover, then commanded his ordinance team to detonate.

Although Phyllis Benetti crouched behind a massive rock, she thought the concussion would blow her apart. The explosion unleashed a gusher of dust, temporarily blocking vision of the cave entrance. When the cloud dissipated, Phyllis Benetti looked into the mouth of the cave and gasped. An army of monstrous Peacemakers bearing laser weapons poured from the hole the soldiers had blasted.

The Peacemakers easily beat back the soldiers. Cofield took command from a makeshift post on a hillock across from the cave entrance. He quickly summoned other patrols who had scattered over the Trinity area. By the time reinforcements moved in, the sergeant and half his men were dead. Almost a quarter more were wounded.

The fresh troops entered the battle with bewilderment and confusion as they squared off against the fearsome Peacemakers.

One of the squadron leaders, engaged in fierce combat with the Peacemakers, radioed Cofield. "Colonel, I'm pinned down. Our only shot at these creatures is an air strike!"

"I agree, lieutenant," answered Cofield into his walkie-talkie. "I'm contacting Holloman Air Force Base now. I'll ask them to scramble a fighter squadron!"

The colonel made the contact, then ordered his troops to fall back and take cover.

Eight minutes later, a wave of F-14 Phantom jets washed the desert floor with fire. The thunderous assault confused the Peacemakers and frightened the few humans who fought with them. It only took two sorties by the jets to rout the attack unit that had ambushed Cofield's men from inside the cave.

"It all looks quiet down here, colonel," came the lieutenant's voice over the walkie-talkie.

"Then send your men into the cave."

Archibald Porteous looked down at Ernst Singlelaub, who was strapped to an operating table in the Processing Center, being readied for his transition into a Primary Being.

"Dr. Singlelaub, we simply want to ensure that you continue to make a great contribution to Trinity II," he said apologetically.

Vadim Arnov hovered to the left of the table, hostility clouding his face. Hyman Stelmetz stood brazenly beside Porteous at the right. "Come now, Porteous, you make it sound as though we're going to torture him," Stelmetz mocked. "We shall do the doctor a favor. He will function at his prime."

Singlelaub remained silent. At a moment of crisis, no one could emit more acerbic comments than he. Now, though, he lay on the table, mute, his eyes shut tightly, his face expressionless. He was exploring the new world of the Spirit, to which he had awakened. Ernst Singlelaub was praying.

Stelmetz addressed the medical team waiting to effect Singlelaub's transition to a Primary Being. "Begin the procedure," he said coldly.

Stelmetz, Porteous, and Arnov moved away from the table as the medical personnel encircled it. "Let's watch from the gallery above," Stelmetz suggested.

As Singlelaub was being blanketed and the surgical equipment laid out, the three men walked up a stairway into the viewing gallery.

The procedure for transitioning a person into a Primary Being began with the insertion of growth cells that enlarged the cranium to receive a greater brain volume. Stelmetz, Porteous, and Arnov watched as the team shaved Singlelaub's head.

Suddenly, the gallery's phone rang. Porteous answered it. "It's for you, Arnov," he said, extending the receiver to the Russian.

"What? How far have they penetrated?" Arnov's ashen face told Stelmetz and Porteous there was a crisis.

Arnov leaped to his feet and handed the receiver back to Porteous. "We've been invaded! U.S. Army troops have discovered the entrance at the surface. They're about to enter the cavern!"

Stelmetz barked an order into the microphone that linked him to the operating room below. "Stop the procedure! Summon a security unit to lock up the patient!"

Porteous was almost in a panic. "We've got to get out of here!" he shouted.

"Shut up, fool!" Arnov yelled. "Follow me. I have an escape plan!"

The three men scrambled out of the gallery and into the corridor between Sectors Four and Five. Arnov led them down a passageway opening onto the service road in the center of Trinity II.

When they came to the road, Arnov glanced to his left, toward the surface cavern entrance. The troops had not yet made it that far.

"Where are you taking us?" Porteous asked.

"There is a tunnel leading out of the disposal area," Arnov answered. "It leads to Nogal Peak, sufficiently away from Trinity that we shall be safe."

Stelmetz and Porteous followed Arnov toward the massive, truck-sized doors that opened into the smaller cave containing the incinerator. Just as they got to the entrance, they heard gunfire at the opposite end of the cave.

"We must hurry!" Arnov screamed.

He led Stelmetz and Porteous toward the wall of the small cave. Quickly, they climbed a small outcropping of rock, slipped through the narrow crevice that led into Nogal cave, and disappeared into the tunnel, unseen.

Colonel Lynn Cofield was at the head of his troops now, leading the fight.

"I believe they're falling back, sir!" shouted the lieutenant over the fury of fire.

"I hope so," Cofield answered. "I don't know how much noise the cave walls can take without collapsing."

The American troops began advancing. Some soldiers paused over the bodies of slain Peacemakers, staring at them in awed curiosity. Gradually, the Trinity II defenders succumbed to the greater numbers of United States Army soldiers.

"Cease fire!" Cofield hollered at last into his walkie-talkie. The command was relayed throughout the cavern. The guns stilled. There was no return fire. "Give this place a complete search, but be careful about snipers," Cofield ordered his commanders.

Over the next two hours, Cofield's squadrons spread out through the strange world of Trinity II, herding docile Primary Beings and Producers into a big holding area in Sector Three of the Applied Science Zone. Wherever they found humans, the troops took them captive.

Phyllis Benetti and her photographer joined Cofield on an inspection tour. Deep in Sector Five of the Research and Development Zone, they found a large conference room where soldiers were holding prisoners.

Suddenly Benetti recognized one of the detainees. "Mark Tilman!" she cried, running toward him.

"Wait a minute. What are you doing?" Cofield called to her.

"It's Tilman, the reporter from the *Star*," she shouted. Looking down at Tilman's bound hands, she asked, "Mark, what's happening here? Have they hurt you?"

"No, I'm OK. Just untie us." He motioned toward Trina, who was standing beside him. "We've got to find Ernst Singlelaub."

"I assure you we're in agreement on that," said Cofield. "Have you any idea where he might be?"

Phyllis Benetti untied her former coworker and Trina as Cofield walked toward them.

Tilman hugged Trina tightly and shook his head in reply.

Cofield gave Tilman a walkie-talkie and instructed everyone to fan out and search.

Three hours later, Singlelaub still had not been located. Tilman, Trina, Phyllis Benetti, and Colonel Cofield gathered again in the hospital conference room.

"We've scoured the place," said Cofield. "Where could he be?"

"All we can do is keep looking," said Tilman

315

with resignation. "Trina and I will search here in the Research and Development Zone. There may be some other experimental subjects we can help."

Twenty minutes later, Mark and Trina found Ernst Singlelaub still strapped to the operating table, his mouth muzzled with heavy bandage strips. He had been locked in a room where experimental subjects were held prior to surgery. Tilman unstrapped Singlelaub and ripped the strips from his mouth. Using the walkie-talkie, he asked Cofield to come to the conference room in the hospital area.

By the time Cofield got there, Tilman, Trina, and Singlelaub were already seated at the big rectangular table.

"Colonel Cofield, I'd like you to meet Dr. Ernst Singlelaub," Tilman said.

"I'm happy to meet you, Doctor. And I'll be happier to hear your explanation for all this," Cofield replied, taking a seat.

Cofield's words cut like a scalpel, puncturing the tumor of dark information that grew in Singlelaub's brain. Singlelaub had to confess to excise the poison that had been in his psyche for so many years.

Ernst Singlelaub went far back in time. He revealed his complicity in the murder of General Royston Wade during the Pearson administration. He detailed the Roman Solution and his dreams for mastery over the nation. He told how the failure of that plan had brought him to develop Trinity II, to seek the evolution of the Survival Society. After an hour, Singlelaub finished.

"Dr. Singlelaub, I'm sorry about your daughter and the consequences you'll have to bear. But you've stood by while a man was murdered. You've betrayed your country by entering into an alliance with the KGB. You've developed a system down here where many people have died. I'll have to take you in. You'll have to stand trial."

"I know," said Singlelaub, his voice cracking. "But before you take me away, please allow me to see my daughter one more time."

"All right," Cofield answered. "You may have ten minutes with her."

Megan's hospital room wasn't far from the conference room. As they reached the door, Cofield started to enter with Singlelaub.

"Alone, Colonel. Let me see her alone," Singlelaub begged.

"I don't know."

"Colonel," Tilman said, "I've spent some time in the last few days with Dr. Singlelaub. There've been some, uh, changes in him. I think you can trust him."

"Ten minutes, Dr. Singlelaub. That's all!" said Cofield, trying to retain command of the situation.

"Thank you." Singlelaub disappeared into the room alone, closing the door behind him.

Outside, as they waited, Tilman and Trina embraced. Each poured the feelings of the moment into one another. For Tilman, there was regret mingled with the relief of their rescue. But he knew that he was reluctant to walk away even from a crisis if it meant walking away from Trina.

"Thank God," he whispered in her ear. "I thought we were both going to die in this cave."

"I know," answered Trina. "I was frantic when they separated us."

"That's what I was just thinking about," Tilman said, taking her chin and gently lifting her face toward his.

"About what?"

"About being separated," Tilman replied. "It must never happen again. We haven't known each other long, but when two people go through together what we've been through, it's worth a lifetime."

"I feel the same way," Trina said, peering intently into Tilman's face.

"I don't want to spend another lifetime without you," he continued. "Will you marry me?"

Trina smiled. "Even if it means living forever in a cave! Yes, Mark, *yes*."

Deep inside the cave housing Ernst Singlelaub's experimental city, he entered the hospital room where his daughter lay and walked slowly to her bedside. He leaned on the bed, studying the sleeping form of his daughter. Her beautiful, sharp features and snowy skin made her appear to be a carefully crafted statue.

Ernst Singlelaub thought about the confession he had just given Cofield. He looked at Megan and realized she was the only thing of beauty ever to come from his life. He thought of the years of prison ahead, the years of separation from Megan. Suddenly, Singlelaub realized he might never be at her side again. *If only she could wake up just once, so I could tell her how much I love her*, he thought.

Singlelaub's legs began to weaken. He slumped to a kneeling position beside his daughter's bed and clutched her hand, praying as he wept. Soon the prayer gave way to speaking her name again.

"Megan, Megan my child . . ."

Singlelaub buried his head in the sheets stained with his tears. He didn't see nor hear anything until a weak voice whispered, "Father, you're crying."